"DO YOU HONOR ALL YOUR CONTRACTS THIS WAY?"

As Helen spoke, she struggled under his strong lean body until she freed herself. "The great Luis San Roque," she stormed at him, "who's supposedly never forced a woman to his bed is now trying to!"

Astonishingly he smiled down at her with amusement and said confidently, "I won't have to force you." Gently he drew her near and lowered his mouth to hers. His lips wandered to her throat, to the soft curve of her breasts, while his hands caressed her warmly, persuasively.

Helen's good sense warred with her longing for him, but his touch soon melted her resolve, and she trembled with desire.

"You see, my beautiful one, you cannot deny what's between us," Luis whispered, drawing her deeper into his arms....

WELCOME TO...

SUPERROMANCES

A sensational series of modern love stories
from Worldwide Library.

Written by masters of the genre, these longer,
sensual and dramatic novels are truly in keeping
with today's changing life-styles. Full of intriguing
conflicts, the heartaches and delights of true love,
SUPERROMANCES are absorbing stories —
satisfying and sophisticated reading that lovers
of romance fiction have long been waiting for.

SUPERROMANCES
Contemporary love stories for the woman of today!

MARIAN JONES

BONDS OF ENCHANTMENT

A SUPERROMANCE FROM
WORLDWIDE

TORONTO · NEW YORK · LOS ANGELES · LONDON

Published June 1983

First printing April 1983

ISBN 0-373-70068-7

CHAPTER ONE

HELEN'S ROOM AT THE COMPANY HOUSE was full of crated paintings. The houseman had obligingly packed them all for Ron to take to Chamartin Galleries in San Diego when the company plane left on Monday. Helen came out of the room plaiting her magnificent copper waterfall of hair neatly into one long braid and entered the big Spanish kitchen. She was a tall girl, reed slim and graceful, a striking contrast to the round dark Mexican woman working by the tiled oven.

"Have you seen my brother today?" Helen asked Guadalupe, the housekeeper-cook, using Spanish almost as easily as English.

Guadalupe, as imperturbable and expressionless as an Olmec sculpture, said, "No, Señorita Helena," giving her name the soft Spanish pronunciation. "I think he is still at Guerrero Negro."

Helen made a face. Ron would kill himself with overwork if he charged ahead all the time at the pace he had worked this summer. His routine explained why he never had time to write home to Garnet Beach or spend time there with their father. When she returned home next Friday night she would tell dad all his worries were over: Ron wasn't in trouble somewhere. He wasn't a con man, a hippie, a dropout or a bum. Ron was carving himself a well-earned spot in an exciting country. At long last he had found the opportunity to use all the brilliant promise their father had despaired of ever seeing fulfilled.

"I'm going down to the south cove to swim and paint, Guadalupe," Helen announced. "I put the Sunday roast in the oven. It will take a long time to cook, big as it is and frozen. The salad's made. I'll be back before sundown."

"It's too hot to leave the house and walk that far," Guadalupe warned, but she was used to this crazy American girl who worked like a man, dressed in her brother's cast-off shirts and was taller than the houseman or her own son, who worked in one of the mines. "Take your hat, or your pretty eyes will develop a squint from our bright sun!"

She waddled after Helen with a wide-brimmed old field laborer's straw. "Sunday is a day of rest! You two *gringos locos* never stop working, never have parties or fiestas. More better when el señor comes and things are a little lively!"

"I'll bet," Helen muttered.

El señor, as everyone called him, was, according to Ron, typical of the world's wealthy exploiters. He had a yacht on the Riviera, a hacienda outside Mexico City, a castle in Spain, an apartment in Buenos Aires, and came around just often enough to be sure the *peones* were producing the means to his soft life.

El señor was arriving on his seasonal inspection trip the following Sunday. Helen would be two days gone, her work finished. It was a blessing her job was to end before he arrived, for her outspoken manner could easily jeopardize Ron's future in the company.

He might be el señor, the man next to God in the *peones'* eyes, but in her own eyes he was closer to the devil. Memos with his slashing rusty-brown-ink signature, "Luis San Roque Q."—the *Q* for Quintana—had streamed across her desk all summer. The man practically demanded miracles, but the branch office hadn't even the basic tools to do a proper job.

This she had pointed out to him via memo, even though she had managed to do the job this summer without the necessary tools. She had prepared a whole portfolio for the great visit, and when she could catch her brother, she had drilled him on presenting it, even though Ron had dismissed the idea with a casual, "Why bother!"

Essentially, the portfolio included an outline of tools and equipment needed to coordinate the branches of Guerrero Negro, El Arco and Pozo Aleman with that at Isla de Cedros more efficiently. It included sample catalogs of the best equipment available and budgetary suggestions on purchasing.

The first such presentation, which she had sent him directly, had been ignored. Undoubtedly he thought that because she was a woman she could be easily dismissed. His attitude rankled, but Helen was determined not to be upset by it. Let him think her impertinent, as she thought him chauvinistic. Probably el señor, male chauvinist in a male chauvinist's country, would assume this second portfolio was a product of Ron's brilliant effort rather than her own.

It didn't matter, she told herself again. Ron was welcome to the credit for any business skill she had. She wasn't necessarily seeking to promote herself; if her ideas proved effective, that was reward enough for a summer that had started her on a path she had once dreamed of and now was determined to follow as soon as she possibly could. The whole summer had been an example of serendipity—pure, crazy, unexpected luck!

THE BEGINNING OF THAT good fortune had been her accidental meeting with Chamartin, the gallery owner, two months earlier. Driving with his wife the length of the Baja peninsula from Tijuana to Cabo San Lucas, Chamartin had happened on her just as she had come up from the cove with a finished watercolor. The travelers had needed water for the auxiliary tank of their camper, and Helen's offer of an ice-cold drink had been accepted with a look of absolute bliss from Mrs. Chamartin.

When Helen had come out on the patio with limeade clinking in a pitcher, Chamartin was studying the watercolor she had left behind with her box of paints.

"You did this?" he'd asked enthusiastically. "It's excellent! Have you more I can see?"

Willingly Helen had brought out the paintings she had done in her first three weeks there, when she had really been drunk on the impact of Punta Temereria. Reflected in the paintings was the essence of this farthest western fragment of the great Sonoran desert, the geometric hills of white salt, the listing mining shed, the glorious starkness of the area. Here the ever changing water went from Pacific blue to grassy green when the combers rose in great glass walls before breaking into spume. Then at times the angry gray of a *borrasca* far at sea could be felt in the thundering surf and seen in the turbulent sky.

Helen had explained to the Chamartins why she was there only for the summer. "My brother, Ronald Forster, manages the branch mining operation here, and he has some administrative duties at Guerrero Negro, El Arco and Pozo Aleman. Ordinarily I'm a teacher of business machines, accounting and typing in Garnet Beach. It's an unincorporated suburb of north San Diego County, near Oceanside."

"I know the Garnet Beach area," Chamartin had responded. "One of the new developments for upper-middle-class beachfront lovers. A paradise for developers." He had mentioned friends in Del Mar and Oceanside whose names she knew, although she didn't travel in their circles.

"We're just one of the poor old original families," she had explained. "My father had his own small business in town until he and my stepmother were in a terrible auto accident. She's been hospitalized ever since, and my father has been a semi-invalid."

"What are you doing teaching school when you can paint like this?"

"Making a living," she'd answered briefly. "Painting is a hobby."

She hadn't mentioned that she also moonlighted nights and weekends during the school year for a local independent grocery store, gratefully accepting their minimum wage in order to swell finances badly strained by medical expenses.

"Ron got me this job," she had told them. "The man who worked here before me was bitten by a scorpion and died. Ron thought I might be able to put things into some order and possibly teach my permanent replacement how to keep it that way, but so far he hasn't been satisfied with anyone who's shown up for the job."

She hadn't mentioned, either, that the job had been like a summer in Europe as far as she was concerned. The salary was fabulous, and if she was careful she could drop the exhausting moonlighting job doing the Blue Chip Grocery's books and spend more free time painting during the coming year.

"Mathematics and business procedures?" Mrs. Chamartin had mused, sipping a second glass of tart limeade after gulping down her first. "Math and art often seem allied, you know; like art and medicine. But you are more the artist, for it's easy to see that you love beauty. You're rather like a specimen rose growing in a surprise spot one would never suspect. Look at her, Cham. She reminds me of my Montezuma rose—that copper hair and flawless skin and the golden eyes. Have you ever done a self-portrait?''

"No," Helen had mumbled, unused to being complimented; she was more accustomed to being teased by Ron. Her softly golden eyes glowed with pleasure and her face flushed a bit under her summer tan upon hearing the compliments about her looks and her artistic talents.

"If I could have my heart's desire, I'd stay right here and paint forever," she'd told them, "but I know my father needs me, so I can't stay forever."

"You're good, though. Really good."

"Am I?" Helen was naturally shy about her work. "My stepmother would love to hear that. She's always encouraged me."

Mama Jessie was the prime reason for her need for money. With some difficulty Helen was adding six hundred dollars a month to the insurance that was supposed to cover her injured stepmother's nursing-home charges. And there was no guarantee her share of the costs wouldn't rise in the coming year as every other cost spiraled upward.

Chamartin had given her his card:

CHAMARTIN GALLERIES
FIFTH AVENUE, SAN DIEGO
COAST HIGHWAY, LAGUNA BEACH

"We'll stop by on our way back north and take these paintings on commission," he'd told her, "and also any others you may have finished by then. I may be able to do something for you." He'd looked shrewdly at the painting again. "In fact, you may do something for me. Your works might not be immortal, but they have a quality ordinary people can appreciate in a painting."

Chamartin Galleries had sold the first batch, including the oil of the main office of the mine at Punta Temereria. The check was no fortune, but it represented a nice round figure for the one oil painting and what seemed to Helen to be fantastic prices for simple watercolors. Chamartin particularly liked Helen's gouaches and temperas and ordered "all you can send." That suited her; somehow oil had never been her favorite medium.

Now, at the end of the summer, there were many more pictures, and even without their sales, the first batch of paintings and her temporary job had made her two and a half months there immensely profitable.

She slung the two canteens of water over her shoulder, tucked a towel in one side of her belt and a clean rag on the other side and picked up two flat watercolor cases containing her paints, palette and pads of watercolor paper. She secured her stylish glasses on the bridge of her nose and whistled for the dog, Perro, her companion on these jaunts.

This time of the afternoon the heat wasn't bad, and Helen had become acclimated to it anyway. She swung down the rutted track that served as a road, unobstructed by the abundance of buckhorn, cholla, devil's-hands and hedgehog cactus. Where the low bluff canted off the track she made her way to the cove down a footpath someone had hacked away from the side of the cliff.

Whoever had carved the steps never seemed to use the little beach. Helen hadn't seen another living soul there all summer, though the swimming was exquisite. Young surfers from San Diego would eventually discover Punta Temereria, even though it was hundreds of miles south in the middle of nowhere, and when that happened she could say goodbye to blissful tranquillity. For now, though, it was her own lush retreat.

She put her painting equipment on the sheltered shelf of rock, slipped out of her old baggy shirt and hung it on a jutting overhang. Off came the macrame belt she had made with shells from this beach, and the faded slacks with streaks of paint that wouldn't come out no matter how much Guadalupe beat them on washday. She noted how shabby her faded cutoffs and halter had become; they would just about last until she returned home before falling apart from constant wear and tear. Her lissome body was golden from the sun and her rosy tan made her eyes, fringed by unusually dark lashes, seem even more glowing. But their beauty was camouflaged most of the time by the eyeglasses she wore.

Finally she removed her glasses and put them in one of her cases, because she wouldn't need them for swimming. She wore them mainly when she painted, worked with columns of figures or drove the car. Her beautiful luminous eyes were unfortunately cursed with nearsightedness.

Straight into the waves she plunged, turning over and over like a rock seal. She delighted in the crisp salt tang of the water, which never failed to strike her body initially with tingles of cold no matter how hot the day.

A short time later she reluctantly left the water and went back up the beach to her rock shelf. On the way she took all the pins from the wet braid of red hair at the nape of her neck and shook it loose to dry. It went from a dark wet tangle in the shade of an old penny to a full fiery mane of spun copper as the sun dried it. The wind that came up every afternoon blew her hair about her shoulders, shielding her from the damaging rays of the sun.

She opened the paint box, put on her glasses

and began to wash in the sky, the water and the point. For living contrast she blocked in some of the little terns running along the water's edge. They hardly ever wet their delicate feet, but when they did they seemed surprised that they hadn't quite gauged the line of seafoam on the incoming tide.

This afternoon Helen had the idiotic feeling that the beach didn't belong solely to her, even though it stretched as usual to empty infinity in the distance. She felt someone else was near. She looked up and down the beach, polished her glasses on the painting cloth, looked again and even searched behind her, above on the bluff line, but the only person in this little world was herself.

"Perro?" she called out. The dog was down at the water's edge, sniffing and barking out at the horizon like a great dummy. She couldn't hear him over the roar of the combers, but she could see all the energy he put into the futile act. Then she saw the dolphins that Perro had spotted.

Dolphins were common enough in the area, traveling up and down the coast to and from Scammon's Lagoon, where the gray whales went to mate. This great school—twenty to fifty, perhaps even a hundred or more—followed their leader in a long orderly line. It was unusual for dolphins to come so close to shore.

Helen wiped her glasses again to free them of the salt spray that continually fogged them. She didn't want to miss a moment of the phenomenon.

As each roller lifted to break, the late-afternoon sun shone through the curve, making the wall of water a clear startling lime green against the quicksilver, gold and blue. Outlined in the concave wall were the giant dolphins enjoying the sea even more than she had enjoyed it herself—dolphins pausing for a play period as they headed south to the lagoon.

She had never seen them so close and so clearly. Their size was magnified by the action of the sun on the water as they leaped with grace and precision, frisking, diving and turning in the air.

As incredible as the scene was, there was an even more startling sight that made her gasp as she set eyes on it. Vividly in the curve of a giant breaker, she saw a man swimming with the mammals.

At first she couldn't believe her eyes. She thought wildly, *someone from one of the fishermen's boats has drowned!* Then she realized the man was in no difficulty. He swam unconcernedly among the giant dolphins, deliberately playing with them. The dolphins were quite aware of him, even friendly.

She stood almost trembling in the hot sun,

struck by the scene before her. A memory came to her of all the old fables she had read about dolphins befriending ancient mariners in trouble at sea. This man actually wrestled with one big creature, rode it out of the water and then down the curve of a breaker.

At last the dolphins were gone, south around the bluffs. So, too, disappeared the swimmer. Still Helen stood transfixed on the beach. Finally she took off her glasses, wet again with salt spray and uselessly fogged. The wind blew her hair wildly, and she tried to tame it with her arm as she stared into the water, longing for a replay of the remarkable vision. She realized that there would come a time when she would think back on this moment and believe she had imagined it. The thought saddened her.

Then, unexpectedly, the man himself rose out of the sea, shaking his hair free of water. Perro, normally, friendly only with those he knew, galloped down the beach and jumped up at him in a frenzy of companionship.

Even from where she stood, the man on the beach seemed extraordinarily tall—taller than any of the men she recognized from the mine, though there were new ones being hired all the time. He did not look the sort to be a mine worker.

He came up the beach unhurriedly. She saw he was as lean as a whip but well muscled, and of a glorious teak brown color she would never be able to capture in any painting medium. He looked taller than her by several inches, which made her feel for the first time in her life that she was a perfect height. In fact, she thought, were she to stand barefoot as she was now, touching him, her head would just rest in the hollow of his neck, or in the protective curve of his shoulder. Heavy black eyebrows slashed across his forehead and his black wavy hair blew into an unruly tangle in the wind.

Strange, in a land of mustachioed men, he was clean-shaven but wore the long sculptured sideburns popular among the Mexican men. As he approached she saw that he was a mature man, perhaps in his mid-thirties. He was exquisitely handsome, though his features looked as if they'd been carved with an adze rather than a fine sculpture tool. His look was more primitively masculine and mysterious than sophisticated and polished. He wore swim trunks, unlike the Mexicans, who generally wore their *pantalones* or swam naked, if at all. Most of them were so chary of water in this arid region that they never thought of swimming.

Fuerte y formal, she thought, a Mexican expression for a truly macho man. Strong and with dignity. How truly it fit him! This man's overpowering first impression had a dizzying effect on her. She felt faint in his presence. Coming from the exotic, almost mystical scene earlier that had stamped him as one with the sea, he had a hypnotic hold on her. Though she was aware she should never stare openly at a Mexican man, she could not tear her gaze away from his. Their eyes simply met and held with a force so strong it frightened her.

She stood rooted in the sand, fending her shining hair partially away from her face with one upflung arm gazing directly at him. Even with her glasses hopelessly fogged and held in her other hand so tightly as to warp the frames, she could still see as he passed that his eyes were as gray and stormy as a *borrasca*.

He made as though to pass by her with Perro gamboling about his feet, but stopped instead directly in front of her. She knew she ought to come out of the paralysis and turn away to prevent this outrageous moment by Mexican standards, but she didn't. He stared intently into her eyes with a beautiful arrogance that matched everything else about him. Her heart pounded, her breath was short and her lips parted as if she would speak. Finally some inner instinct marshaled her good senses and she stepped back, breaking the moment.

He passed by then, so closely that his warm breath brushed her cheek and the smell of him— the sea's salt on his body—enveloped her. He had produced an alchemic explosion in her that aroused and thrilled her to the center of her being, leaving her breathless. She watched, weak and stunned, as he strode away up the beach, climbing the bluff to disappear from sight.

Helen finally drew her breath in one long painful shudder. Never in her twenty-five years had she been so physically and emotionally affected by anything or anyone. The past half hour had seemed like a dream—intense, unforgettable, timeless. Everything about the mysterious man had left an indelible impression on her. She felt so full of his memory that she could not mourn his departure.

As her composure slowly returned, she was left with the incredible realization that here was a man she could almost instantaneously choose to follow into the salt mines, the mountains or one of the mud huts where many families lived out generations of lives. It was a moving discovery for someone who had never been in love and had little knowledge of passion. She felt that if he had pulled her to him she would have welcomed him and responded with ardor.

Who *was* he? A vacationer, a passerby on his way to Cabo San Lucas, Scammon's Lagoon or some other point on the peninsula? No Mexican Indian from the mines had that royalty of bearing. But why torment herself with thoughts of him anyway, she chided herself. After all, he was gone. She realized with some measure of sadness that she would never see him again.

Quickly she picked up her watercolor pad and saw that the painting she had begun was ideal for the inspiration she was now compelled to record. She had already caught some of those shining glass-green breaker curls, and the dolphins were so etched in her mind that they flowed quickly through the painting in deft brush strokes. The man swimmer seemed to leap silhouetted from her brush exactly as she had seen him with the sea creatures. Dreamlike as it was, she felt she was capturing the whole feeling of the experience, the whole enchanted scene. She knew what the title must be: *The Master of the Dolphins*.

When at last she put down her brush, it was too dark to do her signature. She packed the pad in its slot in the paint-box cover and loaded her equipment for the hike back to the company house.

Surprisingly enough, Perro hadn't really deserted her. He was waiting for her in the sand near the bluff.

"Good dog!" she said, which he understood only by the approval in her voice. She put down the big box and scratched his ears. "*Bueno*, Perro!" she repeated in Spanish. He licked her salty hand before preceding her up the cragged steps of the cliff to the rough path to the road.

This might well be her last painting at Punta Temereria, she realized. A week from today she would be back in Garnet Beach, getting ready to begin her classes at the high school the following Tuesday, the day after Labor Day.

At least she wouldn't have to go back to the Blue Chip Grocery. Hallelujah! Deposited to her account at the bank in Garnet Beach was every single salary check for the summer, and it added up to a beautiful sum! Ron had really proved his potential at last and become the brother she had always wanted and thought never to have. How proud their father would be when he realized the full extent of Ron's accomplishments in business. At last he was hardworking, responsible, decent. Dad had always doted on Ron and been so disappointed when Ron seemed headed for trouble, so disheartened at the lack of any word from him. Helen's reports about Ron's success this summer would do him more good than a clinic full of doctors and medical miracles.

She would tell their father that she had constantly offered to do more to deserve her fabulous salary but Ron had told her to stick to the somewhat routine office job, keep things running smoothly and put the unfortunate dead man's files in order. Creating order from her predecessor's chaos was a fair challenge in itself and did pay for her keep, he insisted. Besides, she accomplished twice what the other man had achieved.

There would be no worries for a long time about making payments to the nursing home or for the part-time housekeeper who saw to their father while she was away at school. He had little idea of how much she disliked the prospect of spending the rest of her life handling figures and running business machines. That was the trouble with having learned a skill too well. Perhaps, if the summer painting sales were more than a fluke, she might even be able eventually to devote her time fully to her real vocation. Though her dad said artists always starved, she dared to hope that someday. . . .

But no, she reminded herself; that could only be a dream. She would never run off to the islands and paint like Gauguin when her father needed so much help and her stepmother required permanent twenty-four-hour nursing care. The accident that had crippled her father and put Mama Jessie in the nursing home six years earlier, just as she was about to graduate from university, had crippled her dreams, too. On the other hand, dad had seen to it that she could take a year of graduate school and turn the undergraduate minor she hated into the mainstay of the family. If he had not managed that, they would all be worse off than they were.

This summer Ron had shown he was finally ready to accept some of the financial responsibility for their parents. He had chucked in six hundred dollars toward Mama Jessie's expenses in June, when Helen first flew down to Punta Temereria, again in July and again just this week. He had done it all three times without being asked—and in spite of the fact that he still wouldn't call Jessie ''Mama.''

Helen understood Ron's hang-up about their stepmother. He had been a big boy when their first adoptive mother—the mother he had accepted as his own—died unexpectedly. But he had never accepted Mama Jessie as the former's replacement. Helen, so much younger and missing her mother so terribly, had been grateful for Mama Jessie and had grown to love her deeply.

If Ron would just stick to this career position there was no telling how high he might climb. As she walked back to the company house Helen thought, *I must have a talk with him soon, perhaps tonight.*

One or two little things needed to be brought to his attention. He had to conquer the bad attitude he still had toward all authority figures. Perhaps both of them had absorbed some of their father's rugged individualism. Dad had always hated working for anyone but himself; he never liked tugging the forelock. Nevertheless, the way Ron talked down his employer in front of the Mexican help was bound to cause him trouble.

"You can bet that wealthy mine owner jets around the world on the sweat of his workers. *He* doesn't work; *he* just rakes in the pesos while we poor devils do the dirty work. He's busy sipping champagne in Rio, Mexico City, Paris, London or Tokyo."

"Shh! Ron, you know Guadalupe understands English," Helen had warned repeatedly.

"Who cares?"

"The mines couldn't have been organized and expanded so greatly without real know-how at the top," she'd pointed out; but Ron had set his chin at that and jeered.

She must speak to him more seriously about that kind of thing, she reminded herself now. He couldn't continue to talk openly in front of the Mexicans that way without jeopardizing his own position. Ron should resign if he had real reason to believe the owner was exploiting his help. If there was something he could learn from San Roque, then he should learn and work. Loyalty had to go hand in hand with all the effort put into the job or Ron could lose every gain he had made. She must make her brother see that in spite of his faults, the owner had definitely managed to inspire fanatic loyalty in everyone else at Punta Temereria.

El señor was obviously accustomed to acquiescence. Any hint of opposition obviously infuriated him, as the arrogant memos to his temporary female office manager at Temereria had certainly indicated.

Helen's opinion of the absentee employer was essentially neutral. She had curbed her own impulse to agree with Ron on occasion just on the basis of those irritatingly dictatorial memorandums. He could be rash at times; best to keep his calm and forget such men as el señor existed. She would soon be gone anyway.

She walked down the *corredor*, the open outside room that formed a shady barrier between the heat of outdoors and the cool interior of the house. Then she sauntered into the big room, the *sala grande*, and stopped short.

They had visitors.

Ron, in his best linen suit, stood facing her, drink in hand. A little smile nervously flickered around his mouth, over which drooped a golden blond mustache. "Here's Helen now!" he said with excessive enthusiasm, taking a quick, almost convulsive sip of his drink.

The three other men in the room rose and faced Helen courteously. Total attentiveness to a woman in a social situation was part of Mexican etiquette.

Helen felt self-conscious as she stood towering over the oldest of the three Mexican men by at least three inches even in her flat huarache sandals. He was probably no more than five feet seven. The youngest of the three wore a black mustache in the style of Ron's, so popular with most of the men down here on the peninsula. With him she would be at least eye to eye in her heels. The third man lounged against the mantel of the fireplace.

When her golden eyes met his gray ones, she almost fainted. He was the man with the dolphins, the man on the beach. He gave no indication at all of recognition, but her pulse quickened just from his mere presence in the room.

"We were beginning to be concerned about you," Ron said lightly, "but I told them my owl-eyed sis was too tall and too tough for *bandidos* to tangle with. Besides, all the *peones* think her red hair makes her a witch, and they leave witches alone."

Helen could not help the quick glance she flashed at the dolphin man. Would he give some indication of agreement that she looked like the red-haired witch Ron described?

He turned on Ron with an instant gesture of censure that said plainly, "How dare you!" and she saw Ron wilt into silence.

"Didn't Guadalupe tell you where I'd gone?" She set down her paraphernalia self-consciously. Paint-spattered and showing the effects of the sea and sun, she knew she must have cast a rather peculiar first impression on the visitors. She didn't look the height of chic!

Gravely she waited to be properly introduced, though she was quite sure she knew the identity of the man leaning against the mantel, the same man she had seen on the beach. He had to be Luis San Roque Q., whose signature she had filed a thousand times this summer; the owner of San Roque Enterprises. El señor. She should have known.

She also should have guessed that the powerful signature crossing her desk all summer could only reflect part of the man. It had given no hint of his overwhelming masculine appeal—or his unpredictability. It was perhaps fitting that he should arrive at Punta Temereria one week early, when least expected. After all, he was the last thing she had expected to see rising from the ocean this afternoon.

Her face flamed as she remembered the beach and how he had assessed her without the false barriers of drawing-room convention. Then she paled at the memory of how she had silently responded to him. Her pulse had quickened, her senses opening in alertness, her breathing growing unsteady. She hadn't disguised her attraction then and even now she could not hide it.

She braced herself to face the disturbing situation. . . .

CHAPTER TWO

"Senorita Yolanda Betancourt Ibanez," Ron said in his excellent Spanish, "my sister, Helen Forster."

Only then did Helen see a young woman seated on the sofa. She hadn't noticed her because she was tiny, hidden in the big pillows, and Helen herself had come into the room from behind the couch.

The visitor was incredibly beautiful, curled up on the couch as only small women can curl and tall women cannot. Her slim legs were elegantly clad in the sheerest of stockings and her feet were shod in strappy heeled sandals, an utterly impractical choice in this far reach of the Sonoran desert. Her complexion had been touched by only as much sun as she had allowed to produce the shade of a fresh rose petal in her cheeks. A drift of black curls matched her velvet-dark eyes.

Here was a woman any artist would beg to paint, particularly if he specialized in portraying beauties. Helen appreciated the woman's perfection and felt dowdy beside it. In the midst of Mexico's stark reality, Yolanda Betancourt was unreal. She belonged in a great salon, on a marble staircase under crystal chandeliers. Helen found Yolanda's glorious grooming such a contrast to her own utterly disastrous hodgepodge of ragged coverings that she let her sense of humor relax her and her firm sense of self-worth remind her she couldn't be expected to compete.

Yolanda acknowledged the introduction by briefly shutting her purple-shadowed eyes. She lifted a hand tipped with vivid inch-long nails to her lips and inhaled on a cigarette.

"Her father, Paolo Betancourt, our company attorney..." Ron continued.

Helen soberly acknowledged the older of the two men with full Mexican etiquette.

"Felipe Estrada, business manager of San Roque Enterprises...."

She extended her hand cordially to the business manager, saying warmly, "We've got to know each other on paper rather well this summer, haven't we, Don Felipe?"

"And the owner, our employer and boss, Señor Luis San Roque Quintana."

Did he recognize her as the woman on the beach, with her hair pinned up sedately and her glasses on her nose, dressed inelegantly in her old shirt and pants? There was no sign that he did.

She didn't extend her hand. He only lowered his head for the briefest acknowledgment of the introduction, then pierced her with the most evaluating of gazes. Her heart beat strongly as he took her measure for the second time that day... and she took his.

Ron had faded to a curiously subordinate role as San Roque took over the duties of host. "A drink for you, Miss Forster?" he offered in beautiful English.

"Yes. Bourbon and water, please." She took one of the *limons* that Guadalupe provided and squeezed the sweet green citrus into her drink.

"Reynaldo says you return Friday of this week to San Diego County in California?"

"Yes. I'm sorry to go. It's been a beautiful summer," Helen politely returned in correct Spanish, since it was the language of their employer and the country in which they worked.

"Here?" Yolanda Betancourt laughed at Helen's words.

Helen only smiled. "I'm something of a solitary, Miss Betancourt. Sun and sky, rocks and water, suit me. And I've enjoyed the challenge of an interesting job at an excellent salary, along with the opportunity to paint."

"What is there to paint?" Yolanda asked curiously. "There are no trees or flowers. Everything is stark and ugly here."

"This land has its own beauty. Saguaro, iron-wood, yucca and paloverde; there are so many desert plants if you know what to look for. Staghorn cactus, pincushions, hedgehogs, ocotillo, beaver tail, fishhooks—all cactus, but I don't know the Spanish names for most of them."

"I mean trees and flowers. Those you name are even scarce here. The only place where there is less vegetation to be seen in Mexico is the Viz-caino desert!"

"Scarcity makes even the smallest plant pre-cious," Helen said serenely. She put her drink down. "While you all enjoy Ron's inexhaustible store of funny stories, I'll go help Guadalupe with Sunday dinner and change into something a little more appropriate." She looked with admiration at Yolanda's beautiful ivory silk dress.

"My dear, there is no need to change on our account," Yolanda assured her.

"It's on my account. I'm sand to the bone and know I look a disgrace. I'll be more com-fortable if I look respectable for my employer and his guests."

Señor San Roque raised a dark slash of an eyebrow. "Why is it necessary for you to assist Guadalupe? She has been cook here for more than a decade."

Ron laughed self-consciously. "Well, ah,

Helen's not much for Mexican food. It's her hobby, keeping her hand in at preparing American food on her free time. I told her it wasn't necessary.''

Helen's smile became a little stiff. Far from telling her American food wasn't necessary, Ron insisted on ''decent'' food over the weekends when she was free. She personally preferred Guadalupe's marvelous skills and had learned a whole new cuisine from her during the summer.

Ron had always been fussy about food. She remembered how when she was little he could drive Mama Jessie right up the wall demanding what the mother she could not remember had cooked for him. Her father had excused Ron then as always by reminding Jessie that he was adopted as an older child and had been through a lot before coming to the Forster household.

''The poor kid went through more than you or I could ever imagine before Helen and I adopted him. We wanted a baby, but he looked so pathetic, poor little kid. Then three years later we got little Helen from the same agency; she was just an infant. But you know kids— even if they're brother and sister by birth they can be as different as night and day. Where Ronnie's concerned, he's had reason to be a little difficult. He just needs all the love we can give him.''

That meant that Mama Jessie had to indulge Ron. This summer, what with his being so terrific, Helen had been glad to cater to her brother's fussy taste.

"Perhaps Señor San Roque and his colleagues would prefer Guadalupe's choice?" she asked calmly.

"Not at all," San Roque said. "Whatever has been planned. We realize we have arrived a week early. Yolanda wished to make a trip to Ensenada, so we changed our itinerary. Besides, it will be interesting for Yolanda to see how *norteamericanos* eat."

Helen, unconsciously graceful, casually gathered up her equipment and her paint rags and towels and carried the lot to her room, where Guadalupe obligingly brought water and a basin for bathing away the salt and sand. She changed into a white silk blouse and her one good silk wraparound skirt, which did not begin to compare with the magnificence of Yolanda's attire but did reveal her lovely figure in an understated fashion. She brushed her hair, twisted it back into a fat chignon, polished her glasses and slipped into her highest-heeled sandals. She could never be tiny like Yolanda, so she would be tall and proud of it.

In the kitchen, Guadalupe, who had herself picked up a number of Helen's own culinary secrets, welcomed her with a broad smile. The roast beef smelled delectable, and Guadalupe was ready with the broccoli and ingredients for the creamy golden broccoli sauce that had been Mama Jessie's family recipe. They unmolded the salad of deviled eggs and gelatin that Helen had prepared early in the morning and centered it on a salver. Guadalupe had made rice, as well, white and fluffy in the big iron pot.

"I made flan for el señor," Guadalupe told her.

"And *buñuelos* for me!" Helen felt light-headed, as though she were about to inherit the earth.

"For el señor," Guadalupe corrected calmly.

"Any man who likes *buñuelos* and flan can't be all bad," Helen commented.

"*¿Por favor?*" Guadalupe looked scandalized.

"It's an American expression that I suppose doesn't translate at all well," Helen apologized. "It means I approve of his sweet tooth. Did that translate right?"

"*¡Ah! ¡Sí!* El señor very good for a boss!" Guadalupe used the word *patrón*, which had a much more worshipful meaning in Spanish than any of the other words for employer might convey.

"I'll leave the rest of dinner and the details of the dining room to you, Guadalupe. Everything looks as though you have it well under control,'' Helen added, then went to join the others.

The table looked exactly right with San Roque at its head; he belonged at the head of any table. Ron sat at the foot of the table, a subordinate seat to the one he had held all summer. Nevertheless he looked quite dashing, as Helen had thought proudly earlier, and except for his understandable nervousness he held up his part of dinner conversation beautifully.

Ron had always been a great talker. She remembered hearing her father tell Mama Jessie that Ron had been talking a blue streak six months after being adopted by him and his first wife, the Helen Forster for whom Helen herself had been named. When he had first come from the agency, an abused child, he had been militantly silent. Only when he grew sure of himself did he become loquacious. He was sure of himself now, she thought.

Helen herself was more than usually quiet. She hardly said a word. The powerful attraction she had felt for San Roque persisted to such a degree that it silenced her. She felt ill at ease in the company of the elegant Yolanda Betancourt and overcome with the same ridiculous attack of shyness she had felt when her father introduced her to her favorite movie star at the Del Mar racetrack the summer she was twelve.

Whenever she glanced at San Roque she couldn't help recalling the sight of his lean body silhouetted in the crystal light of the great breakers, tussling with the giant dolphins. She was struck again by his magnetic appeal and her pulse thudded alarmingly.

She knew she was vulnerable and deplorably naive around men. That naiveté could not be exposed.

She had always felt so much responsibility to make good, to earn her father's pride, that she had single-mindedly devoted herself to her studies in high school. Not that she had too much chance to be popular. A girl who is as tall as the tallest boy, even taller, has a built-in problem in adolescence, and Ron had never let her forget it with his teasing.

Three refugee Vietnamese students had won the class honors that year, but Helen had earned a modest scholarship to college and was determined to make her family particularly proud of her when she graduated from university. By then university attendance had meant a part-time job in addition to studying and keeping up the scholarship. She'd had little time to date and felt guilty when she relaxed for even a moment. That stiffness had not endeared her to the less serious college boys, and the serious ones had seemed somewhat in awe of her. Yet she had yearned a great deal, she acknowledged, for some magnificently princely boy to see the tender heart behind the shy exterior.

This man, San Roque, was such a prince; but he was, of course, so far removed from her world as to be almost a...a holograph. Yet solidly he sat there reigning at the table, the king of everything he surveyed, and certainly already the property—if such a man could ever be such—of the absolutely beautiful princess, the regal Señorita Betancourt.

Only once did Helen let her eyes meet San Roque's, and when that happened their gazes held again and the tension between them was almost a live electric charge.

Throughout dinner he carried the conversation. "Do you play chess?" he asked Ron. "I see you have a game set up in the lounge. After dinner perhaps, a challenge?"

"Sure thing!" Ron answered, and inwardly Helen cringed.

"You use the King's Indian defense, I notice," San Roque continued.

Ron looked at him blankly, but before Helen could come to his aid he brightened. "Oh, I thought you were talking about the onyx set on the game table. But if you mean Helen's little plastic toy set by the window—she plays around with it and some ham radioman. Isn't he an old crippled guy in Sausalito, Owl?" he asked nervously, breaking the *buñuelo* into little piles on his plate.

San Roque turned his attention to Helen.

"It's a very good fighting defense," Helen said carefully, wishing Ron would eat his flan and return from his unbecoming fidgeting at the table.

"I don't have much time to waste playing with her; that's why she carries on with this circuit operator," Ron explained, making her running tournament with the radioman seem like a childish game. "She's been bugging him to get her set up with another player. She says she needs more challenge to improve her game."

Helen kept silent. It was true that was what she had told Ron. Their father had taught the two of them to play chess as children, but even growing up she had been able to beat Ron easily, and he would not play with her, only with their father, who allowed him to win in a way he had never allowed Helen to do. Perhaps she was not a chess master, but Ron was a poor player, though she did not like to say so even to herself because it seemed somehow disloyal. He had always been a little jealous of her intelligence, expertise and stability because while dad loved Ron devotedly he tended to hold these characteristics up to him. "You could learn from your sister," dad had said on occasion, much to Helen's chagrin.

"Perhaps," San Roque observed, "I should challenge you, Miss Forster?"

Ron looked upset, and Helen recognized the warning he flashed at her. He was afraid her considerable skill at chess might antagonize his employer and possibly hurt his own position with the company. She smiled reassuringly at her brother and put San Roque off.

"You play a game of chess with our visitor, Ron," she suggested. "I need to get the last of my paintings ready for you to take with you tomorrow when you fly up to San Diego."

"You'll overload the plane with all that junk!" Ron responded deprecatingly but with a sigh of relief that she hadn't risked the chess challenge.

"Just a couple more watercolors," Helen assured him.

"Why don't you show our visitors some of your stuff? It isn't bad for an amateur."

Ron proceeded to explain Helen's recent artistic success. "Someone came by when she had been here a couple weeks and told her she had talent. He suggested she send stuff to him up in San Diego and said he would try to peddle it. Darned if she didn't sell a couple."

"Which takes her out of the ranks of 'amateur,'" San Roque corrected. "I would like to see your work," he said, looking at her steadily with his sea-gray eyes.

"I'm so sorry. They're all crated, ready to send north."

"What about the one you did this afternoon?" he persisted.

"Not finished," she said, her voice firm. She would just as soon strip naked in front of the whole group as reveal the passion with which she had painted that picture. There really were final touches to make on it—such as her signature. She could quickly tuck the painting in with the others and it would go off with Ron in the morning, safe from what she surmised were San Roque's too perceptive eyes.

"Where do you send your artwork?" Yolanda asked.

"Chamartin Galleries. San Diego and Laguna Beach."

"Chamartin?" Yolanda's eyebrows shot up. "Well! Your Punta Temereria bookkeeper must really have some talent, Luis. . . ."

"You know the gallery?" Ron asked, surprised.

"But of course! He handles some of the best artists of your western area of the United States. One of his clients had a retrospective in Mexico City recently and has been quite the social rage. I met Mr. Chamartin when he came for the exhibition."

"I'm only a beginner, a Sunday painter," Helen demurred.

"That's right!" Ron laughed. "The rest of the week she's a working fool in that mine office. Never saw anyone make order out of chaos so fast. She's been worth every cent the company paid her, I guarantee you."

"Perhaps we might persuade Miss Forster to remain at her post here," San Roque suggested, "if it is made worth her while?"

"Helen's leaving," Ron said flatly. "She's got my dad to look after. And her school contract. In fact, Helen, there's no reason why you shouldn't pack up tonight and go with me in the morning. See Chamartin yourself about your paintings. Take a few days to rest up before you have to face packs of howling adolescents."

"You know I can't do that, Ron," she responded. "There's the payroll to get out, and the rest of the filing. I have everything organized right through Friday and I wouldn't want anyone else to come in and find any loose strings."

"I think you ought to have at least a week of some sort of vacation," Ron persisted.

"I've 'vacationed' all summer. Just the change of scenery and the different routine made it a vacation. I've had plenty of free time. I'm quite ready to go home, but not until I've given value for value received and worked out my contract here."

"But the house here is crowded. Señor San Roque could use your room," Ron argued.

San Roque made a quick end to the possibility of an early departure date. "Miss Forster has been paid through Friday. I will see her job here completed before she leaves, even if she has to work both Saturday and Sunday following. She would, of course, be compensated in a manner that would not displease her, if that should be necessary. When you return we can discuss any change in her departure date. You do intend to get back by Wednesday, Ronald?"

"Wednesday noon, if the contracts from Western Salt Company in Chula Vista come through," Ron said, subsiding somewhat sullenly.

"Ah, yes," San Roque replied thoughtfully. "I had almost forgotten those. Then we must do without your company tomorrow and Tuesday? Very well. Wednesday we can do our business. In the meantime, Felipe, Paolo and I can manage and we will see to Cedros. Now for that chess game, Miss Forster. I have a desire to see how you use the King's Indian defense against a player other than your brother or a radio operator from...Sausalito, is it?"

"But I—" Helen saw that Ron was preoccupied with Yolanda and her father. He had totally forgotten that she might win and jeopardize his job. Perversely, she wanted to play chess with San Roque no matter how nervous it made her brother.

She went to the table with the onyx chessmen, but San Roque, at her side, took her by the elbow and led her to the small table with her own tournament chess set—the one Ron persisted in calling a "plastic toy" as though the game could be played professionally only on the expensive decorative board. His hand on her arm excited her and her flushed cheeks and accelerating pulse rate threatened to betray her. Surely he must be aware of how she was reacting—almost as a teenager would with a sudden and devastating crush; only this was more disconcerting and painful than any adolescent yearning had ever been. She was momentarily bewildered by her own galvanic reaction to him, until his rich voice brought her to her senses.

"I would prefer to continue the game from this point, in order that you may practice your use of the Indian defense, Miss Forster, as I see you have been setting the board for that series of plays."

She flashed him a look of surprise, for it was perfectly true. He must be a really dedicated player, she decided, to recognize it without the book she needed. She'd had so little time for dating that the chess games she played with her father had been a rare source of recreation. In fact the game had taken up her free Friday nights when she took her father to his chess club at the recreation center. She couldn't help developing an enthusiasm for the game from her frequent exposure to it.

The match went on longer than she had expected. San Roque was a killing opponent.

"You should not have left your queen at home," he reproved her at last. "There is now no defense left you. Rook to Bishop Eight and check. No matter how you move, I have won King and Pawn."

Helen studied the board soberly. "So you have," she said gracefully. "You've finessed on every side. There's nothing for me to do but resign."

"I am pleased to see you recognize your master," he said, rising as she did from the table.

She instantly froze. "I recognize a *chess* master, not *my* master, *señor*," she corrected him. "It is obvious that you are a more experienced player than I. But circumstances can change, and I do not acknowledge you or any man to be my master."

He looked at her with eyes that said more than she wanted to hear; but before he could devastate her with an unchallengeable response, Ron stepped in, laughing in the self-conscious way he had assumed that evening. "My sister's ever the schoolmarm putting us in our place. Look, didn't you want to finish or fix up some paintings for me, Helen?''

''That's right, I did. You'll all excuse me? I go to the mining office at dawn, where it's cool enough to get in a few good hours before the day officially begins. It means I retire early at night.''

Ron followed her down the hall to her room. ''I want to talk to you before I take off tomorrow morning.''

''Come on in,'' she said, setting the watercolor box out.

''There's no sense in your being here alone the next few days and riling up San Roque,'' he warned.

''I'm sorry. I suppose I did get rather on my soap box. I didn't mean to.''

''You know how the men are down here,'' Ron continued. ''He's the kingpin of all he surveys, so watch your step, speak softly and everything will be all right. I've done nothing but sing your praises.''

''You didn't have to sing my praises. My work has spoken for itself.''

''I know that, but go easy now. You've earned your salary fair and square.''

''Of course I have,'' Helen responded. ''What are you trying to do—scare me into thinking I could get fired in my last week?''

"No, not that. Just take it easy," he persisted.

"Stop being so nervous. You've run yourself ragged all over the peninsula—Guerrero Negro, El Arco, Pozo Aleman and back—all the time. He couldn't ask for more from you, so you haven't anything to worry about, either," she assured him.

"I just wanted you to know you've done a terrific job. We can be a mutual admiration society."

"Right. And he should have hired men to assist you."

"Don't worry about it." Ron shrugged off her remark.

"I can't help it, considering the number of men he hires everywhere else. Can't the new men at Pozo Aleman and El Arco do their own jobs after three months at it? You shouldn't have to do so much of their work after all this time!"

"Let it lie," he told her.

"I could have helped you more all summer if you'd let me," she said a little crossly.

"Women can't run all over the place unaccompanied down here. You've done more than the fellow before you, and you know it. But that's not what I want to talk about right now. I—well, here." He handed her a fat sealed envelope.

"What's this?" Helen weighed it in her hand.

"You know how it is with planes. They sometimes go down with all hands and that sort of thing. What I want is for you not to open this unless something like that happens. Just put this envelope with your passport and your other papers; if there's an emergency, then open it pronto."

"For heaven's sake!" she protested. "Do you really feel some kind of crazy premonition about this trip?"

"Oh—not a premonition exactly. Just call it 'conscience insurance.'" Ron sounded very uncomfortable and she found his concern incredibly touching. She had never seen this side of him before.

"I never helped out with dad much, as you know. And as for Jess—well, she's not our responsibility and there was insurance from the accident."

"Ron, the insurance hasn't been half enough for years, and you know it!"

"All right, but there are government arrangements. You don't have to kill yourself when she's not any real relation. If it comes to that, neither one...." He stopped when he saw the furious objection that was about to erupt from her. "Anyway," he continued smoothly, "I know you don't have much cash since you've been having your salary sent right to the bank.

If there's a—you know—emergency, you'll have this. Hey, don't look so alarmed! When I get back Wednesday, or whenever, you can give me back this envelope unopened. Then I'll double the cash inside when you go home. My contribution to the cause. Just give me the privilege of tearing up my note unread if I'm not dead or involved in a disaster.''

"All right," Helen agreed hesitantly. "But you sound so serious!"

"Right now I have this kind of unreasonable fear of being suspended more than a foot off the ground. That's all it is. Let it lie.''

Poor Ron! He seemed to have so many fears, Helen realized. They had never discussed his early childhood and for all she knew it lay tightly forgotten at the back of his memory, though it seemed often to affect his adult behavior. She would have comforted him if she had known how, but Ron had always gone into a roaring panic when anyone tried to reach him.

"Promise you won't open the envelope unless it's a bona fide, number-one emergency?" he pressed her.

"I promise," she said, laughing. "And you promise to deliver my paintings whether the plane crashes or not?"

"Shake on it.''

"Let me slip this last one in with the others and my parcels are ready," she told him.

''Put them outside the door and the houseman will see to loading them on the plane
tonight. I have to get back to the mucky-mucks.
G'night, sis.''

He was gone, leaving her with the envelope
and a feeling of foreboding she didn't understand. Somehow she knew he hadn't expressed
his real reason for coming into her room to talk
with her.

CHAPTER THREE

RON WAS GONE by the time Helen was up and walking to the mine office in the early dawn. She heard the plane wing north with him, accompanied by the beauteous Yolanda, the contracts for the salt company in Chula Vista and the paintings for Chamartin. By the time Helen could talk to Chamartin on Saturday she would know if anything might come of her latest painting efforts or if the summer's first sales had been flukes.

Already she regretted so hastily sending *The Master of the Dolphins* to Chamartin. What if he sold it? She must write a note this very morning and tell him not to sell it, though it was an unlikely sale anyway. Paintings did not sell with the snap of a finger and she would manage to get it back over the weekend; but just to be safe—or, as the Mexicans said, *"Por si las moscas"*—she would send a note and have it taken off the market.

She relived the emotions that had gripped her as she painted that picture. They were more

poignant to her now than when she had experienced them—as wine becomes more mellow
with time. She wished illogically that she had
kept the painting with her as an emotional
solace; at the same time she was glad it had gone
with the others. For the time being it was out of
the reach of inquiring, too perceptive eyes. But
once the painting was returned, she would keep
it as a reminder of this summer for as long as
she lived. She could not sell an experience that
held so much emotional value for her. No
stranger could appreciate the painting as she
did. There was an innocent passion evoked in
the scene that was too intimate to be displayed;
a depth of fantasy and delight that was hers
alone to savor. She feared being ridiculed for
the emotions she had experienced, and she
would not above all relinquish that beautiful
moment in time.

Remembering Ron's warnings to "go easy"
with the owners, she felt a crazy desire to laugh.
Never mind her "riling" San Roque; he had her
plenty riled himself. She could hardly think
straight when he was in the room with her; the
masculine appeal he exuded literally frightened
her in her inexperience and made her lash out to
prove she was not really affected.

Ron's warnings were well meant, though mo-
tivated, she realized with amusement, by his
concerns for his own career. Her job would last

only through Friday, while his could go on to something big, if her quick evaluation of the scope of the owner's sphere of influence was correct. It was easy to see Ron would not want to muff an opportunity to hold an important position one day.

Helen's musings were sporadic as she worked to get the weekly payroll out. She had been at work approximately an hour when the three men arrived.

"We did not manage to get to the office quite as early as you, Miss Forster, for we wanted to see Yolanda off at Guerrero Negro strip."

Helen looked covertly at San Roque. Was he engaged to Yolanda Betancourt, or close to an announcement of one? The woman was so beautiful she could probably make any man love her. How could Don Luis not succumb to her appeal? Helen felt a strange ache in her throat as she busied herself, not wanting to look at him anymore, for he might see an impossible dream in her own eyes.

"We will not disturb you greatly," Estrada promised. "We will be inspecting operations here; also at Pozo Aleman, Guerrero Negro, El Arco and Isla de Cedros." He removed some of the big ledgers. "A matter of personnel requires we take these books. You might work on those Cedros."

"Eugenio Ochoa has the Cedros books on the island, Don Felipe," she said.

"Well, then, we will see to them on Wednesday. You should have sufficient to keep you occupied with the Punta Temereria accounts payable and bills of lading."

"Certainly, if that's what you wish. You'll be needing these ledgers, too. And one Ron has in his office. I'll get it."

After the three men had taken the materials and left, Helen worked steadily until lunchtime.

Ron's files were in a terrible jumble, as though he had stood and randomly thrown everything in the office into the drawers. Loving irritation accompanied her efforts. Such a gross exhibit of poor business practice was not very sensible of him. Good thing she had found it before the three men had.

She was still trying to make sense of his records when she saw it was time to get out of the heat and take the twelve-to-two afternoon siesta.

She walked back to the company house and, much to her surprise, found the three men in the main lounge, papers spread everywhere.

They were intensely absorbed in their work, but San Roque was aware that she had entered. He paced back and forth, a sheaf of papers in his hand, then halted. His storm-gray gaze met hers, piercingly cold and preoccupied. Still, the mere eye contact staggered her sense of balance. Mentally she steadied herself, meeting his look with open question, a vulnerable willingness to accept and fulfill whatever commands he might voice, but he remained silent. Obviously they were in the midst of work that precluded social graces or need of her services. She nodded and went to the kitchen.

"When did they ask for *comida*, Guadalupe?"

"They do not take the midday meal here, Señorita Helena. They say they fly to El Arco and will dine there. There is only you, but it is ready and hot."

She sat alone at the long table in the dining room and ate. Looking out the window, she could see the coast stretch away south to infinity, unbroken except for diminishing pyramids of salt. She wondered if she would ever see this coast again after Friday. She loved the lonely arid desert of the Vizcaino. She had never felt alone until today, even with Guadalupe waddling back and forth and the three men working silently in the *sala grande*.

San Roque and Betancourt came into the dining room with unsmiling faces. "We are leaving for El Arco," Betancourt said abruptly.

It's the heat, she thought, wondering why San Roque and the others seemed almost hostile this morning. Had she really antagonized him the night before?

They're used to air-conditioned hotels in metropolitan centers. They work in luxury fortieth-floor offices with no inconveniences. This unremitting desert at the back of the world must be hard on everyone who isn't used to it, she told herself.

"Here are the payroll books for Guerrero Negro. The following personnel are to be eliminated." Betancourt handed her a list.

Helen took the paper and examined it with shock. Aguilar, Alman, Almanza, Adargas, Aquito, Andreas—the list went on interminably.

"So many? All to be terminated? With how much notice, Señor Betancourt?"

"No notice. They are not to be on the payroll this week." He looked obliquely at San Roque, who remained silent and aloof. "Their final pay was last Friday," he said.

"No termination notice? What about—"

"Simply prepare termination records to clear the books."

She stared at him in astonishment and incomprehension. In the midst of hiring, all this firing! She opened her mouth to ask a question, but he anticipated her.

"This matter need not concern you. Your only concern is that the men are no longer employed by San Roque Enterprises."

She took the record with a troubled heart, and Betancourt followed San Roque out of the room without further word.

Baca, Bacuita, Baiez, Baños, Barbosa—she knew none of the faces to put with the names, and for this only she was thankful. The poverty of the Mexican population here was appalling. Only the mine jobs kept them from starving or going back into the stark mountains of the interior, where for generations they had led a primitive, impoverished life and had little or no concept of any other world. Ron couldn't know of this, for he would have notified the men to be terminated before last Friday. They must have been told this morning when they came to work in Guerrero Negro, and she couldn't help imagining their uncomprehending despair, greater by far than her own confusion as to why this was happening.

It simply didn't make sense to be terminating so many workers. Here, and at Guerrero Negro, the mines had put out a call for more and still more men. Nevertheless she was left with no one to question and no recourse except to follow orders.

THAT NIGHT the men returned late from El Arco, after she had retired. Early Tuesday morning Betancourt—again acting for San Roque, who made no appearance—gave Helen more names of personnel to be expunged from the operation at El Arco. She shuddered with the impact of knowing what the mine layoffs would mean to the entire peninsula. So many people depended on its lifeline. How could such men as San Roque, Betancourt and Estrada, in their silk custom-tailored clothing, come here and broadcast such devastation!

The list of terminations was even longer when the three readied the record from Pozo Aleman. More than a hundred families would suffer. The new list on the office desk staggered her.

This time San Roque delivered the orders, watching her with narrowed eyes. "In the morning be ready to fly across to Isla de Cedros."

"I've never been over to the island. You do realize I've had no direct responsibility there and am to leave here on Friday?"

"I am aware of those facts. You will go on the regular daily plane. It departs from Guerrero Negro at seven o'clock in the morning. You are aware, of course, that the women on Cedros never wear trousers."

Her cheeks flamed. She had on slim white pants, her high sandals and a cool cotton overshirt. "Of course, Señor San Roque." She added quietly, "I know that customs on the island would mean wearing a skirt if I went there."

The tension of the evening was more pronounced than it had been during the day; in the frenzy of slashing workers from the payroll the men had assumed a demeanor of general hostility. Helen knew she should keep her mouth closed and simply do her job, but she determined that on the way to Cedros she would find the opportunity to ask San Roque point-blank what was going on. She had a terrible need to understand why and how he could be so arbitrarily cruel. Her impression of him now was so different from the image she'd had of him on the beach, or even that first evening at dinner. The current between them was as strong as it had ever been—but it was no longer pleasant. Something had happened. What, she could not be sure; but he was a changed man.

In the morning the houseman drove her to Guerrero Negro by herself to catch the regular daily plane to the island. It lifted off on schedule into a sky covered with a blanket of gray clouds. The pilot flew straight out to sea over Scammon's Lagoon, and Helen looked down at the Sarafan Dunes and the little town of Guerrero Negro—the Black Warrior—at the edge of the hostile peninsula to the southwest.

In less than an hour she saw the island, roughly twenty miles long and half as wide. She had heard of the wild goats, the deer, the mountain lions, the springs and forests of cedars, but she wasn't prepared for several villages and a real city. All she had imagined were piles of salt on the coast and a few sheds, as at Punta Temereria. Here below was a real city and two other villages she could see spaced along the coast.

The plane flew low, announcing its arrival. She saw a swarm of red cabs begin the run out to the airfield on the southern tip of the mountainous island.

She was not unaware of the scope of San Roque's interests here. Because Scammon's Lagoon was too shallow to load salt into ocean-going vessels, the salt was lightered out to Cedros, where in huge piles it awaited Japanese and other foreign freighters. There was also a large steel-fabricating plant that had something to do with the other kinds of mines San Roque Enterprises operated. Light industries associated with the mining of salt were handled cottage fashion. She had imagined this to be all there could possibly be in such an isolated spot, but she saw even from the air that she had greatly underestimated the island. A sizable shrimp and fishing fleet as well as pleasure craft were anchored in the harbor. Some of the yachts were from well up the Pacific Coast out of California's Laguna, Balboa and Oxnard marinas.

A sleek company car waited for Helen, quite in contrast to the elderly red cabs. She recognized the name of the driver from company records: Vergel Diaz.

"We don't seem to be going into Cedros City to the mine offices, Vergel."

"No, Señorita Forster," answered the driver. "We go to Casa San Roque."

Helen wasn't surprised to learn there was a company house on the island, but she was astonished at the placement and size of this one. It dominated the mountain high above the city, was surrounded by cedars and was not a rough building like the one at Punta Temereria. This was a real family home, hewn of island stone, part of the land.

"You're sure I'm to report here? Not to the mining offices?"

"Very sure, Señorita Forster. You were to report to Casa San Roque. El señor ordered it personally."

"I didn't realize they had such an ornate company house here!"

Vergel Diaz turned to look at her with quiet amusement ill concealed. "This is not the company house, Señorita Forster. This is the home of el señor."

He helped her out of the car at the stone steps leading up to the great house. She went up to the great carved wooden doors with brass bands and fittings that must have been polished only that morning. A woman who was Guadalupe's twin in appearance greeted her.

"El señor gave orders that you were to make

his home your home until his arrival," she told Helen at once.

"I thought I was to work at the mining office."

"He was very clear. The house was to be at your disposal. Have you had *almuerzo*?"

Helen normally never ate a big late breakfast; she hadn't adopted the Mexican custom of two morning meals and lunch. On the other hand, she had left Punta Temereria early and had time only for some of Guadalupe's whipped chocolate. "I *am* rather hungry, so I'll have whatever you care to bring. Thank you," she responded politely.

While she waited, she looked curiously around the huge room. It was a library—and the contents were hardly those of a provincial home. There were several thousand fine books on the shelves, many in tooled-leather bindings. The majority of the titles were in English or Spanish, but many were in French, and a few in German. A good reader could be kept busy for years just with the English books. On the great polished table she spotted current issues of many magazines she was surprised to see anywhere in rural Baja, much less on this island.

Also on the table was a tournament chess set like her own "plastic toy," well used. One of the classic books on chess rested by the board. The player was one who studied the chess masters, Alekhine, Petroff and Caro-Kann, and practiced their famous offensives and defenses. Thoughtfully she picked up a pawn and looked at it, wondering how she and Ron had come to be pawns in this empire.

She looked into the room next to the library and immediately felt at home. From its window she could see the airport. In the rose garden just outside, an old gardener puttered. A thick goatskin rug was placed invitingly in front of the fireplace, and the sofa was piled with plump cushions. The fire in the grate warmed the chill here on the mountain island.

The housekeeper came into the den with a tray, which she set on the table by the window.

Helen was indeed hungry after the early-morning flight, and she dug into the succulent Mexican food with good appetite. She picked up a book from the table, and it fell open to a marker. As she sipped the hot fragrant coffee she read the marked page. The author, Pablo Neruda, was a Chilean whose name was only barely familiar to her, but the book's owner had evidently been impressed with the sentiments that were carefully underlined.

I still have an unshaken faith in human destiny...that we shall understand each other...move forward together. That is my undying hope.

She was suddenly filled with anger that a man who could underline such words would so ruthlessly destroy the livelihood of so many of his countrymen.

"El señor is in the library if you are finished with your *almuerzo*, Señorita Forster," the housekeeper interrupted her.

In the next room—and he had let her sit here, not knowing? She hadn't even seen his plane fly over the island.

She followed the housekeeper back into the library, and the Mexican woman discreetly disappeared.

San Roque sat behind the big library desk, eyeing her thoughtfully as he toyed with a gold pencil.

"Sit down, Helen," he said, surprising her by speaking perfect English. Except for briefly on Sunday night past he had, with the others, spoken only Spanish.

She sat silently, wondering if she should take her stenographic pad from her shoulder bag, and decided it was best to do so. She poised it on her knee, ready for dictation of duties in Spanish or English.

"You have asked questions about the personnel," he said without preamble. "The payroll was the reason Paolo Betancourt, Felipe Estrada and I flew to Punta Temereria early. We had uncovered a large corruption, and the trail led directly there."

"I don't understand what I can do—"

"This summer," he continued, looking at her closely, "you and your brother seem to have falsified records of four hundred and twenty nonexistent employees at my mining operations in Guerrero Negro, Pozo Aleman and El Arco. The shortage comes to some $263,000 American."

Helen was glad to be sitting in the leather chair, for she probably would have fallen over with the shock. His blunt accusation was delivered in such a mild conversational manner that she could not believe her ears.

"My brother and I . . . ?"

Slowly it sank in. She felt her face drain of all color, and she gasped before she could begin to find her voice. Utterly shocked, she stammered, "Falsified records?"

His own calm voice added to her trauma. "I can assure you, Helen, I will not be robbed by my employees!"

"You are accusing— It's not true! Ron would never—never—"

He came out of the great swivel chair behind the desk and loomed menacingly over her. "Your brother had my confidence and trust. In his position of trust he employed nonexistent people. Evidence is here in front of you to show he collected their salaries in cash and converted those pesos to American dollars with which he has absconded over the border into the United States on one of my own planes!''

"I—I don't believe it," Helen stammered, still in shock.

"Then you are calling me a liar?" His gray eyes flashed dangerously.

"You may be saying what you believe to be a fact, but it is not the truth!" Helen's voice found firmness, and she stood up, holding her head high. "I don't intend to dispute the possibility that someone has defrauded your company, but it couldn't have been Ron. It couldn't have been!"

"I have testimony to the contrary. Your brother deliberately falsified employment records beginning shortly before you came to Punta Temereria. No one else could have perpetrated this fraud. He alone handled the payroll, transported and distributed money at each operation. He acted as paymaster in every plant except the one here on Cedros, and staggered the paydays so he could make rounds. You covered all his transactions with your records this whole summer."

Again she could hardly get her breath. "Ron must have returned to Punta Temereria by now. You owe him the courtesy of talking to him. He'll make you understand what an outrage this accusation is!"

"Your brother never reported to Western Salt Company in Chula Vista on Monday. After he delivered your paintings to the gallery, he took a plane north to Los Angeles and from there apparently went on to an unknown destination. He does not plan to return to Punta Temereria at all. It will go less drastically for you if you let me know where he is to be found.''

"How could I know? My God, I—"

"He could not have carried out this elaborate plan without your help and knowledge. Leaving you behind was a calculated risk, which has misfired. I intend to recover my money from one of you!"

A terrible premonition came to Helen as she frantically rifled through the portfolio of damning evidence that San Roque had placed before her.

Was this what Ron had meant when he had spoken to her Sunday night and intimated disaster? Had he meant that he was leaving her to face this?

She pulled all the papers out of her shoulder bag and with shaking fingers extracted the long fat envelope Ron had entrusted to her—the envelope he had made her promise not to open unless he didn't return and she was confronted with an extreme emergency. She stared at the envelope with great apprehension, as though to open it would unleash disaster. But she couldn't delay forever. She tore the envelope open and removed the contents, a note folded around a packet of bills.

Sorry, sis. Didn't plan to leave you here alone with no cash, and didn't plan on the boss's coming back early and catching either of us. Use a little common sense and you'll persuade him you had no part in it. It's not your fault, so everything will turn out okay. Chin up, kid. Maybe you can use this to get home and forget any inconvenience.

"Oh, my God," she moaned, dropping the paper and bills on the table as though they had burned her hands. The big bills were easy enough to total. Three thousand dollars in American currency.

She had been an unwitting accessory all summer! She had made out all the records for men she had never seen, men listed for her by Ron. How many of the names she had added to the payroll this summer had been real, and how many were fraudulent? She felt dizzy as she realized how easily her brother had managed his regular thefts of payroll money.

Ron took the payroll to the other operations as acting manager at El Arco, assistant at Guerrero Negro and paymaster at Pozo Aleman. He had said he was serving in these positions, at any rate.

He had collected the salaries of the nonexistent men. Could that be why he had run back and forth so frequently, working night and day, so that she had rarely seen him? It had never occurred to her to question the marks illiterate workers made to acknowledge receipt of their cash salaries. After all, Ron had delivered the money and supposedly they had signed in front of him.

"Whatever he's done, he's my brother!" She choked back tears of outrage and disappointment as she lifted her trembling chin. "I know you must be wrong. Ron wouldn't leave me here knowing I had nothing to do with an embezzlement—knowing you would discover the deception. Wait and give him a chance to explain, to straighten it out," she pleaded. "He wouldn't just...leave me behind!"

She remembered sickly how anxiously he had tried to get her to leave with him when the officials had shown up a week early. She knew her words were hollow.

"In any case," San Roque responded stiffly, "you will remain here on Cedros until my company's property is back in my hands."

"You...you know you can't just keep me here! I have had nothing to do with your company disaster!"

"Hardly a disaster," he said, looking at her steadily. "I merely refuse to be robbed by my employees."

"What good would it do you to keep me here? It wouldn't help you get your money back, no matter who stole it!"

"It suits me to believe that you will be a fair exchange if the $263,000 is not placed back in my hands."

"That's crazy!" Helen protested. She put her hands to her temples to try to press order into her mind. She could only remember her brother warning her not to "rile" the owner.

"There is three thousand dollars on the desk." She indicated the money Ron had stuffed into the envelope. "My salary this summer has all been deposited to the bank in Garnet Beach, but I'll sign it over to you. Naturally, as long as you are convinced my brother is a thief, I will turn over every cent I've received from your company. When you find out he is innocent—and you will—I trust you will return it to me, because I earned it honestly."

"The money you offer me is a mere sop." San Roque dismissed her offer with a sneer.

The remaining money owing in the theft could just as well be all the money in the world as far as Helen was concerned. "Señor San Roque, you are a modern businessman," she said earnestly. "A practical man. I cannot see you attempting to exact revenge like a primitive. Keeping me here will truly serve no purpose. Besides, you are taking your anger out on the wrong people! The ones who will suffer most from your action in keeping me here will be my father and my terminally ill stepmother.''

Her brain had begun to function again and she breathed more calmly. ''If you are right about my brother—and I don't admit it, for I can't believe it—surely you see that he won't suffer if you take out your anger on me. Aren't there more reasonable alternatives?'' Her eyes met his with fiercely blazing determination, even though she was still almost paralyzed with the enormity of her predicament.

''What reasonable alternative can you suggest?'' he challenged her. There was a crackle of electricity between them that seemed to penetrate to her nerve endings and make a feather of feeling on her cheek.

''I have brains, education and expertise. These I can offer in a working reparation.'' She lifted a hand warningly. ''I still do not believe my brother has a part in this unfortunate and shocking situation. But I'll continue working for you willingly, Señor San Roque, and make up the missing money myself!''

He smiled at her brave words, as though she had made a great joke. He circled her at the distance she had created between them, but not warily, more as a purchaser might inspect a new acquisition. Angry though such deliberate appraisal made her, she held her head high and kept her face calm.

''In other words—'' he sounded mildly

amused ''—you propose to work off the debt as an employee, expecting me to trust you even though your brother and you were employees while all this was happening?''

"Yes, I do expect to be trusted, because I'm absolutely honorable! Surely your careful investigation has shown that in every area of my responsibility in Punta Temereria there were no discrepancies whatsoever. Through my efforts the operation has been vastly improved from its former state of chaos."

"It is true that the Punta Temereria office is in excellent and commendable condition. Speak on."

"I know I can serve your company on many levels. I can take responsibility fully, as competently as any man who might consider himself ideal for the same position my brother held."

Her brain went into high gear as she prepared to fight for as advantageous a situation as possible.

He smiled mockingly. "You propose to be of value as a bond servant?"

She looked him in the eye and did not flinch. "Señor San Roque, I can give you references that will make you take all my statements seriously. If it weren't for the accident that crippled my father and put my stepmother in the convalescent hospital, I would have had a prestigious career position. Five years ago, when I completed my graduate studies, I received several offers from companies that wanted to train women for Affirmative Action programs in the States. Since I have been teaching in my hometown, so as to be available to my parents, I've been given a great deal of responsibility by two school districts. I've handled pilot programs in business practices for our Mexican students who aren't yet bilingual. The State of California is seriously considering incorporating my last pilot project into the entire school system. I can cite you many skills I have that would be advantageous to your company."

San Roque studied her silently for a moment. "If I were to consider your outrageous proposition—and I caution you I only toy with the idea—you would turn over your salary in entirety until the debt was paid."

"Or temporarily—until my brother is found innocent of your insane charges," she corrected, then faltered. "With one minor exception...."

"I see I'm about to be proved correct in my instinct that you would find a way to obtain personal benefit from our negotiation," he remarked sarcastically.

Undaunted, Helen continued, "You'll have to deduct from my salary the monthly cost of my stepmother's care in Green Oaks Nursing Home, and the salary of my father's housekeeper.'' She was not intimidated on her stand. ''His pension doesn't allow for anything but the most basic of his expenses and he has to have help in the house. He's in a wheelchair.''

''Your salary as a schoolteacher cannot have left you with much money for your own needs,'' he observed quietly.

''My salary as a schoolteacher wasn't all I had to rely on,'' she replied with dignity. ''I worked at a second job, as well. I did books for small businesses in Garnet Beach. That, Señor San Roque, was why I so gladly came to Punta Temereria for the summer. The money I earned here made me believe I might breathe more easily this coming year. But that is water under the bridge. What arrangement can we make here and now that is agreeable to you and possible for me to live with?''

She felt color returning to her cheeks, even a feeling of what could be termed confidence. ''Have Felipe Estrada or Paolo Betancourt examine the work at Punta Temereria. In spite of the crisis, the relatively short time I was there and the fact that I was working in my second language, I was of value to the operation above my position of bookkeeper.''

Luis San Roque looked out of the great arched library window at the harbor far below them, across the city of Cedros. His back to her, he rested one impeccably clad foot on the low broad sill. His thumbs hooked into the back of his belt and he tapped his fingers as he considered. At last he turned, silhouetted against the arch of the window.

"There is one option I might consider," he said, and hope sprang into her heart. "I have been considering the promotion of Eugenio Ochoa, here on the island, to more extensive responsibilities."

"Yes?"

"There is no way, you understand, that you, a woman, could handle all the responsibilities Ochoa carries. The culture of the island precludes it; the culture of this country, also. I myself would not permit it. But if you, under his supervision, were to assume certain of his present responsibilities, freeing him in many other ways as much as fifty percent of his time—"

"Seventy-five percent or more!" Helen cut in firmly.

"—as much as fifty percent of his time, we could come to some arrangement that would not be entirely displeasing to you."

"I accept any reasonable suggestion," Helen said promptly.

"You are not in a position to demand fairness from me."

"But you are in the position to make a practical offer for an equitable return," she said boldly.

"Perhaps." He frowned at her. "You would have to remain on the island. I will not take the chance that like your brother you would disappear beyond the borders of my country, depriving me of my rightful restitution while you skip away in derision to join him."

"You have my word!" she said indignantly. "I have never gone back on my word. I—I'm even willing to remain here on the island if necessary."

He strolled away from her so that she could not read his reaction to her offer. Then he turned, grinning wolfishly, and stopped directly in front of her. She stared at him mesmerized, uncertain of his intentions, and willed herself not to flinch when his hand went up and touched her copper hair, as though he had just noticed its metallic gleam. He pinched a strand of it loose, curling it around one tentative finger and bonding her as his prisoner. "What other bail can you offer?"

His voice was deceptively soft, his eyes darker than she had seen them and more suggestive. "Perhaps there are other ways of discharging your brother's obligation to me—ways not so practical, perhaps, but softer, more pleasurable."

His other hand came up and his fingers brushed her cheek, stopping to caress her lips as softly as a moth might touch a rose. Her mouth trembled in spite of an inner command to be firm. She finally spoke—trying to ignore his fingers with every ounce of strength at her disposal. "I would not think you a man who had to stoop to such a method of gaining a woman for your bed, *señor*."

"You are a *gringa*," he said musingly. "The situation has its appeal."

"I doubt that the reality would be anything but a hollow restitution for you," she said, her voice quite steady. She was actually dismayed, for she had never imagined this of him. "It would be an empty experience... for us both."

"I wonder," he said, and his thumb gently held her chin as his mouth came down over hers and his tongue traced the quivering outline of her lips. Her mouth and throat filled with the sharp tingling taste of him, herbal and salty sweet. She swallowed convulsively and drew a long shuddering breath, barely restraining the urge to touch her tongue to his and respond fully. She stood statue-still, her eyelids closing against the intimacy of the sensations he aroused in her.

He released her finally in his own time. "Perhaps your word is your bond, but I am a man of contracts in a world that recognizes contracts."

"Write one, and I will sign it if it is fair," she told him.

"Your brother's breach of ethics and morality relieves me of all obligation to be fair. But we will consider such a contract later.''

"Still you mean to keep me on this island as a prisoner?''

"You see, you already chafe at the prospect of remaining here on bond.''

"I'm sorry. I chafe more at the prospect of losing my contract and tenure with the State of California teaching system while you decide whether or not to offer me a fair way to repay the debt my brother seems to have brought on me.''

He considered her words for a moment, then declared, ''During the next week I will attempt, with my staff, to find your brother and elicit an explanation from him directly. You can investigate the operation on the island. I will return at the end of the week with my decision.''

Helen asked, ''May I give some sort of notice to the school board that I will be late in taking up my contract with them? I feel sure that you will find my brother within the week. Let me safeguard my job!''

"I am not a monster," he answered. ''Write what letters you wish.''

"Aren't you afraid I might ask for help from the consulate?'' she said, and instantly regretted it.

"I intend to personally censor your mail, incoming and outgoing. Be circumspect if you want all of your letters to reach their destination.''

"You wouldn't!" she said, shocked.

"Indeed I would," he responded mildly. "You will find writing materials there in the desk." And with that he picked up a portfolio and moved to the other side of the room.

Helen sat down somewhat distractedly. It was not too difficult to write a simple note to the board of education, even though the results of the request were of course up to them. The letter to her father was more difficult.

Dear father,
  I am unable to come home as scheduled—

She crumpled the paper and began another, so as not to alarm him.

Dear father,
  I won't be home Friday, but don't worry.
If you should need to get in touch with me,
Call Señor Luis San Roque, the head of San
Roque Enterprises, at the address in—

"If my mail must pass through your hands, what address shall I use?" she interrupted her letter to ask.

"My Mexico City corporate headquarters," was San Roque's cool reply.

—in Mexico City that I gave you earlier this summer. Señor San Roque will forward any message quickly to where I am working. Your bills are all paid this month and will continue to be met. I am going to write you at least once a week without fail if I am not at home by the end of September. Please, dad, this is vitally important: when you hear from Ron, who has left the company, have him get in touch with Señor San Roque immediately, as it is a matter of the greatest importance to my future. Show him this letter.

I am well, and I know Mrs. Parish will take good care of you. Please keep in touch with Aunt Edna.

Love, Helen

She folded the sheet of paper, addressed her envelope and stood to hand them to San Roque. But she held them back for one last attempt to soften his rock-hard attitude. "Are you absolutely resolved that I must remain here as...a prisoner? Couldn't we work it out in a more civilized fashion?"

He seemed to hesitate and she could hardly breathe, waiting for him to bend even a little. At last he said quietly, "I consider my offered option to be extremely civilized."

She sighed and handed him the letters.

He actually read them, much to her dismay. When he had completed both he put them back in their envelopes and asked, "Who is the Aunt Edna you refer to cryptically within the second letter?"

"You compliment me. I am not quick enough to invent a secret code to alert my father to danger."

"Actually, I want to know how many other obligations you may have assumed that would prevent your paying back my money from your future earnings."

"Aunt Edna isn't a financial obligation. She's my stepmother's older sister, and she's in good health and independent despite her years. She lives in a small house in Oakland, California. I write her regularly, and my father was supposed to keep her informed all summer about my stepmother's condition, but he's a poor correspondent and needs to be reminded. Since I can't possibly let Aunt Edna know how Mama Jessie is from here, he must. Are you satisfied?"

"Quite," he said, tucking both letters into his jacket pocket.

She drew a deep breath and pressed her lips together to keep from screaming her frustration and fury. The situation was clearly hopeless.

"No tears?" he asked.

"I wouldn't give you the satisfaction, and it wouldn't change your mind anyway."

"No, you would not cry. You are a fighter. Neither will you beg me, but you would enjoy striking me with those clenched fists of yours!" With a quick movement he grasped her wrists and twisted her arms to show that indeed her fists were doubled fiercely. She struggled in a futile attempt to wrench out of his grasp, but ended up in an even more helpless position, her golden eyes flashing fire. The terrible ignominy of her plight fed the flames of anger within her.

Yet, perversely, she was dizzy with the desire to let this man overpower her any way he chose. His mere presence in the room was enough to make her ache with primitive longings. At Punta Temereria she had wanted to embrace and be embraced by him; here on Cedros she wanted to strike out at him, yet at the same time she was disturbingly aware of the staggering effect he had on her.

But she had to keep her cool. There was no one here to come to her rescue. Her father needed her at home, and if she didn't maintain her self-control she was lost.

"Don't be deceived," she managed to grind out between her teeth. "I wouldn't hit you with simple fists. I would like to use the nearest deadly weapon."

"There is a loaded pistol in the top drawer of the desk," he said, laughing at her, holding her easily.

"Don't think I wouldn't use it if I thought I'd be able to leave the island afterward! I'm determined to prove to you that my brother has stolen absolutely nothing from you."

He released her and allowed her to nurse her wrists, but his compelling eyes still held her his prisoner.

"I am glad to see you are sensible." He turned to his desk to gather up some papers. "Now it is necessary for me to leave you. My housekeeper, Soledad, will show you to your room, where I have taken the liberty of having your personal belongings delivered. If you wish to explore the island while I am gone, either she or my houseman will walk with you. Vergel will drive you wherever you need to go. Do not go about unaccompanied." He gave her a formal little bow. *"Mi casa es su casa."*

Then he was gone and she was alone in the library of this great luxury prison except for the housekeeper and the houseman. A short time later she saw the helicopter lift off into the sky and head east, back to the peninsula.

CHAPTER FOUR

THE HOUSEKEEPER SHOWED HELEN to the room where her few belongings had been placed—a room so large that she was almost overwhelmed by it on first impression. Everything that had been at Punta Temereria had evidently been removed and flown here the moment she had left that morning.

She stood in the center of the great room and surveyed her quarters—the most elegant prison cell she could ever have imagined. Compared to the house at Punta Temereria, which was luxurious for that part of the peninsula, this was a palace.

The cool gray green carpet underfoot was soft and thick. Hand-painted floor tiles were exposed outside the border of the rug. Everything in the room combined to suggest an atmosphere of understated luxury and tranquillity.

Ordinarily Helen was not overly fond of heavy carved Mexican furniture with its overtones of Gothic gloom, but in this room, on this island, in this house, the style was the only right one. It was perfect furniture in the perfect setting.

Each piece, created by a master craftsman, was delicately embellished with hand-painted flower designs in exquisite taste. The carved bed, chests, wardrobes, chaises and chairs were also extraordinarily scaled to tall persons. When she sat on the chaise she realized for the first time in her life how cramped she had always been in ordinary furniture intended for small, shorter-legged people.

"The room was made for giants!" she remarked to the housekeeper, bemused by its scale.

"It was the room of the old *señor* and Doña Isabella. The old *patrón* and his lady were tall like you. Can you not tell they were tall from seeing el señor, their son?" Helen did not answer; she was only too aware of San Roque's height and how it complemented her own.

She explored the suite and found two smaller rooms opening off the big bedroom. One was a small lounge, and one had served as a great walk-in wardrobe but was now used for storage. There was also a bath and a set of closed, locked double doors leading to another room.

"Where do the closed doors lead?"

"These rooms were all the heart of the house once, Señorita Forster," Soledad explained. "The sitting room was for Doña Isabella, mother of el señor. Don Luis said to make it proper for your use, as you wished. The double doors led to the *lugar de retiro* of the father of el señor, Don Adelberto; but Don Luis did not think you would need that room. Many rooms have been closed off since the old *señor* and *señora* died. First Doña Isabella and then Don Adelberto; he could not live without her." The housekeeper shook her head sadly.

"This is too much space for me," Helen told her as the woman laid away her embarrassingly meager supply of clothing in the drawer of one chest and the corner of one wardrobe. She put her paints in the storage room and came out to feel delightfully dainty again in the great central room. A beautiful arched window opened onto a balcony ornamented with wrought iron, overlooking the city and the lovely bay.

She took off her awkwardly high sandals and slipped into her well-worn huaraches. "This is truly a beautiful home," she commented to the housekeeper.

"A great house, Señorita Forster. Would you like me to show you through? I can open rooms—most are closed away at present."

Soledad guided her up and down three levels of the house, pointing out each site of events in the family history.

"Here is the nursery of young Don Luis. This is where the old *señor* stayed after his wife died.

He was a changed man after Doña Isabella died in a *borrasca*. She was worried for the family of the gardener and had gone to bring them up to the great house for safety when the storm struck. She was pinned under a tree, and when the old *señor* found her he went half-crazy with grief. Nothing was ever the same after that day. Not for any of us.''

Up and down the housekeeper wandered, with no pattern. Helen was quite confused by the circuitous excursion. She tried to imagine how the house might have looked in its heyday, and it boggled her mind.

''The works of some of the best Mexican artists in this century are hanging in the *galeria* on the landing,'' she commented with some awe.

''El señor has the excellent taste of his mother and the head for business of his father, but he never stays here anymore. Many of the most beautiful things are stored away.''

Soledad opened another door on the second level. ''This is where he stays when he comes to the island.''

Helen caught just a glimpse of a room Spartan in its simplicity, a room with the look of infrequent use. There was a narrow bed, a desk, a small book-filled credenza and a huge refectory table that took up most of the space. On it were swim fins and a great pot of blooming orchids, two briefcases and a portable typewriter.

Soledad then took her down to the kitchen, where relatively modern appliances stood next to an old-fashioned wood-burning stove and Mexican bread oven.

"I think I would like to go to the mine office," Helen said. "Is it possible?" If she had to work out the debt, she should begin quickly to be worth her hire.

"Vergel will take you there if that is your wish. But now is the hour of siesta and no one will be there. I will fix you the *comida*, the noon meal, and when the men have returned to their work at the office Vergel will drive."

"But I can't eat a thing after the meal you fixed such a short time ago," Helen protested with a laugh. She liked Soledad already.

"You barely touched your plate. No wonder you are so thin!"

"That is what Guadalupe complained of all summer. She succeeded in putting several pounds of weight on me with her good cooking."

"Although Guadalupe is my cousin," Soledad said, "I am older, and a much better cook than she."

"Then I shall become a *gorda* in no time," Helen said with a mock sigh, "because Guadalupe was the best cook I have ever known."

WHEN THE HOURS OF SIESTA were over, Vergel drove Helen down into town to the mining office, a long low complex of buildings at the hub of the wharf area. She now surmised shrewdly that this Cedros operation must be one of the key offices of the corporation because of its location.

Eugenio Ochoa, a brown, round-faced young man dressed in neat tropical white, welcomed Helen with some obviously repressed questions in his honest brown eyes.

"I have told el señor of the excellent cooperation we received this summer from La Punta," he reported. "You come from the *Estados Unidos*, so you will find us provincial."

"The island must be a fine place to live and work," she said. Under other circumstances she would have found everything about Cedros tremendously exciting. "I will not miss the advanced equipment of a big city."

Eugenio showed her around the company office and described the general island operation. She suspected he had no idea why she was really here, and absolutely no knowledge of her brother's defection from the operation he referred to as "La Punta."

He did voice some grumbling comments about how hard it had been to reach Ron. He obviously attributed his difficulties in that respect—as Helen had—to Ron's hard-charging constant work in the field.

Everything on Cedros was orderly and nothing like the chaotic office situation in La Punta when she had arrived. There seemed to be a heavy backlog, but she saw that much of it could be blamed on old-fashioned methods.

"It is difficult to find and train the office workers we need," Eugenio apologized. "Few will come here, even though Don Luis pays well. The islanders keep to themselves and do not think overly much of outside ways."

"So I have noticed," Helen commented with an eye on the antiquated office equipment.

"Neither will they go for training to the north, nor even to Mexico City."

"Why is it so difficult to train islanders here, right at home?"

"Train them here?" Eugenio had not thought of that. "Why, there are no teachers and no facilities, Señorita Forster." He thought long and carefully. "The young men also think to see the world and become important. Those who are adept go, but they do not return. Those who remain here do not have ambition. Also, none speak any other than the island language and Spanish."

He smiled pleasantly but with reserved friendliness. "I understand why el señor wishes to hire an American who speaks both languages." He also had the expression of one too polite to add that he found el señor's hiring of a woman far from approved custom.

Helen decided that by the time San Roque returned, whether or not her brother had surfaced and shown his innocence, she faced forfeiture of her position with the schools in Garnet Beach. There were many teachers waiting to snap up new openings. Though San Roque must eventually come to rectify his mistaken judgment, he would owe her the chance to make up for her lost teaching contract. Eugenio Ochoa would be her ally.

Two Japanese merchant marine officers arrived to see Ochoa and obviously did not care to include her in the conference, nor could she add to it. She excused herself and went out onto the quay.

A three-masted sailing vessel was being serviced there. Although it wasn't the largest pleasure craft in the harbor, it was a lovely one. Two officers of the crew gave orders to the stevedores, but Helen could hear them converse together in English. They were obviously American.

The realization that she might have few if any further opportunities to alert outsiders to her circumstances propelled her to approach them quickly on impulse. "Are you on your way north to a California port by any chance?" she asked.

"No. We're sailing around Cabo San Lucas into the gulf and over to Mazatlan to pick up a party of South Americans," she was told.

"My name is Helen Forster. I seem to have

got into some rather rotten difficulties here. Could you get a message for me to the American consul in Mazatlan?''

"Sure!" the one in charge agreed obligingly.

She rapidly described her predicament as a kidnapping. "It's important that the consul know I'm here—and that they know that Luis San Roque Quintana, of San Roque Enterprises on this island and Mexico City, is holding me virtual prisoner. He's decided that...that my brother is a thief, and he's intent on holding me for ransom. While the consul need not call out the U.S. Marines, I do want to be sure they contact me personally here on the island. I don't want to turn out to be a permanently missing person. So do promise to get this message to the consul, won't you?''

Hearing the story, the two men exchanged startled looks of incomprehension. At their suggestion she hurriedly wrote out the particulars of her situation. Eugenio Ochoa came out of the office to take up business with her again on the departure of the Japanese businessmen, and she rapidly concluded her conversation with the crewmen of the sailing ship.

Feeling relieved of some of her helplessness, she went back with Eugenio. "You can have Vergel drive you around the city to point out landmarks and give you the opportunity to orient yourself," he suggested. And she gratefully took him up on the offer.

Most of the city was neat and prosperous except for one area—a *colonia* built up the side of what had at one time been a cliff. Residents of this burrow were able to reach their tiny wooden nests only by climbing the most hair-raising set of rickety steps Helen had ever seen. Despite the extreme danger of negotiating this aerial ladder, children gaily trooped up and down. "Good heavens!" Helen commented on first seeing it.

"Barrio X," said Vergel tersely. He had no intention of stopping.

"Wait," Helen said. "I thought the island was prosperous. That is a ghastly and dangerous slum!"

"No one can do anything with the *colonia*," Vergel explained disdainfully. "Most of the residents live on the handouts of sailors and will not work." He added, "It is not a place for a lady to pause."

"If I am going to work for the company here, I need to know the whole island, not just the pleasant, attractive parts."

"Ah, that is true." Vergel nodded wisely.

"This area is a blot on the island's image, but I will find out more about it later if I am to be here."

They drove on, and Vergel took care to point out with pride the beautiful coves and coastline.

"We are all but born in the waters of our island," he told her. "Even the smallest child is good at diving for abalone and lobster."

She could see much of the island was geared to bounty from the sea.

"For ladies like yourself, the best place to swim is not the common beach but in one of the coves near el señor's own house, where there is a waterfall. It's a fine swimming place."

The island was so enchanting that Helen could almost forget for that afternoon the unfortunate reason for her presence there. But at the back of her mind loomed two dark questions: how could Ron have so callously used her to suit his scheme, and why didn't San Roque understand that she was as much a victim as he had been?

It was not in her nature to dwell on negatives. During the tour she mentally planned ways to better her bargaining position at her next confrontation with San Roque. In the meantime she must make herself as indispensable as possible to Ochoa in the island's operation.

As they returned up the winding, breathtakingly scenic road to Casa San Roque, she had plenty to occupy her mind and keep her from succumbing to despair.

CHAPTER FIVE

"WHAT DO YOU DO THERE, Señorita Forster?" asked Soledad, who stopped busying herself at turning down the great bed when she saw Helen come out of the huge bathroom carrying some dripping hand washing.

"I've rinsed my one decent skirt," Helen answered. "I thought I'd find a warm place for it to dry by morning."

Soledad was scandalized. "But you are not to do the laundry! You must leave it to me!" And she bore the skirt away with small clucks of disapproval.

In the morning the skirt was carried in looking crisp and fresh, and Soledad also brought an excellent *desayuno*, the typical fruit and coffee of the first of the four meals the Mexicans considered normal during their day. She fussed at Helen for not wanting more, in order to give her the excuse to prepare it. Unlike Guadalupe, who tended to be easygoing and unconcerned with American habits, Soledad was determined to take care of her guest in spite of herself.

Cedros was in many respects no different from other Mexican cities, Helen found, but its total isolation from the mainland made it unique. She was driven to work, where the day had begun with everyone in the lower echelons cleaning around the complex. Coffee and fruit was brought into the office where she was assigned and everyone came to make polite greetings. All the old typewriters stopped their clatter at the hour of noon. The office emptied out to complete silence, and the buildings became deserted as all employees headed for home for siesta.

Vergel knocked discreetly at the door of Helen's office. "You must not work so long, Señorita Forster, that you do not take siesta."

"I had an enormous breakfast and don't need lunch—"

"But everyone has left, and it is not right that you do not leave, also," he told her.

"Vergel, there is no law that demands everyone must go home to spend two hours. If you want to go, do. I'll be fine right here," she said firmly.

"I cannot let you stay alone, Señorita Forster!" Vergel became agitated. "El señor said I was to take care of you, and I must take you home for the midday meal."

"I won't run away!" she replied with some asperity. Vergel looked so blank that she felt guilty. "Can't I walk along the quay?"

"You cannot do that!" His black eyes went round with anxiety. "The sailors wouldn't know you were a lady. They would accost you as though you were one of the women from Barrio X!"

"But the women who work here in the office go out there," she pointed out.

"Ah, but they are from the town, not foreign lady executives. No, it would not be right, and el señor instructed me to see that you did nothing that was incorrect."

"Well, then, you shall take me to *la casa*," she said, surrendering. "And come again for me just before the end of siesta." She gathered her notebooks and the papers she had been studying, resigned to working in the den off the library.

As THE DAYS PASSED without word from San Roque or her brother or anyone else, Helen became increasingly anxious. Ron had to know by now that she hadn't made it home. He had to have contacted their father. He must realize she was being held virtually as hostage in his stead. Could he deliberately leave her with hostile and powerful strangers, in danger of the universally dreaded Mexican jail?

Then she succumbed to despair and anger. She had always looked up to Ron, loved him unconditionally, and now she wondered why she had. Whatever unhappiness he harbored from his childhood could not explain away his actions here. They were adults now and should stick together.

San Roque, even more cold-blooded than her brother, would not care why Ron had deserted her so unfairly. She wanted to pummel San Roque to a pulp, to scream, shout and sob; but none of those courses of action would move him an inch. In fact, he would be amused by the futile struggle on her part. No—there had to be more rational, hardheaded ways to reach that man, and she would somehow prove to him that he must relent toward her.

His delayed return unnerved her and she was as jumpy as a cat. On Friday of the following week, midmorning, Eugenio Ochoa poked his head through her office door to announce, "The helicopter arrives!"

Everyone went into a frenzy of preparation. Agustin Benevidez, San Roque's secretary on the island, sent his own secretary out for flowers to be arranged fresh in el señor's outer office. Everyone went at a rush down the halls, and the great mezzotint portrait of the San Roque's father and the one of el señor himself in the great oak frames were dusted for the second time that day. There was enormous activity at the files while everything for him to approve and initial, to comment on and edit, was placed in portfolios and arranged for his inspection.

Helen herself was equally anxious, as though her life depended on some forgotten detail. She tried to maintain her coolly efficient exterior, but unbidden the memory of him on the beach that first time and the attraction she had felt crept into her mind and caused her cheeks to flush. She struggled to compose herself with the thought that he might bring news and information about her brother. Fortunately, none of the others thought her agitation at all unusual, for their own concern over his arrival were foremost.

Eugenio, always immaculate in a light-colored tropical suit, fussed with his collar and smoothed his hair.

"Everything is in excellent condition here, Eugenio," Helen assured him to calm his tensions as well as her own. "Señor San Roque cannot help but compliment you on the fine operation you run."

Not entirely convinced he would be free from el señor's criticisms, Eugenio inserted a fresh handkerchief in his breast pocket. "El señor wants everything and everyone to be perfect when he arrives."

Helen tucked the huaraches she had been wearing into her desk drawer. Though they were unflattering, they were comfortable and she wore them to minimize her height around the short Mexican men in the office force. She replaced them with high strapped sandals that she also kept in the drawer, and when she stood in them Ochoa looked up at her with an expression of real dismay. He surveyed her shoes with the expression of one wondering why she should want to be so tall.

She could barely admit to herself, let alone to Eugenio, that the high heels were for San Roque's benefit. Though he had her at a disadvantage in every way, she was determined to stand tall before him, to be as equal to him as she possibly could. The shoes might be a feeble statement of that, but she was grateful for the boost they gave her both physically and psychologically.

Just then Benevidez bustled in and told them they were requested immediately to report to their employer's own office. When they entered the room, carrying the file folders they had snatched up as they were summoned, they found San Roque standing at the window that looked out onto the quay. Once more Helen was astonished at his impact on her. She could have thrown herself on him, wrapped her arms around him and laid her head pleadingly on his shoulder; the effort required to stand coolly at the back of the room, allowing Eugenio to take the lead and the action of any staff conference, was considerable. She felt this magnetism put her at a terrible disadvantage and somehow she had to overcome it. She tried not to look at him too eagerly in her desire to know what was in his plan for her and what news he might have brought from the mainland in regard to Ron.

As he motioned her and Eugenio to sit down, she lost some of her control and blurted, "Did you bring news of my brother—word from him?"

"Why, no," he said in a pleasant tone of voice. He looked at her piercingly, assessing in minute detail every aspect of her. She controlled a slight tremor in her lip as he added, "Did you expect me to hear from him?" Then he turned from her, leaving her dismayed and frustrated. "Eugenio, how have things progressed?" he asked.

"Very well, sir. Except—" Eugenio risked an apologetic glance at Helen "—Señorita Forster never ceases working even a moment. We are all worn out and begin to imagine we shirk our own responsibilities, but I assure you, *señor*, we do not!"

"Señorita Forster has the *norteamericano* work ethic," said San Roque, a small smile playing about his firm lips. He looked at her obliquely and Helen responded with a frown to show that responsibility was no laughing matter.

"Señorita Forster knows our operation amazingly well for having worked less than three months at La Punta and having been here only a matter of days," Ochoa continued. "And *señor*, except that she is a woman who does not know the ways of Cedros, she could handle my job in its entirety and you would have few concerns. In fact," he added unwillingly but compelled by his total honesty, "with her knowledge of modern procedures she could do an even better job than I. Whatever you assign her, there should be no need for your concern. The employees here already look to her for direction. She is not like other women in our office."

"So...she is efficient, eh? Well, now that you have made your assessment," San Roque said with his usual rapid thrust to matters of business, which was not in the traditional manner, "I can make my own decisions as to her value to the company." He took Eugenio's files and smiled cordially, indicating his business with the man was closed. "I will talk with you later, but now I have business with Señorita Forster."

"Of course, Don Luis."

When Eugenio had carefully closed the door behind him, Helen blurted in spite of herself, "You're sure you brought no word from my brother?"

San Roque took a small packet of papers from his tan jacket and placed it before her on the desk. "I have brought your bank statements, forwarded to you in La Punta. There are letters: one from your Aunt Edna, one from the art gallery in San Diego and one to you from your chess-playing friend—a new one, I believe."

She picked up her letters coolly but exclaimed in dismay, "Why, every one of them has been opened!"

"I told you I intended to censor all your incoming and outgoing mail."

"But it's my personal mail! From my family!"

"I should also have assigned a bodyguard to report your contacts away from the office and Vergel, it seems."

"I thought you assigned a bevy of them," she said. "Soledad, Vergel, Eugenio—"

"Not one was told to report to me your personal comings and goings. Not one knows the reason you are here. But the crew of my yacht did bring your message to the American consul in Mazatlan directly to me. All my employees are unswervingly loyal."

Her face flamed and her heart sank miserably at his words. How foolish she had been to trust even American strangers! She should have realized that the beautiful vessel so close to the San Roque Enterprises office on the quay might be his own!

"You are aware that no matter how unorthodox my methods may appear to you, Helen, I must use them to recover my property."

"And as long as you hold me prisoner on this island, you cannot fail to understand my obligation to secure my freedom any way I can!" she retorted. "I did not ask them to take me from the island, Señor San Roque. I asked only that they let the consul know I am here and not by my free will. I would have started an official search for my brother through their channels." She challenged him with a clear and steady glare. "Now, since my brother is still. . .absent without explanation, I am ready to negotiate with you about the temporary plans for repayment of the money."

He returned her look quite as steadily, holding her gaze with his unwavering gray eyes. She could see him calculating her words and the narrowing that dashed her hope of consideration.

"Negotiate? I set terms. You are in no position to negotiate."

"Señor San Roque, I am convinced that if you really want value received we must negotiate."

Amusement replaced calculation in his eyes, and his harshly handsome features appeared to soften in a kind of tolerance as he listened. He spread his hands as if to suggest an open mind.

Helen paced the floor in her agitation as she

began passionately, "During the period you have left me here cooling my heels, I've been up and down every street in Cedros, every byway on the island. I've looked in every file drawer that isn't locked. I've studied every facet of the operation here and in the allied industries on the island. I've read every report to and from this office for the past year. I've asked a million questions of Eugenio Ochoa." She drew a long firm breath. "In short, Señor San Roque, I understand this office better than I understood La Punta. And because Eugenio Ochoa is sincere, honest and cooperative, I also have gained much understanding of your island and its relationship to the rest of San Roque Enterprises."

"Yes?" His features were expressionless, but she knew he was first and foremost a tough businessman. She would have to call upon every shred of ingenuity she had to convince him of her usefulness to his company.

"I feel that Eugenio was kind, saying I could take over his present obligations right now," she continued. "My fluency in written and spoken Spanish more than makes up for what I lack in cultural nuances. You know Eugenio is not fluent in English; he and the other employees on the island barely manage amenities in the language. It is an important second language your staff on a supervisory level should master, even though on Cedros I realize they do not come in contact with those who speak it regularly."

She whirled to confront him; there was a proud thrust to her chin as she warmed to the challenge. "I will take the responsibility for returning the money no matter how long it takes. I think the only point is that I do deserve a top salary, with which I can repay you in a reasonably short term of time. I do have a life of my own to live someday!"

He rubbed his chin, and his eyes were half-closed in a lazy rejection of her claims. "Following your defection attempt, I find your impassioned promises meaningless. I will take stringent measures to ensure you do not disappear at the first opportunity in my absence and so deprive me forever of what is mine."

Her color heightened and she fought down an indignant retort, with the greatest effort she kept her voice from trembling in outrage. "For someone with your extensive influence and money, you are making a medieval issue of what to you must be a relatively small sum of money! Why can't you handle this like a gentleman and a businessman?"

He laughed derisively. "I find it easier to handle as a man!"

"Naturally, I meant as a man—as the decent man I know you must be in others' eyes," she said persuasively.

Again she heard the little cold chortle that unnerved her so. "You do not know me at all, Helen. Decency is no consideration when I have been robbed of my property. I become a primitive, not the gentleman and businessman you seem to wish to deal with. When will you understand?"

His voice had a feral growl and suddenly she felt afraid. He grasped her chin with his long fingers, holding her quite as easily as he would hold one of the small brown island apples. She could not move her head away even a fraction of an inch and was forced to look him in the eyes. The closeness was agonizing.

"Until I have my own property returned, *you* are my property, to deal with as I see fit. I may deal with you as an employee if I wish, or. . . ." He swiftly lowered his head and kissed her punishingly, invading the recesses of her mouth in an unmistakable command to her to respond. The demanding kiss was without tenderness or respect and was as insulting as if he had bought and paid for her in the marketplace. Just as quickly he pulled away and continued, "Or I will deal with you as a man who possesses a woman's spirit and can bend her to his every wish through his skill—without the use of commands."

His mouth claimed hers again, this time with a tenderness of approach she could not retreat from. Slowly and with infinite attention his lips teased hers, coaxing her to forgive the brusqueness of his first kiss. She responded timidly at first, then with ardor, knowing only that she wanted the embrace to go on forever. The warmth of his mouth on hers made her come alive in a way she had never experienced and could never explain, beginning a chain of reactions that swept through her veins in a million explosions. She uttered an involuntary moan, intensifying the pressure of his lips on hers; then, realizing all resistance was pointless, she sagged a little against him, held up only by his supporting hand.

Slowly he released her, and his hot gray eyes told her the moment that had passed would come again if he willed it. She drew back from him, shaken, hardly able to believe the sensations she'd just experienced. Beneath his gaze and passionate touch she had felt vulnerable, aroused. And she knew it could happen again.

She lifted a cool hand to wipe her brow and smooth her hair. Swiftly her composure returned, and driven by some perverse demon within her she returned to the issue at hand.

"Señor San Roque, you are a wealthy man, and you would never miss the money you are using as an excuse to humiliate me. You have squandered it easily in a night of gambling, or in a trip with friends on your yacht, or in—"

With an arrogant shrug he interrupted, "The amount of the embezzlement means quite as much to me as an amount a thousand times smaller would mean to you. Do not imagine that wealthy men do not know the value of every dollar. I will not begin with you to build a reputation for being an easy mark."

"You won't be cheated." Helen's confidence, which had slipped a moment before, began to return. She held out the binder she had brought in with her, turning it around so he could follow her finger as she pointed to charts and graphs. "Since you are an astute businessman who recognizes value, you will see immediately that I am proposing a practical, civilized, *fair* program of reparation."

"Then, considering the basis of language, you should realize French and German are equally important languages to the business here. And Japanese—especially Japanese. Also Swedish and Norwegian at times. German and Japanese are principally more important than English."

"Japanese? Well...." Her confidence ebbed a little again, but she recovered. "If that is a language you require, I shall find a way to learn!" She played a trump card. "My grandfather was of German descent. As a little girl I heard the language enough that I'm sure it wouldn't take much effort for me to master basic communication. As for French—I spent a summer in France as an exchange student in high school. I always hoped to go back and visit my French foster parents, so I studied French in college to keep up the skill.''

"Very well; I recognize your linguistic abilities in three and a half languages. It is a promising plus that the average North American does not possess. You seem to have skills that should not be summarily dismissed. You shall be credited with three-fourths of the salary of Eugenio.''

"Wait!" she objected. "I've also made a study of your office personnel.'' She flipped a page from the portfolio to emphasize her point. "They work hard, they're loyal, they do the best they can; but with antiquated procedures and equipment they are far behind the times. It would take a special business college to bring them up to scratch. These shortcomings make it impossible for you to realize your company's potential and compete in today's world. Where I taught, I gave my students the training that no staff here has. You may not realize it, Señor San Roque, but my specialty in teaching was with culturally deprived students of Mexican background. I devised the school's pilot project for upgrading students' skills and it led to such high employment statistics for the graduates that it was considered a phenomenal success. You may check this out!''

"I have," he said simply.

She gave him a startled look but continued firmly, "I can train your employees during siesta, after employment hours, before the workday begins—taking no time from your operational hours. I can set up classes for others in the city of Cedros who may wish to participate. I can teach all your supervisors how to do business in English, and all your office staff to use modern office machines and computer equipment if you will have some installed. All this can be of great value to your company.

"I propose that you pay me by contract. But I can also work for you under salary as manager of the island operations under the tutelage of Eugenio. You must recognize that my real experience in the field more than makes up for my deficiencies in the other areas you've remarked on. I propose that you pay me Ron's salary. You paid Ron twice as much as Eugenio because Ron was a clever American. Well—" she straightened from her portfolio figures and looked directly at him "—I am clever, better trained than my brother and extremely honest."

She thrust the binder nearer to his relaxed hand on the desk. "I have set up all the guidelines in this prospectus."

She stood back and watched him as he considered the proposal. She tried to look cool and calm, determined not to show any insecurity. As he stood reading page after page of the plan he fired off sharp questions, all of which she answered in as assured a manner as she could. She had prepared for this moment as completely as she could ever since he had left the island. As they confronted each other over the binder on the desk, the very atmosphere between them seemed to crackle.

"Sit!" he ordered finally. Then he, too, sat down, swiveling his chair so that his back was to her and he could concentrate on the material she had painstakingly prepared.

She sat down and attempted to relax, but she feared she had failed. She gazed over her letters, which at least gave her the appearance of composure. She hoped when he turned back to look at her he wouldn't see any sign of her anxiety.

At last he swiveled the leather chair and put the binder back on his desk. "Perhaps I have accidentally acquired more good fortune than I have lost. You should have been kidnapped sooner to this island. You may actually have some real value to San Roque Enterprises."

He looked at her with grudging approval and she saw she had won a battle.

"Well! Thank you," she said, fighting to keep sarcasm out of her voice and more than a little amazed at his ability to give due credit. "Then it is settled?"

"I am prepared to contract with you for your

training program—though I do not think you will find it as simple as you make it seem on paper. I will authorize what you need. This island is long overdue for modernizing."

"Good! I—"

"There will be other obligations I will require of you."

"Other obligations?"

"You are to serve as my official hostess. The house has not been fully opened for many years, and I have not entertained as I might. When I bring guests here to Cedros, you will have the responsibility of entertaining them. That in itself will be taxing role."

She was taken unawares by this new proposal and it flustered her.

"Señor San Roque," she said, "I do not think I am suited to being the official hostess of a great home. I...." She stopped because she was beginning to stammer.

"The servants will handle details I do not dictate personally. But the presence of a Señora San Roque is necessary when guests are invited for extended periods."

"A Señora—"

"Exactly."

"You can't mean you expect—"

He came from behind the desk just as she stumbled back, stunned, and he put out a hand to steady her. As soon as she had recovered her balance, his hand dropped from her shoulder, allowing her to find her own distance from him.

"If there is to be any contract at all, you must accept all the conditions attached."

"Which are . . . ?" She could hardly breathe.

"Considering your attempt to reach the American consul and because I will not have you, like your brother, take it into your mind to disappear beyond the borders of this country and cheat me out of my rightful property, there must be the strongest of contracts."

"But you have my word!" she said, frantically searching for the slightest loophole. "I didn't ask to be rescued, only to be . . . to be under some surveillance by the consulate!"

"Nevertheless, the next step would have been rescue from the island and then flight back to the United States."

"I accept the debt as my charge! I don't condone my brother's disappearance or his theft—if that's what it is, and I am not certain of this. . . . But apart from that—it is me you are dealing with here and I have never gone back on my word!"

"I am a man of contracts in a world that recognizes the value of them. I must have my guarantees."

"Then write your contract. I'll sign it."

"My contract includes the condition that you

will marry me and remain here on this island with your affairs completely in my control until your full debt is discharged.''

She drew a short shocked gasp of breath as she shrank back in utter dismay. ''Marriage! You are out of your mind!''

His dark brows drew together in an angry frown. ''I am in full control of all my faculties, Helen. Marriage would effectively prevent you from making a scandal through the American consulate by deciding you are being held improperly against your will. It will make any possible complaints uttered by your family of no validity if investigated. It will make you more bindingly subject to Mexican law.''

''But I have given you my word and you can have an employee contract,'' she protested.

''I had such a contract with your brother,'' he pointed out dryly.

Helen shook her head decidedly.

''You are a modern woman,'' he snapped, ''not some shrinking little virgin sheltered from the world.''

''Strange as it may seem to you, with your apparent attitude toward modern American women,'' she said, flushing and utterly unnerved, ''I have never....'' She swallowed. ''In your eyes I am indeed a 'shrinking virgin.' I will continue to own my own body and soul, no matter who claims my time and loyalty!''

"You have been sensible, Helen. But I find your last remark exceedingly foolish."

"Find it whatever you like," she said, coloring furiously.

"You were meant to be with a man, whether you are now a virgin or not." He sounded smug as he watched the color ebb and flow in her cheeks, leaving her alternatively pale and flushed with outrage. "So you do not bed with men? Well, you will one day soon. You are far past the age of being coy about it. All the more reason to make sure your mind stays on the business of reparation, not personal pleasure."

"I may be past the age of being coy, as you put it so nicely," she gritted, "but I'll never sleep with a man I do not love. And I'll never love a man who doesn't consider me his equal—which makes your suggestion and this particular condition of the contract out of the question!"

"The marriage will be a business arrangement only if you feel more secure in that knowledge. To further ease your anxious mind, I rarely come here to the island."

She still shook her head stubbornly. "You have my word I will not attempt to contact the consulate again until the debt is repaid. That should be enough," she insisted. She spoke slowly in her excellent Spanish, just as he had spoken to her in English, to be sure he understood.

"You have my word that it will be a marriage of convenience. Is that not enough?"

Desperately she stalled. "One of the elegant women of Mexico City, Paris or Buenos Aires could be much more suitable and convincing as your wife. A woman like. . .like Yolanda Betancourt!"

"If I wanted Yolanda Betancourt I would have chosen her."

"Then why complicate your life with a wife of convenience? However," she compromised as gracefully as she could, "I am willing to be your official hostess as well as your island manager—without marriage."

"You will be silent! I will make all conditions. I am willing to credit you with fifty thousand dollars a year—to start. There will be a marriage contract. Your finances will be handled by my business manager, Felipe Estrada. Your salary will be deposited in an account after he has deducted expenses for your father and stepmother as necessary. All else will be applied against the amount your brother stole."

"This is crazy!" Helen could not believe the conversation. She collapsed into the leather chair, completely stunned.

The salary was far more than what she might expect to end up earning at the top of a career as a teacher. It was so much more than she had expected San Roque to agree to, even after protracted bargaining, that she stammered, "That—that is more than a fair offer."

"The salary is contingent on the marriage contract. You can remain here on Cedros without hope of leaving until your brother's debt has been paid—or you can marry me. That is my last word."

"I'm prepared to give up five or so years of my life—even more—to pay my brother's debts," she told him. "What satisfaction can you get from placing me in such an impossible position?"

He looked at her with eyes like twin daggers, and again she shrank back. "Does it humiliate you so to think of the mere possibility of being forced to share a bed with me? Does it offend your sensibilities? Demean you?"

"I didn't mean to insult you in any way, Señor San Roque. But such an arrangement is fraught with problems I don't even wish to contemplate. If in this marriage of convenience there comes a time when you wish to...to be with me, and I cannot dissuade you, a child could result. That child would be the needless victim of the situation!"

"So you think I might want to take you to bed?" He smiled wolfishly.

"You know what I mean!" She feared he knew exactly how attracted she was to him despite the fact that under the circumstances she ought to find him offensive. She did not flinch under his disconcerting grin as she continued to challenge him. "I assume you've waited almost two decades to choose a proper wife, and you wanted a woman you could love and cherish. I am quite aware of the Mexican view of marriage as a permanent and enduring contract. Your unbending determination to regain your lost funds would make any marriage a mockery!"

"And you want no mockery, no sacrilege?"

"I do not!" she stormed at him defiantly. "I won't be bought and sold like a slave. I will only accept a reasonable employment contract that is soluble when completed."

"You, then, have your own ideas of marriage as a commitment?"

"I do!"

He laughed. "Very well. I have no intention of forcing you or any woman into bed; I have enough who are only too willing to volunteer for such occasions. I promise you no intimacy you do not want, you determined woman. Serve as my hostess. The marriage will be only a civil one. I will sleep in other beds as I am accustomed. I do, however, expect you to show such affectionate behavior as may be necessary in public. You understand? For appearances?" He tapped his gold pencil on the desk impatiently. "Does that relieve your anxious virginal mind?"

"I don't know," she said, biting her lip. In spite of everything that had happened, he was still so powerfully attractive to her that she was thoroughly frightened. She knew she was of no consequence to him, just a means to an end—a way of recovering his property. And in the interim he was quite capable of using her in any way convenient to him. This knowledge disturbed her.

"My time can belong to you," she said slowly. "And my talents. Those alone."

"Let us agree on that at least," he answered amiably. "I am not the oger you apparently have decided I am. There will be time for you to paint here as you did at La Punta. Much inspiration is to be found on the island. The social occasions at the house will not be unpleasant interludes, and when you are a successful hostess I will not be ungrateful. Your family will not go uncared for and may actually end up in happier financial circumstances than formerly."

This man had the maddening ability to change her mood from panic to hope. "I sometimes sell my paintings," she said, "as you may have noted from the correspondence I received today. I'll put the profits of such sales into the account owed you."

"Treat the sale of your paintings any way you prefer," he told her, carelessly tossing his gold pencil onto the desk top.

"Take this money draft that came in the letter from the gallery," she persisted, handing it to him.

"Do you intend this to go on the interest or the principal of your debt?" he asked with a lift of one eyebrow.

"Interest?" She had not even thought of this problem adding to her indenture, but was suddenly horribly aware of the astronomical Mexican interest rates. "At what percentage do you intend to assess interest?"

He smiled, teasing her. "You are prepared to argue again, I see. To avoid that time-consuming process, I am willing to be magnanimous. No interest will be assessed. It will take you long enough to settle the debt, and I am interested only in the principal. You owe me only the amount taken. Now you can breathe again."

She felt ill at ease once more with his mercurial attitude. "I don't want any disagreements."

"All will be arranged in our contract," he assured her. "Let us by all means spell out every facet so that neither of us can be cheated or misunderstood."

"It's my life you're jockeying about, Señor San Roque." Her voice trembled slightly in spite of her resolve. "I intend to fight for every bit of it. I know in my heart that my brother will come to his senses and I won't be restrained here long under these conditions. Until then I will live up to every stipulation in a legitimate contract.''

''You are wise to recognize that the wait may not be temporary.''

''I can work with facts as they are, not as I want them to be.''

''Then you must recognize the first fact is that you and I must go to the *alcalde*, where the civil marriage ceremony will be performed immediately.''

''There is no other way?'' she asked faintly, saddened somewhat that the ceremony would take place so coldly in the office of the justice of the peace, and not a church.

''No other way.'' He put his hand on the buzzer to summon Ochoa, but paused. ''Tell me, Helen, is it necessary for you to make yourself so extraordinarily tall? It intimidates Eugenio. He is sensitive enough around me, but for a woman to tower over him must be devastating.''

''I wouldn't hurt his feelings for the world,'' she responded indignantly.

''Then you must be attempting to be as tall as I,'' he said mildly, looking down briefly at her shoes. ''I must warn you, Helen, you can never tower over me. It was not meant that way by God or nature.''

She colored again. ''I wasn't trying to—''

"I believe you were, but let it pass. It is only that I would not have Eugenio feel uncomfortable."

"You may place it in our contract," she said, "that I wear only flat shoes. My huaraches are in my office. I'll get them."

"You have one trait that blesses and curses you, Helen—your *norteamericana* determination to beat a man. I shall enjoy seeing the struggle within you!"

CHAPTER SIX

SOLEDAD DROPPED A RESPECTFUL CURTSY to Helen as she and San Roque entered the front hall. "Señora San Roque! Don Luis has requested you approve the new staff who are waiting in the back hall."

"New staff?" Helen echoed, momentarily confused to hear herself addressed as Señora San Roque.

The brief civil ceremony had been a shuffle of papers, a rapid exchange of Spanish in the office of the justice of the peace, and a never ending line of handshakes from crowds of people who had appeared, it seemed, from nowhere.

"*Sí*. Maria Cruz and her sister, Maria Lourdes, have been employed along with Zonia Torres to do laundry and polishing. Also, there is the new chef, a man from Ensenada who was with the Britellin restaurant. A very grand man!"

"But you are so skilled!" Helen responded in surprise.

Soledad smiled. "Many years ago, when the

leave within hours of my wedding. I asked Soledad to bring us some supper."

"I'm not hungry," she said quietly. Except for a sip of the wine the justice of the peace had insisted they have at the registry, she had not eaten since breakfast.

"You are hungry and exhausted. You have had a long day during which you became an executive of San Roque Enterprises, a bride and mistress of the San Roque household. You also spent a busy morning at the office."

"I am not tired," she protested, refusing to admit to either condition.

"Since your time now is at my disposal," he reminded her, "you will remain at home for the rest of the day and the weekend. There is much I have planned."

"Planned?" She reached for her stenographic pad. "If you will give me your instructions—"

He took the pad and pencil from her nerveless fingers and tossed them both at a wide-mouthed urn by the stair newel. "When I am here—" he held her hands prisoner with each of his own lean dark ones "—you will give no appearance of being a businesswoman. You will be simply a woman...the woman you were meant to be."

She looked alarmed, but he paid no attention. "Your brother denigrated you and forced you to feel less than you are as a woman. Your husband will not let you be less than a queen in her castle." He smiled to reassure her and to her relief he released her hands.

He walked around her, inspecting the white nylon skirt that she had laundered so often during her stay on the island.

"The first item of business will be to provide you with decent clothing."

"I think my clothing is sufficiently...decent," she said in a small voice.

"The wardrobe expected of Señora Luis San Roque Quintana is of a special variety."

"I'll go into Cedros and find a seamstress. I doubt that the stores can fit me because of my height." Her shoulders were stiff and her golden eyes cool.

"You may do that if the necessity arises, but the director of the house that does the wardrobe of Yolanda Betancourt will arrive by company plane tomorrow morning with material and samples."

"I can't afford—" she began in some dismay.

"These clothes can be considered uniforms, which of course are always provided by an employer," he said with a glint of amusement at her discomfort. "Come, Helen, do not look so distressed. The prospect of a wardrobe of some quality would delight any other woman. Consider it a small fringe benefit of your durance here. There must be some such pleasures in our arrangement or you will not be able to produce the results you so confidently predict will accrue to my investment.''

''I like beautiful clothes. But there's no need to go to such expense as a designer when I am only to be here on Cedros. I can save the money—''

His hands bit into her shoulders as he interrupted her, ''One day I trust you will learn not to argue with me! Get some necessities in the village. You can wear them until you're furnished with proper clothing, such as befits a great lady. I do not want to see you in that rag again: it has served its purpose and scandalized Soledad sufficiently.''

His angry grip relaxed, and he rubbed her shoulders soothingly. She couldn't be annoyed with Soledad for making it known to San Roque that she had only one work skirt. After all, she told herself, he did have a right to dictate her general appearance under the circumstances. Nevertheless, the bitter facts of her predicament were hard to swallow.

''What is it that you are dying to say and choking back?'' he asked with his maddening smile.

''Nothing at all, I assure you.''

''Out with it or you will make yourself ill with keeping it bottled up.''

''I had nothing in mind, except....'' In spite

of herself she began to smile at the wicked thought that leaped into her memory "I was merely thinking of a small French quatrain—but you wouldn't want to hear it."

"I assure you I would like nothing better than to hear it."

Boldly she snapped it out:

> "Je suis Francoys, dont il me poise,
>   Ne de Paris empres pontoise,
>   Et d'une corde d'une toise
>   Scaura mon col que mon cul poise."

He laughed, a delighted sound, totally free from his usual restraint and control. His teeth were white and even. "I am surprised at you, Helen! Such ribald verse from poor old Villon coming from your inhibited lips!"

To her immense surprise he quoted it back to her, translating it from archaic French into perfect English. The short pauses he took allowed him the chance to make the verse rhyme.

> "I am Francois...luckless jay...
>   Born at Paris...by Ponthoise Way.
>   My neck...looped up beneath the tree,
>   Will learn how...heavy butt may be!"

She chose to restrain her admiration and challenged him again. "Perhaps you would prefer a more conservative prisoner's lament, written by a great American abolitionist:

"High walls and huge the body may confine
And iron grates obstruct the prisoner's gaze
And massive bolts may baffle his design
And vigilant keepers watch his devious ways:
Yet scorns the immortal mind this base control!
No chairs can bind it and no cell enclose!"

"Enough!" San Roque cut her off, laughing. "You have proven to me you are something of a bluestocking already, and you need not go to greater lengths. I do find your ability to see a bit of humor in the midst of your anger and frustration an interesting facet of your character at least. I have no fears that you will be an uneducated conversationalist."

She looked at him with quick suspicion; she seemed forever thrown off balance by his mercurial changes in mood.

"We may as well not be bored while I hold you for ransom, eh?" he said wryly, not allowing her to dismiss the question. She was forced to nod grudgingly.

The housekeeper prompted their adjournment to the dining room, where San Roque poured coffee and served Helen a bowl of the steaming *caldogallego* Soledad had brought in.

Helen tried to decline, but he was adamant. "If you do not sample Soledad's culinary efforts you will hurt her feelings."

She tasted some of the hearty broth and was unable to resist its infinite delicacy and delicious appeal.

"You were hungry after all," San Roque teased when she had finished. "Apparently I can judge your temperament better than you can. Are you through with your meal? We need to be about our errands." He rang for Soledad.

"We are going to the village where you will do some shopping. It is the duty of a husband to approve the selection of the wardrobe of his wife. So let us be off," he said, guiding her out the door. "I am only investing in your appearance for the image of the house of San Roque, you understand?" He smiled at her teasingly, and she did not immediately move out of his casual embrace as they waited for Vergel to bring the car.

BY THE TIME they returned to the great house, Helen was truly physically exhausted. She surveyed the results of the evening shopping sortie as Soledad shook out items and clucked over them.

"If Don Luis brings a proper dressmaker here, I will again enjoy caring for a true wardrobe. These are pleasant little things for a country whim, but not to be classed with Doña Isabella's clothes in the old days. Soon...." Soledad anticipated resuming duties she had obviously loved.

"I think some of these are absolutely beautiful!" Helen exclaimed as she held up a floor-length wraparound, hand-loomed linen skirt in a warm shade of brown banded in green Indian block print. It had a delightful swing to it and looked as chic as a designer original from an expensive boutique. She had bought a full-sleeved green satin shirt to complement it, and when she held the shirt up to her softly bronzed skin the color brought her hair alive like a flame. The contrast of the satin and the linen was sensational, a strange and exotic blend of textures.

The island dandies bought such shirts to wear to the *cantinas* and impress the girls. Ron had laughed at the shirts when he had seen them on young mainland men. "Obvious," he had called them, and perhaps they were meant to be by the wearers; but when the shirt caught Helen's eye, San Roque grinned and told her to indulge her daring taste. It looked marvelous, and San Roque had given a sign to the shop manager to wrap it for her.

"While it was meant for a young man, it is obvious you mean to wear it yourself. It only points up the impossibility of your ever being

mistaken for a man." San Roque gazed wolfishly at the way the collarless satin décolleté
neckline molded and accentuated the curves of
her breasts.

She could have managed perfectly well with
just one outfit, but he had insisted on buying
several, patronizing every shop in the city.

"Did he not replenish your lingerie?"
Soledad muttered. "I told him it was in sad condition."

"Of course he didn't!" Helen was about to
say when she remembered it was a Mexican husband's prerogative. "Señor San Roque was interested only in making me presentable. No one
is going to notice how plain my lingerie is."

"Ah, well," said Soledad wisely, "no doubt
the lingerie will arrive later from a better source,
then. I do not suppose a husband will notice
lingerie at this stage of your marriage. You
must, however, think about later, when he *will*
notice."

"Soledad—" Helen said crossly, then swallowed the words. The old woman was so pleased
for her employer and so excited about the developments that it didn't seem right to be cross
with her, nor proper to give her even the
slightest hint that the marriage was hardly a
romantic or passionate one. The servants would
know soon enough, for they quickly sensed
those things.

Soledad took her keys and unlocked the doors of the entrance to the *lugar de retiro*. "It has been years since the rooms were opened. This, as I told you when you first arrived, was the suite of the parents of Don Luis. Don Luis uses this den as his room when he is on the island."

"I didn't realize his room adjoined the one I was in," Helen responded, startled. His room next to hers? No! Everything he did, every circumstance seemed to conspire against her. There was no chance for her survival if he decided to demand what was now his by rights; he was quite capable of taking her in spite of his contract. She could not forget the moment on the beach that had overwhelmed her with its blatant suggestion of desire and passion.

Soledad did not realize her charge was dismayed. "I knew when you came, Doña Helena, that it would be but a matter of time before the doors were open again and there were two hollows on the pillows of the great bed in the mornings."

"There's a draft through these rooms," Helen said, trying to ignore Soledad's revelation. "We'll keep the doors closed and use the doors in the halls." She calmly shut the double connecting doors. She would see they were properly locked again as soon as it was possible.

Unaware of Helen's agitation, Soledad continued happily, "Yes, there is a breeze in these rooms, but you will be glad of it when hot weather comes again next year. Already it is growing colder. Soon will come the time of the *huracán*, the great storms. Then we will place cedar shields over the windows to prevent damage from flying tree branches." She laid out a drawnwork skirt and its beautifully intricate camisole top. "Will you wear this tonight? It is appropriate, for it is a wedding dress from the state of Tehuacan."

"A wedding dress!" No wonder San Roque had smiled when Helen, merely looking at it, marveling at the detail, had been pressed to try it on. No wonder he had insisted she take it even when she demurred.

"I think, tonight, the brown skirt and green satin shirt," she said with a stubborn set of her chin. "It's beautiful!"

"But, Doña Helena, this dress would please Don Luis! There is a portrait in the library of young Doña Isabella wearing just such a dress."

"I certainly don't think I resemble Señor San Roque's mother," Helen protested, remembering now with surprise that in the portrait his mother had indeed worn almost the same kind of dress. Why had she been attracted to it herself? "No, not that dress," she ordered firmly.

The great doors between the rooms were pushed open and San Roque appeared wrapped in a dressing gown, wiping water from his black hair with a thick towel. He ignored Helen's embarrassment at his appearance and surveyed the two of them as well as the dress in Soledad's hands.

"I want you to wear the dress from Tehuacan," he said almost as though the women's conversation had been overheard.

Soledad smiled broadly and again brought the drawnwork dress with its gauzy pleats from the press, where she had reluctantly placed it.

I suppose I must allow him to dictate what I wear, Helen thought, chafing at the imposition of San Roque's whim. With careless propriety he returned to his own room and Helen, sighing with relief to be released from the spell he seemed to cast on her whenever he was near, let Soledad drape her in the gauze.

She descended the staircase to the dining room wishing she had insisted on her right to free personal time, with specified hours in the contract. But, on second thought, that might have defeated her goal to be paid for as many jobs as possible.

She entered the library knowing she looked lovely. She had spied herself in the great hall mirror and been entranced by the romanticism of her dress. The sight of her own beauty had flushed her cheeks. Perhaps it was just as well he had wanted her to wear this special dress. In some strange way, it made her feel powerful and at the same time softly feminine.

San Roque, elegantly attired in a gray silk suit, waited for her in the library. He looked perfectly relaxed as host and master of the manor. "Ah!" he commented. "The dress was created with you in mind." His smoldering eyes swept over her and she felt her power dissolve to helplessness.

"It ought to sweep the floor, but I am too tall," she said, attempting to disregard the effect his words and eyes had on her.

"Who said you were too tall? Your brother? Other little men? You suit my taste and I appreciate the glimpse of pretty ankles. Will you have mineral water or sherry?"

"Bourbon and water," she said boldly.

He frowned.

"Unless you object," she added, deliberately placating him as a good employee ought.

"Certainly not," he said amiably. "Many of my business colleagues from the United States like Scotch or bourbon, and I keep a generous supply for them. Women generally choose sherry. I prefer mineral water or a very dry sherry before a meal I know has been prepared with distinction, for these do not spoil the palate. It is merely a matter of true sophistication."

"I will have the mineral water, then," she

said cooperatively, since she did not really like bourbon and water. She matched his relaxed manner outwardly, but inwardly she was tense.

He poured. "This is not the Perrier most guests expect. I prefer to patronize products of Mexico and serve Penafiel water from Tehuacan." He passed it to her and their hands touched. Hers shook as she lifted the crystal glass to her lips. He offered her a long dark cigarette from a magnificently chased silver box.

"I. . . I don't smoke."

"No? I should have thought an aggressive career woman like yourself would smoke small cigars." He smiled lightly, teasingly.

She did not smile. "The aroma of a good cigar doesn't offend my sensibilities, but I am not inspired to smoke one myself." She added, "Unless you expect me to smoke them as part of my duties?"

"Heaven forbid!" he said. "A woman who smells of tobacco loses power over a man rapidly, no matter what their relationship. Ah—here is Soledad to announce our wedding supper."

He set down his Penafiel and taking her elbow ushered her into the dining room, where two places had been elaborately laid at the great long table. She wished he would cease his possessive way of taking her arm and touching her back, though she was beginning to adjust to it with somewhat less galvanic reaction than at first. There was no way to protest, for she could not accuse him even silently of taking undue or unwelcome liberties. The problem was that in the present circumstances even his courtesies seemed fraught with danger. He would not understand if she tried to explain. He might even use her fear of him against her if she made an issue of it by flinching.

Although Helen was seated at one end of the table and San Roque at the other, she was more than aware of the gray eyes regarding her, intently assessing her as dinner was served. She could only predict what his next plan would be for her. Though he did not discuss anything but the most superficial of social amenities or the meal itself, her nervousness grew.

The meal began with a beautiful hors d'oeuvre of thinly sliced prosciutto and melon on a bed of watercress topped with a piquant dressing. Hot consommé was followed by a poached egg on a fine slice of pink ham garnished with hollandaise and an artichoke heart. Helen could barely taste the nuances of flavor; her normally healthy appetite had deserted her. She moved the food around on her plate and took small bites, attempting to go through the motions of eating.

Fresh fish, superlatively baked with the merest suggestion of lemon, was served with tiny new boiled potatoes. The main course consisted of roast duckling in a sherry sauce with a tender dollop of creamed spinach and a salad of white escarole.

Throughout the meal San Roque's enjoyment was as obvious as Helen's stiff silence. He ignored her mounting tension. When the dessert course arrived—baked oranges with curaçao—Helen couldn't eat a single bite.

"I would like a word with the new chef," San Roque said, finishing his portion with relish. When the man was summoned, San Roque compliment him warmly. "Excellent!"

The chef said, "*Señor*, when my list of necessary supplies arrives I will be able to handle any request and easily outdo tonight's meal."

"Are you settled? Is your family comfortable in the house in Cedros?"

"Everything is quite settled, Señor San Roque. My tools are also established in the kitchen here."

"You will have all the free time you wish, for when I am not in residence I doubt that Señora San Roque will require your attentions in quantity. At those times your responsibilities will be shared with Soledad. Only when I bring guests from the mainland will your talent and energies be challenged."

It crossed Helen's mind that much preparation had gone into bringing this chef here. His hiring had not been accomplished in one day. San Roque either had been very sure of her brother's continued absence and had planned this kind of bond to keep her here, or had planned changes in the running of his home for some time. She preferred to believe the latter.

"We will have brandy served in the sitting room," San Roque declared.

"It has been, as you mentioned earlier, a long day," Helen pointed out. "With your permission, I would like to retire."

"Of course. I shall be up shortly."

Helen exited gracefully and climbed the stairs to her room. His words were for the servant's benefit, she thought; but if he had any intention...she had the key to lock the door and she would use it.

She took the great ring of keys from the top drawer of the chest and inserted key after key into the lock of the connecting door, attempting to find a match. After what seemed to her interminable failures, she found the proper key. San Roque could not break past this door, she thought. It was as solid and impenetrable as six inches of oak could make it!

Finally she backed away, breathing a sigh of relief. She shook loose the knot of hair piled high on her head and slipped out of the high sandals. Her toes relaxed in the thick carpet as she headed for the bathroom.

When she'd finished bathing, she hopped into bed and began brushing her long hair, curled from the dampness of the bath, and braided it for the night.

Quietly the hall door opened, and San Roque strolled in with easy familiarity. Helen dropped her brush in shock. She had been so concerned with the connecting door that she had not locked the main hall door.

Barely glancing her way, he walked through and tried the handle of the locked door.

"Give me the key, Helen." He held out his hand.

The key ring was beside her on the bed. She sat immobile.

"You are invading my privacy," she said stubbornly. "There's not the slightest need for that door to be unlocked."

"Let the servants guess, if they wish, that this marriage was not made in heaven—but that door remains unlocked, or by God I will sleep with you in the master bed and the sheets will daily bear evidence to keep the servants admiring their master's machismo."

"You wouldn't!" she gasped, her face draining of all color. She was quite sure he was capable of carrying out his threat. Reaching beside her, she grasped the key ring and threw it across the room so that it landed on the carpet at his feet.

In one instant his long stride brought him to the bed. Before she could prevent him, he grasped her by the shoulders and pulled her to him. His mouth came down on hers and he forced her lips apart with his probing tongue.

Then, as quickly as he had caught her off guard, he let her go and she fell back among the soft pillows. Leaning over her in an instant, like a hawk seizing a sparrow or a panther pinioning a rabbit, he pressed her to the bed with his hard thighs. She was unable to move her arms or her body.

"Is this the way you honor all your contracts?" she cried out, struggling unsuccessfully to free herself. Her panic transcended any of the wild longings that had leaped to the surface moments before, suffusing her to the core. She managed to twist her face away from him long enough to manage, "The great Luis San Roque, who never has had to force a woman to his bed!"

Astonishingly, he smiled down at her with amusement hot on the heels of his brutal assault on her senses. His blazing eyes were sardonic and his laugh mocking. Suddenly he drew her close to him and slowly, passionately, lowered his mouth to hers. This time his method was gentle and persuasive, no longer forceful, and it was impossible to resist his touch; she felt as if she were drugged. His eyes gazed down into her own, still angry and intense despite the hypnotic effect of his touch.

She was fighting him, still, unwilling to give all of herself to him. But as his lips wandered from her mouth to her throat to her eyes, she felt her resistance wane.

He teased her eyelids playfully with his tongue, then flicked down to her ear, exploring the whorl of it until she shuddered involuntarily with the thrill of the sweet sensations he aroused in her. All the fight went out of her and her heart pounded furiously as his mouth found her breast and teased the nipple until it swelled with desire. His hands moved caressively down the rest of her body, seeking out her soft hidden recesses, awakening her senses and tapping her deepest needs. She grew unavoidably aware of the intensity of his desire for her and knew how close she was to complete sensual surrender. It was then that her rational mind called a halt.

This can't be happening, she thought wildly. *I won't allow it!* Willing herself to feel nothing, to register nothing, she suddenly went limp.

Her feigned indifference succeeded. San Roque was immediately aware of the change in her and his caresses ceased. He raised his head and looked at her. She stared back, willing her fury, her desire and her fear to be nullified, willing herself to recede from the tidal wave of sensations that had almost overwhelmed her. The impasse she created destroyed the emotions crackling between them. She felt drained and sensed the same had happened to him, though there was no indication of that in him physically.

"Do you see now with what kind of danger you court?" he asked her softly. "Do you want to take more chances with me?"

She was able only to shake her head with great effort and shut her eyes so they would not betray her near surrender to him. She was trembling violently as she continued to shake her head.

He released her, walked across the room, picked up the offending keys, unlocked the connecting door and then dropped the keys almost at the spot where she had thrown them.

"This door remains unlocked from now on," he said quietly, and shut it behind him.

She lay dazed, knowing that if she tried to stand, her weakened legs would not hold her upright. When her heart resumed its normal rhythm she cautiously sat up.

There was silence beyond the door. She could have been absolutely alone in the great house. Shaking with panic and the ragged remains of her resistance, she leaped from bed and ran to pick up the abandoned key ring.

Anger soon replaced her other emotions. She hated him! How she hated him! She realized she hated herself, too, for responding to his caresses so easily, wanting them as much as she wanted to reject him.

Her trembling fingers barely managed to get the drawer of the chest open to drop in the keys. She ran to the storage room and opened her paint box, taking out the sharp knife she used for whittling wedges on canvas frames or sharpening carbon pencils. Clenching the knife grimly, she carried it back to the bedroom. It was a silly weapon, but she felt better for it.

The mountain fog made the room chilly and her shivering, she realized, was not all due to the unwelcome attentions of San Roque. She closed the great leaded windows against the damp of the night and went back to huddle on the bed and stare at the closed double doors. At any moment they might open and he could invade her room again.

If he does—I'll kill him, she assured herself grimly. But at the same time she recognized the foolishness of her threat; for the real villain was her own body with its treacherous urges. What compounding of misery would her succumbing to his primitive machismo bring!

An hour ticked by, and her eyes began to glaze with fatigue and droop. The door remained closed. Finally she placed the knife in

the bedside-table drawer and dozed off into a
fitful sleep. . . .

SHE WOKE WITH A START as she felt San Roque's
touch on her shoulder. He halted her tense convulsive attempt to escape with a firm hand, as a
trainer might gentle a skittish colt. The knife? It
was of no use to her now. What good would it
do to struggle against this man? She lay looking
at him warily, haunted by memories of the evening before. Would he caress her again, proving
to her that she could not resist him? She could
not read his expression, but there seemed to be
no passionate plan registered on his mobile
features.

It was morning. The last wisps of fog trailed
out to sea. There was a beautiful salty damp sea
smell in the air of the room. "Soledad is bringing up breakfast and will wait outside to take
our tray when we finish. Would you rather eat
here, or shall I have her set it in the sitting
room?"

"The sitting room," Helen said in a daze. She
suddenly became self-consciously aware of her
threadbare cotton pajamas and her lack of a
robe. He lifted her gently from the bed and
steadied her until, still paralyzed by sleep, she
found her balance. Then she followed him into
the sitting room, feeling slightly disoriented.

San Roque was cheerful this morning, as

though the night before had never happened. He courteously offered her toast, jam and juice, then helped himself to the food.

Helen sat rigid at the little table, cautiously sipping her juice. It was cold and unexpectedly sweet with a strange exotic tang; she recognized the taste immediately. "Jackfruit!" she exclaimed. "I haven't had it since we were in Hawaii when I was little, and dad owned the stationery store. It's so good!"

"We call it *guanabana*, and it grows on the mainland of Mexico," he said in a perfectly conversational tone that bore no trace of threatening sensual confrontation. "Soledad knows how much I like it."

Abruptly, the conversation shifted. "The company plane has already arrived with the designer and his assistant from Mexico City," San Roque informed her. He indicated she should pour the coffee. "After *desayuno* you will present yourself to them. The plane also brought some lingerie, which I left in the other room. You might like to have proper foundations for the fittings."

Her face flamed, but he took no notice. "Sebastian and his assistant are breakfasting downstairs now. When you are ready, you can be measured, then select materials and designs. Sebastian is, I am told, a wizard. Certainly Yolanda has the reputation of great chic."

"I'm sure she has," Helen said, her voice shaky.

A willowy young man, impeccably groomed with a carefully styled mustache, waited for them in the library. By his side stood his assistant—a beautifully turned-out middle-aged woman with two tape measures hanging around her neck. The library was overflowing with their equipment: boxes, tissue-covered bolts of cloth, huge portfolios of designs.

The young man stood on tiptoe in his soft embroidered leather dancing slippers and clapped his hands with undisguised delight as he assessed Helen's appearance in the brown print skirt and blazing green shirt.

"The House of Sebastian is at the Señora San Roque's service!" Rather than being intimidated by her height, he seemed to revel in it. "Indeed at your service! Were you a haute couture model before your marriage, Señora San Roque?"

"Heavens, no! But I was often in demand as a flagpole," she answered, laughing.

His dark brown eyes sparkled and he almost pirouetted in his enthusiasm. "You will turn out to be my greatest example of the art of Sebastian," he exclaimed, "for you have natural style. Who would have chosen such a successfully warring combination of separates without a royal eye for true fashion!" He circled her as though she were some prize he had acquired, imperiously beckoning his assistant forward with the first of the huge portfolios.

"Such a woman must never be hidden on a faraway island, *señor*," he protested to San Roque in the background as he tore into the brown paper covering the first bolt of material and unfurled it with a snap of the wrists.

Every design was more elegant than the last. The materials were exquisite, and Sebastian's skills soon impressed Helen. His enthusiasm impressed her, too. He plowed through every cloth sample from linen to tropical-weight wool to beautiful raw and Thai silk.

"I can't possibly wear all this in two lifetimes, not even three!" Helen protested to San Roque. "I'll be an old woman before I have the opportunity to wear each item more than once."

"Let me judge your requirements," San Roque replied, unperturbed. "See to it she has proper shoes, as well," he ordered Sebastian.

"But of course," the designer agreed petulantly.

"I suppose you think I should wear conservative shoe heights?" Helen said slyly. "Everyone seems to want to cut me down to size here."

"Señora San Roque, your size is only one of the glorious things about you," said the young man, not at all overwhelmed in spite of being short himself.

"Order what is correct, Sebastian. If the mode declares stilts, then that is quite acceptable to me. I want her properly dressed," San Roque drawled. "I also will need a hairdresser to stand ready to report to the island every Friday at times when we are both in residence."

"I don't need a hairdresser," Helen objected. "I've done my own hair all my life and it's *not* going to be cut!"

"It will be dressed as it ought always to have been dressed," San Roque interrupted. "You may have been a redheaded witch to your brother, but you will be called a titian-haired queen by any visitor to this island." He turned to Sebastian. "You will have my itinerary from my secretary in Mexico City. See that arrangements are made for next week, when we will entertain two of my foreign colleagues and their wives. Since one of the ladies was the subject of an international style magazine recently, I would not like Señora San Roque to be at a disadvantage."

With a dramatic gesture of his pearl and gold ringed hands, Sebastian assured him, "But, *señor*, my reputation would be at stake if your lady did not present her best appearance! If you have your secretary tell me what activities the weekend dictates, I will see that all necessary items are delivered by Friday along with my own brother, who is the top hairstylist in Mexico City!''

AFTER A DAY WITH SEBASTIAN Helen knew what exhaustion could really be. She had been measured and fitted with indefatigable zest. The only person in the house who was not exhausted seemed to be San Roque.

He remained in the background, calmly approving or rejecting the items Sebastian recommended. Only occasionally was Sebastian's protest heard.

At last even Sebastian seemed to have exhausted his store of samples. ''There is, of course, the matter now of accessories and jewels—''

''Never mind jewels. *La señora* has no need of new ones at this time.''

''But of course I realize she has jewels already. The San Roque collection was always one of the great ones. But I suggest this lady was born for emeralds such as Bechtel de México have recently displayed in some fabulous new designs.''

''Sebastian, every redhead wears emeralds if her husband or lover can afford them,'' San Roque dismissed the suggestion. ''And every raven-haired beauty fancies emeralds are her special stone, as well. I do not care to see my wife display jewels merely because I can afford them. She is unique and need not follow the crowd.''

Sebastian raised a well-manicured eyebrow but reluctantly agreed. "Still...it is a shame when emeralds, too, are such a work of nature's art.'' He gestured to his silently attentive assistant to gather up their equipment.

At least San Roque had not gone so far with the farce as to purchase expensive jewelry to decorate her. Helen already felt like an odalisque in such a costly, unending list of clothing.

Never mind, she told herself. *He can dress me in paper clips or a nose ring if it suits his purpose to make me an appropriate hostess for his houseguests. I can carry off the game when he's here. Such elaborate "uniforms" can stay in the closets with Soledad to guard them. The main thing is to work things out so that they can be turned back to him in perfect condition as soon as possible!*

San Roque came up behind her, unheard on the cloud of carpet in the library, and put his hands on the back of her neck. "You are exhausted.'' His thumbs lightly caressed the nape of her neck. "You must feel free tomorrow to do whatever you want. No interference from me.''

"Thank you.'' She wished the gentle massage were not so damnably relaxing, refreshing.

He moved away to stand at the window and look out over his island. She said in a small voice, "Then may I go now?"

"Go on to your room if you like," he said, not turning, his voice harsh in the gathering dusk. "I will not intrude, and Sunday is a day of freedom."

"I—thank you!" she said again, and when he did not respond she escaped to her room.

CHAPTER SEVEN

HELEN SLEPT SOUNDLY THAT NIGHT but woke early, intent on quickly eating breakfast, then going outside to paint. She wanted to begin a watercolor of the city from the beautiful terrace vista. Dawn light was always perfect, with the fog just lifting. She had awakened feeling like singing, and sing she did as she came down the stairs.

Early as she was, Soledad was earlier. The two Marias were already polishing away at the furniture, and Zonia, on her knees, scrubbed the tiles of the great hall.

As Helen came down the stairs, Soledad was directing the houseman in the removal of one of the paintings on the landing.

"Why is that being taken away?" Helen asked.

"It is to be rehung in the *galeria*, Doña Helena. The boys are putting here a picture by our island artist, the old one—El Viejo."

Helen looked curiously at the large framed painting being carried in by two village youths on hand for heavy work. The picture was a seascape and had a nice feeling to it, but it was not a masterpiece. The rest of the collection in the great-hall *galeria* was carefully chosen and obviously valuable.

"El Viejo has talent," Soledad explained, seeing Helen's somewhat critical look, "but he is no mainland artist. The picture is a gift from the islanders to el señor for saving the north harbor. Sea lions and also cormorants live there and breed. El señor would not let the sea creatures be driven out because greedy people wished to have a yacht basin for the *norteamericanos* who sail their yachts this way in the summer."

Helen could see that the painting of the cormorants and sea lions, the rocky promontory and sheltered bay, was indeed a tribute to the natural beauty of the area. How strange San Roque was, she thought as she went out onto the stone terrace that overlooked the city.

There was a haze over the pyramids of white salt and the squat sheds that housed the salt industries along the wharf. The entire wharf was a testimonial to San Roque's industrial reach— from the mainland to the peninsula to this island. Inside the great house the art gallery testified to that same reach, bringing the most sophisticated elements of the city to the isolated island. On one hand he brought the world to the island and made it prosperous; on the other, he preserved the ecology that had existed unchanged on the island's rocks for centuries.

Soledad brought fruit, coffee and hot *bolillos* out to Helen for *desayuno*. As usual, she fussed at her for objecting to such a spread of food so early in the morning.

Helen sketched in the section of the city she was inspired to paint—the part with the church spire rising high, the blue-and-gold ornamentation standing out above the squat wood buildings clustered around it. She forgot the problem of Ron, the contract and the man sleeping upstairs. She washed in the sky and began to lay on pastel shades of houses in jewel colors somewhat grayed in the dawn, and then dry-brushed one of the dark cedars in the foreground.

A bush down the slopes by the cedar rustled out of harmony with its neighbors. Helen looked at it sharply. There was some kind of animal hiding in its depths. A deer?

She polished her glasses and looked again. This time she caught a glimpse of white among the leaves as the bush rustled again.

Curiosity won over caution. She left the terrace, circled around the area and came at the bush from below. "Hello, little one!" she called to the child she caught still crouched behind the bush, peering at the great house.

The child turned so suddenly he lost his balance and fell over in an awkward little heap.

"What are you doing here, *niño*?"

"I came to see my aunt, *señora*."

"Which of the maids is your aunt?"

"Why, Zonia Torres!" he stammered, staggering to his feet. Helen saw with a wrench of compassion that he was crippled with a club-foot. The forked stick with which he supported himself had been flung down the slope in his fall.

"Tía Zonia does the laundry and polishes the silver in the great house," he said, continuing to look up at her. Seeing she was not hostile, he became quite at ease despite his prone position. "What do you do, *señora*? Paint pictures for *el patrón*?"

"*¡Sí!*" she laughed. "What do you call yourself, *niño*?"

"I am Juanito. There is no food in Rafaela's house and no milk in ours. I did not know what to do," he complained slyly. "So. . . I had to come and ask Tía Zonia."

"If you're hungry, Juanito, you may share my country roll while I go fetch your aunt."

"May I take some back to Rafaela?"

"Certainly, if you like."

She left him on the patio ripping into the food Soledad had brought out, and went to find Zonia, now dusting the great staircase balustrade.

"What is that brat doing here!" Zonia exclaimed, both exasperated and embarrassed by the child's temerity in bothering the *patrona*.

"Don't scold him, Zonia. There was no milk at home. Is Rafaela your child?"

"Not mine, *señora*!" Zonia looked shocked. "I am not married, but I am a good girl! Rafaela is the child of a girl who works in the cannery all day and dances all night in the *cantinas*. She was cursed for her sins. My dead sister, her companion in wickedness, was also cursed with Juanito for her sins."

"A darling little boy like Juanito is not a curse!"

"You have seen his foot?" Zonia crossed herself.

"Such accidents are not curses!"

"It is not I who say so, *señora*, but others. Nevertheless, my dead sister and Rafaela's mother danced in the *cantinas* with abandon and had their children without benefit of marriage. Both are marked children!" she ended triumphantly.

"What is wrong with the other child—Rafaela?"

"She does not walk, she does not talk and she must be cared for entirely. Still, she is a patient child under her afflictions, so perhaps you are right, *señora*, and she has a saint within her soul in spite of her mother."

"She is... *imbecile*?"

"Who knows, *señora*, since she does not talk. I think she manages to make her wants known to those she trusts, so perhaps she thinks. Her mother pays Juanito to look after her and be the substitute for useless muscles that do not obey the will. Do you want me to tell Juanito to go away and stop worrying you about her?"

"He has left a helpless little girl all alone?"

"Rafaela will be all right," Zonia shrugged.

"You say she cannot care for herself. I will have Vergel take Juanito and me to see that the child is all right."

Zonia, looking anxious about causing trouble, followed Helen back to the terrace, where Juanito was now delving into her paints.

Zonia screamed at him in terror, *"¡Malcriado!"*

"Don't scold him," Helen shushed her, laughing. "Juanito, you rascal! Hasn't anyone ever told you not to add to another artist's painting? You must work only on your own paper."

Juanito ducked his head. "The little tree wanted to be in the painting, *señora*."

"That's quite true!" She looked with amazement at the cedar now in her painting. "You have talent, Juanito. Do you paint at home?"

"I do not have paints, *señora*, nor paper." He looked yearningly at Helen's supply.

"Well, you shall finish this painting for yourself, later. Meanwhile we have to see to poor Rafaela. Come—I will take you home in the *carro*."

"You need not go to such trouble, Señora San Roque," Zonia protested.

"Is this the *patrona*?" Juanito asked, astonished. "Why did you not tell me, *patrona*? You do not dress like a *patrona*."

"These are my painting clothes, Juanito," Helen explained. "Smeared, aren't they? Take the rest of the bananas and I will have Soledad bring you more country rolls for Rafaela. Zonia, I'll go down as far as the house of Vergel and he will drive us the rest of the way. Juanito can be our guide. Don't worry; I will return soon."

"Do not disturb Vergel this hour of a Sunday!" came an order from above. Helen looked up to see San Roque leaning over the balcony dressed in a polo shirt and slacks.

"You said—" Helen began to remind him that he had ordered her to be driven to Vergel— and also that this day was hers.

"Sunday is his day of rest, too," came San Roque's dictum. "You will make do with me."

"Is that *el patrón*?" Juanito tugged at her, impressed.

San Roque disappeared from the balcony but appeared in a moment on the tiled patio, wearing a butter-soft suede jacket with a scarf tucked into the neck of his shirt. He carried a soft woven Mexican *rebozo* shawl, which he threw around Helen's shoulders, cocooning her against the chill of morning.

"Where do you go to school?" she asked Juanito as they rode in the back seat in grand style while San Roque jauntily assumed the chauffeur's role.

"Me? I do not go to the school. The school is not for me, or Rafaela. They would laugh at us and worse. I would like to buy many paints and paint many pictures, but I would not go to school."

The child was obviously unhappy to come to the end of such a prestigious ride.

"You live in Barrio X?" Helen asked, horrified to recognize the slum she had remarked on earlier with Vergel.

"Not I but Rafaela, *patrona*. Our *casa* is across the way—not one of those bad places!"

San Roque turned his head. "You are not wise to get involved with these children, Helen. The little girl's mother is, to put it plainly, a *puta*."

"Rafaela's mama is not my concern, but Rafaela is," she told him firmly. "She is young, crippled and alone and should be watched over. She can't go hungry."

"She is just up there, at the top, in the oldest

section, *patrona*." Juanito gestured with his forked stick. At the top of the makeshift nests up the side of the perpendicular hillside was a small dark figure. "She is coming to meet us, *patrona. Hola*, Rafaela! Wait!"

Helen was out of the car in a flash, racing up the rickety steps to intercept the child.

As she carried Rafaela down, Helen judged her age to be about four years. The child was far too small to be left to her own devices. The thought of a brain-damaged tot clambering about such a dangerous area incensed her.

"This is the *patrona*, Rafaela! And we have brought you a banana and some good bread! I rode in the *carro del patrón*!"

Helen dried the tears on the tiny girl's cheeks with her own shirttail. "Hush, Juanito! Rafaela's not deaf, are you, *niña*?"

Rafaela shook her head vigorously. Good, Helen thought. The child appeared to have normal intelligence and more than normal determination, so she was not nearly as hopeless as Zonia had pictured her. "Since there's no food at your house, we will go back to mine, and you shall both breakfast with me!" She glared defiantly at San Roque, who said nothing. "At least, Rafaela can eat, but Juanito cannot be hungry. He has already had two oranges, a banana, bread, coffee and a papaya."

"But I am always hungry, *patrona*!" the little boy protested.

"Then you are in luck, for Soledad loves hungry boys and girls. She always tries to stuff food into me."

"Is that why you grew tall like a giant?" Juanito asked.

Helen laughed. She looked up at the rabbit warren and the rickety catwalks on each level. "Where does Rafaela stay? Perhaps we should go up and leave a note for her mother to know she is safe with Zonia."

"You don't have to do that," Juanito scoffed. "She won't be home till tonight and maybe not even then, since a merchant ship is here."

Back at the house, Helen carried Rafaela into the kitchen and sat down at the table with her. San Roque seemed to have been detained by the indefatigably charming Juanito, who, having overcome his fear of *el patrón*, could not extract enough information from him about the *carro*.

"Where have you been, Doña Helena?" Soledad asked curiously.

"Out for a ride with el señor. Can you make some hot cornmeal mush and hot chocolate for Rafaela and Juanito?"

Soledad went about the task without comment.

"Tell me, Soledad, could these children stay

up here during the day when Zonia works and play out back of the kitchen? It would be so much safer than Barrio X."

"If that is what you want, Doña Helena. The children could play in the garden if they did not annoy the gardener."

"You would not let Rafaela annoy anyone, would you, Juanito? And you are a good boy yourself, I'm sure."

"I am very responsible," he declared proudly.

"What if you could come here every morning and have some paints to use, and I promised to pay you regularly for watching Rafaela. Would you never leave Rafaela alone as you did this morning?"

"Even without the pesos, *patrona*, the promise of paint would cause me never to leave her side."

"Except when you are in school," Helen pointed out.

"School costs money, Doña Helena," Soledad put in mildly. "Zonia is not responsible for his education, only for helping to feed her parents and the boy. The sister, Estelita, is old enough to work at the cannery but will soon marry and have her own family to worry over."

"It can't cost much to send such a little boy to school!"

Soledad enumerated costs on her fingers: tuition, books, paper, pencils. Helen added the costs in her head and subtracted them from the sale of one painting. Juanito could attend school for a year for such a little outlay of cash in her life, yet that little amount was beyond what his grandparents and his aunts could afford. She wondered if she might somehow add the cost of that schooling to the deductions she was allowed from the debt payments. Would San Roque disapprove actively? She would chance confronting him with the proposal that the few miserable pesos be allowed.

"You *niños* finish your breakfast and go out and play," she suggested. "Juanito, if Rafaela gets cold or wants to take a nap, will you wrap her in a blanket? Soledad will give you one. Don't let her crawl near anything that might be dangerous."

"*¡Sí, patrona!* You will see how responsible I can be!"

"Calm down. I am no more deaf than Rafaela." She smiled at him while protecting her ears from his loud joyous shout.

Turning to Soledad, she said, "Please talk to Zonia about the children...especially little Rafaela. I wouldn't be able to sleep nights thinking about that child tumbling off those terrible stairs!"

The housekeeper made a hissing sound that Helen now knew signified impatience with the *señora*'s whims. It was also a sign that she had heard and would take care of the matter.

Having changed from her painting clothes to one of the new blouses in her wardrobe, a snowy Mexican cotton layered with fine handmade lace ruffles and a neckline that showed off her lovely shoulders, Helen slipped into a coffee-brown peasant skirt and matching sandals. She was twisting up her hair when San Roque entered her room unannounced.

"Do you object to what I did?" she asked, turning to look directly at him, wondering what his scowl meant.

"Not necessarily. I only wonder if you plan to bring all of Barrio X here to the *casa*. If so, I have more practical suggestions."

"Barrio X is no laughing matter. The place is an ulcer. How can you let it exist?"

"I have no jurisdiction over Barrio X," he told her, his scowl deepening. "And you have not contracted to remodel the island of Cedros, only to teach some of the targeted inhabitants English and business methods. The inhabitants of the barrio perpetuate their problems by accepting that way of life instead of seeking jobs in the salt industry and housing elsewhere."

"Must these two children suffer?"

"Did I say that? If Zonia can keep them out of the way of the other servants and is not unduly disturbed by them herself, I have no objection. In fact I find it confirms my suspicion that you have a strong maternal streak."

Unexpectedly, she was grateful, and she smiled at him genuinely. "Thank you!" Her eyes gleamed with her appreciation.

"You are a strange girl...." San Roque lounged against the wall by the connecting doors and frowned speculatively at her.

"What do you mean?"

"I mean that for casual permission to take in two waifs and make a center for children of sorts, you are inordinately grateful. For a hundred thousand dollars' worth of beautiful clothes you are indifferent."

She gulped a little at the cost of the wardrobe. "I didn't ask for the clothes," she said quietly. "If I'd had my choice that money would have been better spent to reduce the debt I owe. However, I am not indifferent to gorgeous things to wear. I just wonder where your priorities lie."

"Let us mutually agree that those 'uniforms' are needed for the duties you perform as hostess in my home."

"I'll accept that, but it doesn't require me to be grateful. As for the two children—I have *asked* for consideration for them, and I thank you for giving it. The little boy is unusually talented; maybe I can help him to develop that talent. The little girl...well, it's a personal whim, I suppose; but after seeing the situation in which she exists, I'd be miserable if I ignored her.''

"Orientals say that once you save a life you are responsible for that life ever after.''

"Her poor little life could never be a burden to me,'' she stated firmly.

San Roque paused for a moment. "Perhaps you are right,'' he concluded. "And now, when you are ready, Vergel will drive us to the church in the square. It is to be something of a formal introduction for you to the citizens of Cedros. They wish to acknowledge you as *patrona*.''

Helen would not have the free day she had hoped for. But he had done her a favor and she, too, could be generous, even if it seemed a mockery for her to meet the villagers as Señora San Roque.

THE WORD OF SAN ROQUE'S MARRIAGE had obviously run like a wildfire throughout the city, and after the mass in the square it was almost impossible for them to make their way down the broad stone steps to the car. San Roque kept his arm around Helen as they received felicitations and cheers from what seemed to be nearly every man, woman and child in the city, and many from down the island. Gifts of fruit, flowers and carvings were offered, as well. San Roque appeared to know every single citizen by name.

Afterward, as the crowd thinned and the air

of fiesta faded, they were joined by the priest.

"You must take today's *comida* with us, Father," San Roque invited him. He added without looking at Helen, "At a later date there will be a blessing of the marriage in the church; but for now my wife, who is not of the island, would prefer to make arrangements for blessings with her own parish first."

Helen said nothing, though she felt her face flush. The explanation served a purpose. San Roque at least was not putting the seal of his church on the marriage, which indicated some faith with the agreement they had made. He could be sensitive when he wanted to. Again she found herself feeling grateful that she did not have to go against her deepest conviction that marriage blessed by the church—any church—was no light matter to be confused with a temporary business contract.

Later, sitting at the dining-room table with the priest and Eugenio Ochoa and his wife, she again was silent. San Roque and Eugenio talked of business matters, while Magdalena Ochoa and the priest conversed on local subjects. Helen felt alien and lost.

"I leave, then, for Mexico City tonight, Eugenio," San Roque announced. "You will come with me. It is time. We will return on Friday."

"Eugenio!" cried Magdalena, as if all the

pleasure had suddenly gone from her evening.

"You will both survive," San Roque soothed her, impatient with her anxiety. "Do not look so stricken, Magdalena. I will bring him back. You can do good works and pray with the good priest while he is gone. He must learn to be a businessman in a world that looks more and more to Mexico."

"You're coming back next weekend?" Helen blurted. She was aware of the irony that while Magdalena could barely stand the separation of a scant four days, she looked at the time her husband was off the island in quite a different fashion.

"I expect to use this house to the extent my parents once did." He cast Helen a warning look, reminding her of her signed agreement. "There is much to do in a short time and I intend to entertain business colleagues and their wives here."

"After so many years!" the priest exclaimed with pleasure. "I am glad to hear it! Well I remember the days of Doña Isabella and your good father, Luis. You were only a little boy when the house was bright with fiesta. How you strove to emulate your father!"

He continued, "You and your father sorely missed the good Doña Isabella after the tragedy. I recall how Don Adelberto became a driven man, grieving himself to death even while he expanded the family business in his frenzy to forget his loss. His determination turned you into a man before your time."

The old priest sipped thoughtfully at his wine. "I worried and prayed for you, Luis. You became a serious child overnight. Nothing was the same for you after your mother died and I feared your father forgot you were only a boy and could not be expected to lose yourself in work. Yes, I am glad you have brought a beautiful wife to the island and that you are opening the house."

Helen thought to herself that it was no wonder young Luis San Roque had become a powerful, enigmatic adult. He still emulated his father, even to working single-mindedly to build his empire. She felt a strange compassion for the little boy who had lost his mother and father and wondered if Ron's miserable childhood had similarly affected him even more than she and her father ever realized.

The same fire that melts wax hardens steel, she mused; but somewhere in Ron's life there must have lain a more telling flaw. Had he looked back at all to wonder what was happening to his sister here? Could she have prevented the whole crazy scheme he had hatched if she had understood him better? Guilty or not, she was paying and would settle the debt.

CHAPTER EIGHT

AFTER EUGENIO OCHOA LEFT with San Roque on Sunday evening, Helen's first duty was to soothe the distraught Magdalena Ochoa, who was not at all sure she could survive being separated from her husband until Friday morning.

Soledad sourly pointed out to Magdalena, with the familiarity of one whose age entitles her, that if she expected Eugenio to become as important to Don Luis as Magdalena proudly held in her heart, then she must make many sacrifices and be the kind of wife an executive in the outside world needed. Soledad's years of experience as housekeeper to San Roque and his father lent strength to her advice, and Magdalena went through the week in a somewhat calmed state of mind while Helen concentrated on her new situation.

It galled Helen to have to send her personal mail through San Roque, but she had no other recourse. When he left he took three personal letters with him. The first was to her father with the most careful of explanations and announcements. She suspected that he would not be overjoyed to hear of her marriage.

Though she was intensely loyal to her father, she realized he must be upset, perhaps even annoyed, that she had not returned to take care of him. His disability since the accident had made him bitter and fretful. Now, she assured him, his son-in-law would continue to see to his financial needs. She hoped he would approve of her marriage; if he didn't, she suspected he would probably continue to address her as Miss Helen Forster, refusing to acknowledge her changed status.

She made little reference to Ron in her letter: the subject was immensely distressing to her and she was still in the dark as to his whereabouts. She wondered if San Roque had his agents actively looking for her brother or if he was as resigned as she had become to the inevitability of her paying the entire debt.

She wrote a cheerful note to Aunt Edna. The old lady was alone and determined to stay in her little home. The city had encroached on her space over the years and her house was now at the center of the city instead of in the midst of farmland.

Lastly Helen wrote to the old chess player in Sausalito and told him she would be delighted to play chess by mail with the partner he had found for her, especially since the new player guaranteed his capabilities as a teacher who would give her pointers. She could use a little added diversion to preserve her sanity during what was apparently to be a long-term imprisonment.

The additional chess matches would be a break from her duties on the island. She had already begun to plan her strategy for training employees and there was time for a few personal pastimes. She scheduled chess times in her appointment book: "Wednesday, 9:00 P.M.: chess with Don Castle, new player, San Francisco. Thursday: chess with Michael McDonaugh, Sausalito." She wondered what San Roque thought of her chess-playing partners, if he was aware of them at all. So far he had made no disapproving or sarcastic comments.

Handling classes was the simplest part of Helen's new job. An expert teacher, she lacked only students. Early in the week she announced that the training project would soon begin and asked how many would be interested. A profound silence greeted her; the sea of brown eyes in the big room held no expression.

"The classes will be conducted during siesta and you will have a half hour to eat your *almuerzo*. Also, there will be no charge."

Still no response. Was she was going to fail miserably at her contract? She could not fail!

"This is your chance to rise in your careers," she urged.

She had expected some indifference from the few women employed in the office. What was hard to understand was the total lack of interest from the men, who should have been anxious to be promoted.

"Mexico is no longer *mañana* land," she said firmly. "The eyes of the world are on her development. You must be ready to lead, to advance!"

San Roque's male secretary pointed out patiently for the umpteenth time, "But everyone takes siesta." He obviously wanted to be off home as soon as the noon bell sounded.

Sighing, Helen let him go. She gave Vergel a box of her work to carry to the car.

"What is wrong with your people?" she asked him more or less rhetorically. "Here I am trying to help them and they won't take classes even free of charge."

"Why must you teach during siesta, Señora San Roque?" Vergel asked her.

"For one thing, it is a large block of time, and for another, classes after hours would come when everyone is tired and wants to go home to supper. Classes from twelve-thirty to two are ideal."

Vergel did not answer. She had a faint suspicion he knew something he did not care to voice.

"Is that not true, Vergel?"

"I would not want to say, Señora San Roque." He ducked his head and hunched his shoulders.

"But I think you know a reason why I am unsuccessful. Please tell me," she persisted.

Vergel still refused to answer.

"Remember, I told you it was important that I get to know the island. I am not yet a *mexicana* to the core and I won't know where I'm going wrong unless someone helps me."

"True," he mumbled. Finally he answered haltingly in an almost inaudible voice, "At noon we like to.... That is our wives...."

"We like to...?" Helen repeated, bewildered; then realization downed. So that was it! "All the men?" she blurted.

Yes, all the men in the office were married, and all had homes to go to and wives waiting. She remembered something she had read a long time before: that the men of Latin America all felt the best time of the day to make love was at noon.

She stifled a laugh. How stupid she had been not to realize that the siesta had other, more powerful reasons for its hold on the Mexicans and the islanders than just the break it offered from the midday heat of the tropics.

"Thank you, Vergel. I see I have more to

learn than I realized. You have helped me greatly.''

After lunch, when she went back to work, she called Agustin Benevidez into her office.

"About the classes," she said, and watched the rather blank look of resistance drop over his brown face. "About the classes," she repeated firmly. "I know all the men want to go home to their wives. They do not understand any interruption of their siesta. If a man is content to earn only what he can earn today, and not look to the future, he is a fool. Señor San Roque does not keep fools in his employ."

"I am not a fool, *señora*. But I do not wish to insult my wife by not coming home during siesta."

"I know how you feel. But a man with ambition will also sacrifice a certain amount of present pleasure for future benefit—for the good of his children to come after him. The class will not take forever, only until the end of November. When it is over, both you and your wife will benefit from it. You will then be the ideal choice for assistant—well, it is then merely a step to the post of manager. I will not be employed here forever. You may well be."

She added, "Think about it very carefully, Agustin. I need to find someone to be a training officer later, and that person will be my assistant. It would be too bad if I went into town and found an ambitious young single woman to train because none of the men want to take advantage of the opportunity.''

Finally Agustin, who had been staring miserably at the floor, raised his dark eyes and asked, "Every day, Señora San Roque?"

Helen had planned until that moment to hold five days of classes every week, but she knew when to compromise. "Only two days. Either Monday and Wednesday or Tuesday and Thursday for the rank and file. But for the one who wishes to be superior and end as the training officer," she said firmly, "it would be wise to go each day of the four."

He looked so miserable that she relented. "Classes are from twelve-thirty to two o'clock; but from two to four o'clock when el señor isn't on the island on a workday you may take your siesta."

When he didn't say anything she added, "I have put a notice in the newspaper that comes out today. The classes will be open to anyone not employed by the company if there is room for them on the first day."

"But, *señora*—"

"And any person who finishes the course and wants employment... will be hired. The hiring level will be on a par with or above those now employed who do not take the course. Do I make myself clear?"

"Very clear, Señora San Roque."

His black eyes searched her golden ones in a manner that made her say, "That is all, Agustin." Clearly he wondered how el patrón could find anything soft and endearing in such a woman *sin compasión*—without pity. But she knew she had won the battle! When San Roque found out about this skirmish—and he certainly would—how would he take her to task about it, she wondered uncomfortably. Would he consider it unforgivable meddling in the lives of his employees? But she had to succeed in her contract; she had no choice but to force success. She must in order someday to escape the island—and him.

Whatever his personal reservations, Agustin spread her message. When she entered the classroom on the first day, all desks were occupied and the walls were lined with prospective students, not all of whom were employees. She sighed with a great rush of inner relief that she was truly about to earn her salary. She could see hope that the debt would now begin steadily—if slowly—to melt away.

There were more than enough interested students to fill two classes. Helen was pleased at how many young women had come who were not employees, and how well Agustin had persuaded the previously reluctant men to sacrifice their siesta a short time for long-term gains.

"Those who draw the number one on papers in this bowl will take the class on Tuesday and Thursday. The rest, those with number two on their slips of paper, will come Monday and Wednesday. I know the time you spend here is a sacrifice, but it will pay you good dividends if you persevere."

As she went about getting the names of her students she discovered that Zonia's sister, Estelita, had opted for the training.

"Why can we not learn the machines and the English on Fridays, and proceed faster?" Estelita, the most enthusiastic student, wanted to know.

"Because each of you has alternate days to use your siesta however you wish. And Friday is my day to do as I wish."

"That is fair," said Estelita.

HELEN NOW BEGAN HER DAY earlier than most of the citizens of Cedros and worked straight through until the time in the afternoon when the children left school. Then Vergel helped her carry a load of file boxes to the car, to last her through an evening in the upstairs sitting room, and drove her past the school where Juanito had been registered.

Full of importance with his new studies and the status of riding in the *carro*, Juanito held himself stiff with excitement. Helen wondered if the young San Roque could have been more full of pride than this lad, who had plenty of spunk and strength in spite of his weak foot. As soon as Juanito arrived at the great house, he set to painting pictures with his newly acquired supplies, while Helen exercised Rafaela. Then Helen turned the job of the little girl's supervision over to Juanito in order to do her own homework.

Rafaela, accustomed to amusing herself with as little as a bird's feather or a patch of grass, always observing life around her, was delighted to see her companions come home.

"When we are not here, Soledad, could you encourage Zonia and the two Marias to talk to Rafaela?" Helen asked.

"What about?" the astonished Soledad responded.

"Why, about anything!"

"But she cannot answer," the housekeeper protested.

"No. She cannot speak now, but the more you encourage her the more likely she will be to learn. I suspect our Rafaela is more than just bright. All that intelligence is imprisoned within her, just waiting to be released. She needs our help."

Soledad raised an eyebrow and shrugged acceptance of the responsibility. Helen looked at Rafaela crawling determinedly after Juanito and cheered for her. The child was able to maintain determination in the face of all odds. Though unable to speak except with her expressive little features, she had an active mind; of that there was little doubt.

What San Roque thought of the new member of the household, Helen did not know. His face, unlike hers and Rafaela's, revealed little or nothing of himself. Once he had been a sensitive little boy, then he'd retreated within that child to become the proud man he was now, with steely gray eyes so piercing and unrelenting.

"What was he like?" she asked Soledad.

"Don Luis?" Soledad answered promptly, "A small replica of the old *señor*."

"What was the old *señor* like?" Helen persisted.

"He came here to the island already a widower, already the owner of a salt company. He built this great house before the arranged marriage. Doña Isabella was the daughter of a Mexico City importer with whom the old *señor* did business."

"But he loved her?"

"Ah, Doña Helena! He was mad about her. She came to this island just a girl, but a girl used to the glittering life of cosmopolitan Mexico City, and he brought the world to her.

"The old *señor* was a busy man and Doña Isabella the cleverest of women," Soledad continued. "Doña Isabella made the great house a home to draw her husband from wherever his world business interests took him. Great yachts brought guests to their home on Cedros, and in its own way Cedros became the center of the world.

"When Don Luis was born, Doña Isabella's health changed and the old *señor* learned then what his wife meant to him." Soledad interrupted her story to sigh profoundly, then went on, "He had three loves, the old *señor*: his work, his wife and his son. When the *señora* died, the light went out of his life.

"More and more the old man retreated to the island where he had known such love and happy times, and he ran the business from Cedros. In his stead he sent his young son—much too young for such responsibilities—to the capitals of South America and the Far East to stand in for him in business matters. He never did know that the company was not the first love of the boy.

"Left to himself," Soledad said with wisdom born of knowing San Roque all his life, "he would have been a scientist of the sea. He would have lived as one with all the sea creatures. All the islanders respect and love the sea, but Don Luis more than any. Doña Isabella would have made his father understand. She, too, was a sea creature, even though she was originally an *extranjera*. She was as sleek as a seal and as bright as the sunlight on a flying fish. It was she who taught Don Luis his love of the water and everything in it.''

''She sounds like a lovely lady,'' Helen observed rather wistfully, wishing she could have known San Roque's mother.

She went to work on her files, spreading them out all over her room, sitting among them with an intent frown as she planned and made outlines. Lost in concentration, she didn't hear her door open.

''What the hell are you doing at this time of night with office material!'' demanded the deliberately harsh voice of San Roque. How long he had been watching she could not guess.

She scrambled up in confusion. ''I—what are you doing back here?''

''Answer my question, damn it! You will ruin your eyes and crease your forehead permanently, to say nothing of destroying your health.''

''But I—''

''Soledad told me you never stop, and I see her concern is justified. I felt I needed to come back and I am glad I did. There will be a stop to this!''

''What am I supposed to do after office hours when I am alone in this house?'' she burst out defensively. ''Twiddle my thumbs? I want to pay the debt I inherited and pay it as quickly as I can! The more valuable I show myself to be—the quicker I earn the right to be myself!"

"The quicker you will kill yourself," he corrected her. "However, I shall provide opportunities for you to be considered for bonus dividends if it will keep you from bringing the office into my home. I absolutely forbid it in the future, Helen. You are forewarned. When the successful entertainment of my clients and their wives enriches me, you, too, can be enriched. Spend your spare time making sure you will not be too tired to play the ideal hostess!"

She angrily gathered up the papers and stuffed them into the portfolio. "Very well," she fumed, her mouth tight.

"Helen!"

"Yes?" She turned coldly and realized he was confronting her from only a breath away. "What—" she began harshly, but he stopped her mouth with a firm kiss that softened her lips and dissipated her anger.

He held her off a little. "Forget the cruel trick your brother has played—and start to live."

"Have you forgotten his 'cruel trick'?" she demanded. "If so, this farce of marriage can be ended!"

He turned away, now angry himself. "No," he said. "And you will not let me forget, either. So be it!"

He slammed out of the room, leaving her feeling awkward, unhappy and alone. In the center of the room her fallen papers lay forgotten on the floor in chaos. On the bed San Roque had placed unnoticed a packet of mail from the mainland.

Sighing, she picked up the letters and laid aside one from each of the chess partners, though she rather enjoyed her new opponent and recognized the neatly typed envelope from San Francisco.

The letter from her father, in his spidery handwriting, was disquieting.

Ron was in San Francisco, doing well again, her father reported, working for a large investment firm. He had many obligations and could not yet send money, but he seemed sure to rise to the top of the company in no time at all.

An investment company! Helen was horrified. Ron could do the same sort of damage there as he had done in San Roque's employ. He might manipulate the finances of little people far less able to stand the loss. No longer could she naively believe her brother was innocent of any mishandling of funds. She was alarmed that he had so easily found another occasion of temptation to do the same.

Her first concern was followed by another disquieting realization: San Roque had read her mail. He, too, now knew where to find Ron easily enough.

Finally she thought, *if he can be found and made to pay, he should be. He must take the consequences. Perhaps if Luis is able to stop him, some worse results can be avoided.*

CHAPTER NINE

HELEN'S FIRST EXHAUSTING WEEK on the training project was exhilarating. She found herself longing for some approval from San Roque, but she received none.

Friday morning the company plane brought Eugenio Ochoa back to the island at nine-thirty. With him arrived the hairdresser from Mexico City, practically a carbon copy of Sebastian, the designer.

"I don't have time to have my hair done," Helen fumed. "It looks quite respectable as it is." She knew she fought a losing battle, since San Roque was inflexible. He had left for the mainland the night before to meet his guests and bring them to the island.

Eugenio told her, "El señor specifically ordered that you should leave the office no later than noon. Here are files on the guests he brings with him. He also—" Eugenio coughed apologetically "—suggested that my Magdalena take advantage of the hairdresser when he has attended to you. Don Luis wishes Magdalena to

make an excellent impression on his visitors, as well."

"Eugenio, why don't you go home to your wife and say I have invited her to lunch with me later, and we will both have our hair done together," Helen suggested. "Vergel can take the stylist up to the house to refresh himself."

Eugenio was delighted at opportunity to go home. He promised that Magdalena was ready to be picked up [V]ergel on Helen's way home from the office.

When Helen and Magda[lena] were met at the door by Soledad, Rafaela [in] her arms, the housekeeper looked a bit [worri]ed. "You saw the red cabs going down the [drive?]"

"Yes. Have our visitors a[rrived] already?"

"Not visitors—just the dresser and a plane full of clothes from [Mexi]co City! How can anyone work where yo[u h]ave instructed when the room is full to the ce[iling]?"

"I'd forgotten about the cl[othe]s that were to arrive. Let's have a look at the[m]," Helen picked up Rafaela and carried the ch[ild] upstairs with them. Her pleasure in the marv[elo]us assortment of clothes was sobered by the re[min]der that they were, after all, only "uniforms."

Soledad had not exaggerated. [T]he huge bedroom and sitting room were pil[e]d high with every kind of box and package. Magdalena

Ochoa's eyes went round with awe. "It is like heaven!"

"It is like a madhouse! Soledad," Helen requested, "please have Zonia and the two Marias make space to put all these things away."

Magdalena exclaimed loudly as Soledad opened the first big flat box and held up a dress for inspection. Helen nodded, "Yes—that is beautiful." A beautiful costly uniform, she thought. "Perhaps I should wear it tomorrow night. It's important enough to impress the king of Spain. Maria Cruz—Maria Lourdes—please clear everything out of the sitting room. Señora Ochoa and I can lunch in there."

"Do let me take the child downstairs, Doña Helena," Soledad offered. "You and Señora Ochoa deserve a quiet time while the hairdresser prepares."

"The *niña* should not have to crawl about on the floor all of the time," Magdalena interrupted. "It is good for the exercise, but indoors she might have a small chair with wheels and learn to get around more rapidly."

"What a magnificent idea!" Helen responded. "Magdalena, you're going to be Eugenio's greatest asset. Do you know anyone who could make one for her?"

"I think so."

"You hear that, *niña*? Soon you will have your own *carro*!" Helen looked up from the

child and saw Soledad's more than usually sour expression. "Now what is wrong, Soledad?"

"All respects, Doña Helena. The poor child is being spoiled for her own kind. She will not know where she belongs. She will yet fall from the barrio stairs or into the fire or water, and all your attention will have been for naught."

Helen stared, sobered, at the child of whom she had quickly become so fond.

"The mother would let the child stay if you were to say you would be her *patrona*," Magdalena suggested. "Then you would have no problem."

"I shall speak to Zonia and we will talk to Rafaela's mother seriously."

Soledad did not smile, but she no longer looked so cross. "She can have a corner of my room if it comes to that, Doña Helena."

"We'll work out a plan," Helen promised. "And Juanito can continue to watch out for her afternoons and early evenings like a big brother, since he's adopted her."

Thank heaven Juanito was a better adoptive brother to this child than Ron had been to her, Helen reflected. Ron had thrown temper tantrums whenever pressed into the job of supervising his little sister.

After lunch Soledad notified Helen and her guest that the hairdresser was ready. Helen realized how apprehensive Magdalena was and made every effort to put the young woman at ease. "I guess we're both going to endure somewhat of an ordeal, but it is all for the good of the company, is it not?" she remarked lightly.

"That is what Eugenio tells me," Magdalena whispered.

"It's really rather fun," Helen encouraged her. "A woman of style should change her hairdo every six months and keep it that way for two weeks whether she likes it or not."

"Even if it is very strange?"

"Even so!" Helen said. "But Sebastian's brother is the finest hairdresser in all of Mexico and can only make you more beautiful. There is nothing to worry about."

"Is that true? You are so terribly educated. I am proud to have you for a friend, Doña Helena!"

"Then you must call me simply Helen and forget the *doña*, or else it will not seem to me that we are really friends."

"Helena," Magdalena agreed shyly.

The hairdresser fussed over Helen, lifting her hair with reverent fingers. "Color such as this is a gift of God—a color no man has been able to match! And you have the unusual creamy complexion most redheaded women envy! It is a pleasure to enhance your beauty with my scissors and curlers."

He clucked a bit over Magdalena. "Your hair

will have to be thinned and trimmed. But in the end, I promise, you will look chic."

Despite Magdalena's inspired protests the hairdresser propelled her into his chair, and before she could even burst into tears he had her luxurious tresses falling on the floor about her feet. The end result was a new Magdalena. Her cropped hair made her seem slimmer and far more sophisticated.

Then it was Helen's turn. "My hair goes terribly curly without weight to tame it down," she warned him.

"For you, *señora*, only a trim, a shaping and a new style to make you a queen among women!" The hairdresser continued to make expansive promises as his fingers flew, proving his skill.

"Is that really me?" Helen asked at last, looking at herself with unexpected pleasure.

After Magdalena was taught how to maintain her new style, Vergel took her home to dress. She would return later with her husband.

Helen passed Juanito in the hall and was caught short by his appearance.

"Where did that bruise on your cheek come from?" she asked sharply. On closer inspection she found more battle scars. He ducked his head sullenly, suddenly uncharacteristically uncommunicative.

"You must tell me, Juanito," Helen ordered, but it was Vergel who gave her the story.

"The other students tease him, Doña Helena. Because of his crippled foot."

"I do not like the school at all!" Juanito blurted, his face red.

"I will ask Don Luis to speak to them like thunder!" Helen was furious. She could remember the pain of her own childhood with Ron's constant name-calling. He had nicknamed her "Owl" because of her reading glasses and "Stork" because of her height. How it had made her life hell! No one had championed her, though Mama Jessie had tried to stem Ron's cruel little jokes. As she grew into an adult she had realized his cruelty was a product of his own insecurity, but some part of her still continued to believe his criticisms. She had believed them right up until the afternoon she had been introduced to San Roque.

San Roque had silently but effectively stopped Ron's gibes, making her feel special, attractive. She had never felt so pleased with herself as a woman as here on the island. And she had no doubt that a man who would rescue her from her brother's thoughtless taunts would also rescue a small child from the cruel teasing of his classmates.

"We will have to see a doctor about your foot; I am sure it can be fixed, Juanito. Soon you will run as well as any boy in your school. Perhaps better!"

"You can truly do this thing, and mend the curse?"

"It is not a curse! It is nothing but an accident of nature. The most beautiful trees are often a bit different from others of their kind. Also, the most beautiful trees must be pruned and trimmed. Your foot can be mended; it only requires patience and courage."

"*Patrona*, I will allow the doctors to cut me without being asleep if it is required!"

"Juanito, you are a brave boy. Such an operation will not cause you pain at all, I assure you. But you must do exactly as the doctors tell you."

His mood brightened by Helen's promises, Juanito grinned and trotted happily after Vergel, who was off to pick up his employer and the weekend's houseguests.

"Which of your new gowns will you wear, Doña Helena, when el señor arrives with his guests?" Soledad had come up quietly beside her, ready to attend to Helen's needs.

"Something very simple, I think. The wives will have traveled a long way and would not thank me for looking too grand when they may not be at their freshest."

"Not one of the great gowns from Mexico City that el señor expects you to wear as his hostess?"

"Tomorrow I can wear one of the truly grand

ensembles, after the guests have had a chance to match my elegance. Tonight I think the best choice would be the satin shirt Don Luis bought for me last week in the village and the dark green crepe skirt that the designer sent from Mexico City. Don Luis will approve my judgment, you will see.''

Sebastian had taken time to look over the items that Luis had helped her select from the island stores, and had enthusiastically endorsed the dandy shirts. "They are magnificent on a woman such as yourself. With your hair, Señora San Roque, the choice is a tour de force. For an informal evening at home you might combine the green satin shirt with a fine dark green crepe skirt and a cunning gold belt!'' he had recommended excitedly.

Before dressing for the guests, Helen selected music for the elaborate stereo system downstairs. She chose background music carefully from San Roque's excellent record library: Strauss waltzes for the German wives of the Argentinian and German industrialists; Antonio Bribiesca, the noted Mexican guitarist, for Mexican atmosphere.

Soledad helped her into the shimmering satin shirt, the great circular floor-length swirl of deep cedar green and the hammered-gold belt that emphasized her small waistline.

''Your hair is like the flame of sunset above

the trees of the island," Soledad told her, patting every last hair into place proudly.

She was ready downstairs when the guests arrived with San Roque. When he entered his eyes gleamed with approval; he went to her and held her firmly so that her stiffness could not be detected. The kiss he gave her was far too enthusiastic, she thought indignantly, but the guests found it perfectly understandable in a new husband after any length of absence.

Her heart leaped into her throat and she could no more keep from returning his kiss than she could stop the sun from rising. The firm pressure of his arm about her waist as he introduced her reminded her she had to expect such demonstrations of connubial affection. She could not put safe space between them so she willed herself to relax, trying to convince herself that he had not noticed the unwilling response he'd elicited from her even though he himself was playacting for his guests.

The two industrialists were relatively young, and their wives, even after exhausting hours of plane travel, were elegant beauties—willowy fair blond girls, almost as alike as matched pearls. Helen knew she had been correct in not dressing too elegantly for their first meeting, for the wives' pale linen suits were rumpled from their flight.

San Roque's gaze lingered on the décolleté of

Helen's saucy green shirt and the soft rounded curves of her bosom. "I see you are promoting our island's styles tonight, as well as Sebastian's creations," he said. "All arrived in good order?"

"Soledad is beside herself with the joy of being wardrobe mistress," Helen answered calmly. She carefully sidestepped another kiss. *"Sehr angenehm! Wilkommen in Cedros!"* she said to the two women. With a few laughing admonitions to them to speak German *"bitte langsamer,"* the ice was broken.

Ailse, the wife of the Argentinian, Kines, whose beauty had only recently been featured in *Town & Country* magazine, was the outspoken of the two. "Where did you find such a magnificent satin shirt? I am—you should pardon the expression—quite green with envy! One never sees such styles when one searches in a city!"

"I can take you to the artisan here on Cedros if you like." Helen glanced slyly at San Roque. He was looking with amusement at the shirt, and she guessed that he had thought her choosing it to be a statement of rebellion, though that had not been her intention at all. The shirt had been designed for a man, not a woman; but for all that it was exceedingly attractive. San Roque was no doubt both pleased and dismayed by the attention it garnered.

"I love it! So chic!" Ailse continued. "The beach boys at Acapulco wear similar shirts, and I would never have thought of one for myself until this moment, but I would adore one in electric blue!"

"Young men here use these shirts to catch the eye of their girls and hint at what good money they make at the cannery or in Luis's salt works. The brighter the color, the better and bigger the impression."

"And yet it is your marvelous hair that the shirt sets off!" Ailse enthused. "Perhaps blue will be good for my blond?"

"And red for me?" Renate, the German national's wife, suggested eagerly.

"All colors can be bought here on the island. You will be sensations when you go home," Helen assured them with a laugh.

The women were delighted at the prospect of shopping for unusual outfits, and Helen shot San Roque another sidelong glance of triumph. Her first small reputation as a hostess had been made and their guests were already well disposed toward the weekend.

Later, at dinner, she proved she had absorbed information from the guests' dossiers sent down that morning when she commented knowledgeably on Kines's art collection and asked questions about the European soccer team that was Waugenheim's passion. San Roque would be pleased with her handling of her assigned hostess duties, she felt certain.

"Don Luis says we are to sail tomorrow. I enjoy the snorkel and the scuba. Do you, also?" asked Renate.

Helen didn't want to admit she had never been aboard a sailboat in her life, though she had lived on the coast. "I haven't had a chance to go sailing in a long time. I'm looking forward to it just as you are," she added, and realized she really was.

"There are excellent coves across the island where we can dive for abalone and the local lobsters," San Roque told the men. Everyone except Helen was familiar with scuba gear and discussed the prospect of diving at length.

When pressed, Helen only laughed. "I am as happy as a fish in the water, but I've never had the time or opportunity to learn anything about scuba diving. I'm sure my husband will have a lot to teach me, if he cares to put up with projects along that line."

"You will have to be clever and see that he takes time from his business, then," Waugenheim suggested. "This man is a legend in our world of financial dealing. He has never taken a vacation of any note since he became the *wunderkind* of the salt industry."

San Roque handed Waugenheim a whisky and soda and poured Helen a Penafiel as the others sipped their before-dinner drinks.

"One day," he said calmly, "when I find the men I can trust, I shall turn the running of the business over to my managers and devote myself to living." His free hand casually caressed Helen's shoulder and he pulled her playfully closer to him as they stood in an informal circle, chatting easily with the guests.

"Perhaps the time is approaching?" Waugenheim asked roguishly, eyeing Helen, who though calm enough was disconcerted by San Roque's seizing of every opportunity to appear the adoring bridegroom. There was nothing she could do but accept his deliberate attentions. If she blushed often the guests would attribute it to a young bride's modesty and shy reserve in public.

After dinner, in the library, Helen was challenged to a game of chess by Waugenheim. "Your husband says you are an excellent opponent."

"He said that?" Helen asked in surprise. She flashed a glance at San Roque, wondering just what he had said about her to these friends of his. He only nodded her way and continued his own conversation with Kines and the two other women. But of course he would have said that, and expected her to play with Waugenheim, who had chess listed as one of his interests in his dossier.

She was not embarrassed by her game, and she realized when it was over that San Roque had deliberately set up the match because Waugenheim was not a good enough player to confront Luis himself and was too egotistical to enjoy or even tolerate being beaten. Nevertheless, he did not find Helen a poor opponent and the win was enough of a challenge to make him crow a good deal.

When she was at last able to retire to her room, she was exhausted, but she took the time to search the new wardrobe for appropriate sailing gear. One of the first items she found was a pair of white boating slacks, followed by boating shoes and a delightful diagonally striped top in russet and white.

San Roque entered unannounced and she felt at once like a bird frantic to escape. He had stripped out of the embroidered beige cotton shirt and matching silk trousers he'd worn that evening. His dressing gown was open, revealing more of his tanned torso than she wanted to glimpse, and she could tell he had showered again.

"You were worth your hire tonight—even to your choice of clothes," he remarked.

"Thank you." She eyes him warily as he pulled aside the draperies over the great balcony window, and beckoning her to join him on the tiled terrace overlooking the city below them.

"Perhaps we should arrange a bonus—a month off for your fine performance as Señora

San Roque! The wives are delighted, the husbands are happy and the company makes a profit from business transacted in such an atmosphere.''

"Whatever you think is fair," she said carefully.

"On second thought, this is at least a part of what I bargained for." He bent his head and his lips brushed her forehead, but though she immediately tensed he made no further attempt to be intimate. He turned away, his attention on the panorama before them, unusually free of the night fog common to the island. A night bird called somewhere close and the cricket chorus seemed louder than mariachis.

She moved a safe distance away, once more unprepared for his companionable mood, which demanded nothing of her physically or emotionally. He took a packet of letters from his dressing-gown pocket and handed them to her.

"I had no chance to give these to you sooner. I would judge from the chess partner's note that your game is improving."

She flushed a little and shrugged.

"Your father's spirits seem better," he commented. "That should relieve your mind somewhat."

She longed to read the mail from home, but she did not wish to appear rude and end the rather pleasant evening on a harsh note. "Tomorrow I will continue to play the hostess you expect, Luis. Tonight...it is late, and I am tired from a long exacting day.''

"I know about your long days. They are much too long. We will talk later about the hours you keep. Good night, Helen. *Hasta mañana*." He would not intrude on her, she realized; though he did follow her back into the suite to draw the draperies for her against the damp night.

"Until tomorrow," she repeated uncertainly, as he closed the door between the rooms behind him.

She looked quickly at the letter from her father. He was in better spirits, she saw with pleasure. He went on at length about how well Ron was doing in his new position, the compliments he had received from the president of the company and the new car he had purchased—a Mercedes!

Helen laid aside the letter, wishing she dared discuss her brother frankly with San Roque. She had thought so much about Ron since all this had begun.

The letter worried her. San Roque had not indicated whether he was taking any measures to apprehend Ron in San Francisco. Perhaps he could not locate him as easily as she thought he could.

But San Roque was not a man who would let

another get the better of him. She hoped he would be firm but fair. She knew Ron must be apprehended at some point and forced to pay his debt honestly; he had to learn to live in the light of reality, commitment and responsibility. When would that be?

She stared uneasily at the connecting doors of the bedroom. She wasn't prepared yet to talk to San Roque about Ron, though she knew it might assuage some of her fears. No, she counseled herself. What went on between her and her brother was their own business. Meanwhile, she must do as she must.

CHAPTER TEN

WHICH OF THE BEAUTIFUL SAILING CRAFT in the harbor belonged to San Roque, she wondered the next morning. Possibly the one she could see daily from her office window. Somewhere between here and Mazatlan was another yacht, the one with the captain who had not hesitated to tell San Roque of the message she wanted relayed to the consul. So he owned at least two sailing vessels.

She wasn't surprised to discover that the sailing craft she had presumed was his was in fact their destination.

The two German women, looking forward to a day of fun, chattered like magpies, switching from English to German and Spanish without apparent difficulty. The three men, along with Vergel and Genaro, served as crew. Against the blue sky and under the golden sun they sailed out of the harbor that morning and anchored in one of the coves around the island. Out came the scuba gear. Frosty drinks were served by Genaro.

Ailse and Renate peeled off the boating slacks and stretched out on deck in the briefest of designer bikinis. "Are you not going to take the sun?" Ailse asked.

Helen, overcome by embarrassment because she had hoped to avoid this moment, glanced at San Roque nearby at the helm. "Why not?" she finally said, and pulled off her boating outfit to stretch out in her ragged white halter and shorts.

Renate squealed in girlish discovery: "Did you buy those in Paris? That is where the best cutoffs are found, properly faded and shrunk. I have never seen anything so beautifully worn!"

"I did it myself over a period of the past six years," Helen said, relieved that the women at least were not appalled. "They are more than threadbare. They may fall apart before we dock today." She kept an eye on San Roque, hoping the old gear would not disgrace him.

The two women didn't swim but lay about slathering lotions on their bodies and broiling in the island sun. Helen dived off the deck into the water and investigated the activity of the men as they brought up huge abalones.

"Careful!" San Roque warned, surfacing beside her. "You can injure yourself if you handle these badly." He pointed to the abalones' rough outer shells encrusted with sharp barnacles.

Helen ignored his warning and continued to

examine one of the catches in the net bag being
hoisted into the dinghy. San Roque grinned
playfully as he held up an enormous lobster,
and she flipped back into the blue water to
escape the creature's menacing claws.

The great lobsters were left in the box traps
behind the boat. Genaro pounded the abalones
until tender as butter and produced a delicious
lunch from the galley.

When a bank of fog began to lower, the boat
sailed back into the Cedros harbor. San Roque
and the men retired to discuss business contracts
over drinks in the library. Helen shepherded the
women to the city's shops, where they purchased satin shirts to their hearts' content and
the shopkeepers' delight.

The elegant Mexico City hairdresser, waiting
at the great house, wasn't at all delighted to see
what the sun, salt water and wind had done to
his client's hair. But he set to work to repair the
damage and afterward coiffed the two guests.

Helen, with Soledad's assistance, pulled on a
peach-tinted satin gown, slipped into matching
satin sandals and wrapped herself in a lacy stole.
She allowed Soledad to spray her with a per-
fume she could tell was sinfully expensive even
though she had never heard of it before.

After a debate with herself she left her eyeglasses on the dressing table. She would do her
best to be the perfectly turned-out hostess San

Roque desired. Ron's nickname of "Owl" was not an epithet any of San Roque's guests ought to think appropriate for her tonight.

When San Roque opened the connecting doors and came into the room, Soledad looked inordinately proud as Helen stood patiently allowing herself to be scrutinized. He only nodded approvingly, which deflated Helen slightly.

"You have evidently begun a style in the ladies' jet set with your island *currataco* shirts," he commented with his usual amused look. "But I confess I could not decipher your reason for wearing your old swimming attire today when you have such choice."

"But I didn't have a choice," she protested.

"Surely the House of Sebastian did not fail to send swimming gear!"

"It's just as well they didn't," she said. "I would have felt out of place in the kind of things Ailse Kines and Renate Waugenheim wear. Please don't expect me—"

San Roque laughed. He stepped to the chest of drawers and rummaged through until he found and displayed for her several maillot swimming suits, not too dissimilar from what she might have chosen for herself. They evidenced style, while her old halter and shorts suggested expediency.

"Wear what you please," he said finally, his point made. That would serve her for not taking a proper interest in her new wardrobe, his attitude seemed to say. "Your taste and good sense are not in question so far. The woman seem bent on imitating your style." He added with a thoughtful frown, "Tonight is business and you will be on duty as I will. I would like you to mention your training program to Kines. Let Magdalena entertain the wives, and I will keep Waugenheim occupied with other matters."

"Then...you aren't too displeased with the program as I have begun it?"

"When I am displeased you will know." He produced from his jacket a flat velvet jeweler's box. "Wear these to complement your beauty tonight."

She opened the case, and a magnificent necklace glittered out at her. She had never seen opals of such color, worked into a primitive gold design. They were almost crystal clear, a brilliant fiery orange, and it seemed as if smoke swirled within the depths of each without muddying the clarity.

She drew her breath sharply, weak with the impact of them.

"My mother had many beautiful jewels," San Roque told her, lifting the necklace from its black velvet bed.

"What if something happens?" she asked, staring at it in amazement.

"What could happen? Beautiful jewels are meant to be worn." He turned her to face the great pier glass. Carefully he fastened the necklace around her neck and quite casually brushed her nape with his lips, as though to seal the jewels' clasp. His touch on her bare skin was as fiery as the beam of the stones.

"My mother's ears were pierced. I will have the earrings altered into clips." He stood behind her, his brooding eyes meeting hers in the pier glass, his hands caressing her shoulders as he regarded her finished appearance. He had such a disquieting effect on her.

She shook her head. "I wouldn't think of your doing that. It would be a sacrilege to touch them." She shivered. "Especially. . . ."

"Especially what? I would not have thought you superstitious about opals."

"I'm not!" she protested, an angry catch in her voice. She felt helpless decked out in such opulence, as though she were a mannequin in a fine shop window. "It's a responsibility to parade about in borrowed feathers, that's all."

Again the amused smile crossed his mouth, as though she were a gauche *norteamericana* without the sophistication of a well-bred Mexican woman. "You have become an exotic bird in your fine feathers."

"We should go down," she interrupted, hastily heading for the door.

On the stairs she stumbled and might have fallen but for San Roque's firm hand on her arm.

I really should have worn my glasses, she thought. *I can't see three inches in front of my face without them!*

When Genaro served them at the bar, she remembered to ask for Penafiel and explained her preference to the two women, adding now that Penafiel could be beneficial to the complexion. Unseen by the guests, San Roque winked at Helen, who blushed.

"We must take some cases of this marvelous water home with us!" Ailse begged her husband.

"You won't regret it, Señor Kines," Helen supported her. "The water is also known for its effect on the digestion."

As she reached again for her own glass, she knocked it over, causing a great clatter among the bibelots. In embarrassment she rang for Soledad.

"Please get my glasses from the dressing-room table, Soledad. I was foolish not to wear them. So much for making a grand impression!" she said boldly.

San Roque looked mildly surprised at her honest confession.

Soledad promptly brought the glasses down to her. "Now," Helen said, putting them on, "none of us need to fear a glass of wine or water in the lap, courtesy of my blindness, and I need not worry about breaking my neck because I can't see where I'm going.''

"If only Ailse would be so charmingly frank about her need to wear glasses," Kines remarked. "She cannot tolerate contact lenses, either.''

Helen almost told him the real reason she didn't wear contacts: she couldn't afford them. But she suspected this would only have brought contact lenses and replacement sets to the island, and she had no intention of inviting a spate of personal benefits to make up for the gilded prison. She glanced briefly at San Roque, whose expression remained blank.

The chef had prepared a dinner fine enough to feed even the president of Mexico but quite Argentinian in theme. An Argentine dish comprising potatoes stuffed with beef, onions, black olives, raisins and tomatoes particularly pleased Kines. Broccoli pancakes topped with walnut shrimp sauce were without peer, and the incredibly airy asparagus soufflé added an unusual touch. For dessert there was an Argentine flan. All was served with an Argentine brandy. Kines was the most appreciative one in a room full of dazzled diners.

When San Roque ordered the chef to come in for compliments, the man graciously gave credit for the menu to Helen.

"Señora San Roque suggested the menu—and talked me into it."

Helen blushed when the extravagant compliments were shared with her and tried not to be so overwhelmingly aware of San Roque's satisfaction—and her own pleasure in seeing it.

By late Sunday afternoon, when San Roque and the two couples were ready to leave, Helen was exhausted from the unremitting efforts of her weekend hostess duties.

Genaro came down with San Roque's luggage. Helen, in the great hall, smiled without revealing her weariness and savored the prospect of going directly to bed once they had gone.

"Our guests will be leaving immediately," San Roque told her, following Genaro. "It has been a profitable weekend for San Roque Enterprises, Helen. You played your role well. I will finalize all the groundwork with a contract in Buenos Aires this week." He strolled to the big front doors with his arm around her shoulders.

"Then...I won't see you again for some time?" She felt oddly lonely and saw that he read her easily.

The two couples went out to the car, considerately leaving their host and hostess to a private goodbye.

"Oh, I will be back on Friday with more guests," he said, and the small smile played about his lips.

"I haven't wanted to interrupt other matters on your mind this weekend, but I do have some concerns I need to mention before you go," she said, turning to face him boldly. "You remember I received one check from Chamartin, which I turned over to the debt account, except for a sum I needed to use here on the island—"

"Any merchant here will take care of your accounts through me," he said. "If you like, they can fall under the heading of business and living expenses expected to be covered by the employer under such a contract as ours."

"There are some things I want to pay for myself," she responded. "I do not want to burden you with them."

"Such as?" he asked with a frown.

"Nothing that need concern you—"

He grasped her arm almost roughly. "Are you planning to hide money away and bribe someone to help you escape? If so, it is impossible, Helen!"

She pulled her arm away and confessed unwillingly, "Magdalena is helping me get a wheelchair made for Rafaela. I also wish to pay the island doctor to look at Rafaela and Juanito and let me know what help he can offer them. Neither child is your responsibility, but I—"

"The islanders' welfare *is* a San Roque responsibility," he said bluntly.

"Then do something about Barrio X!" she

retorted, and immediately regretted her sharp words. "I really would feel better if you allowed me to deduct the children's expenses from my painting sales."

He extracted some bills from his wallet. "Here is cash. I will take your check, and Estrada can deduct the cash from its face value if that is the way you must have it."

"Yes. I would like it that way. I'll give you a receipt for the cash when you return and you can sign for the check."

She realized she had offended him and regretted having done so after such a pleasant weekend, which had been more like a vacation than a business gathering. He had turned as cold as steel, and she knew she had provoked his anger because he did not even bid her goodbye.

After he and the others left, she made an entry in her receipt book. In just three weeks the debt Ron had dumped on her had been reduced to $249,000. At this rate—although it was foolish to think such a steady rate could be maintained—the debt would be erased in three years and three weeks!

Better than the five years she had originally resigned herself to be indentured. Ron was someday going to be called to pay for this, even if she had to wait until Judgment Day!

She muttered a soft, "Damn!" and mentally ground to a halt. She had forgotten all about her dad and Mama Jessie. To eliminate the debt in three years she would have to earn at least twenty-eight thousand dollars more than she was earning now, both in salary and paintings. Instead of going to bed, she sat down with the company files and began to do work for the next day.

But her usually competent mind refused to concentrate. Instead she was haunted by the pleased expression in San Roque's gray eyes as they had rested caressingly on her whenever one of the visitors had remarked on her appearance or reacted to something she said or did in her role as hostess. It was sad that she and San Roque were unalterably on opposing sides— sadder still that they were worlds apart. Even so, Helen thought dreamily, if Ron had not betrayed San Roque's trust; if all that separated her from San Roque were his position as owner of the mines and hers as employee. . . .

The thought was too painfully sweet to consider for more than a moment. She dared not keep in mind anything but the cruel inescapable fact of the debt that had to be erased.

WEDNESDAY EVENING Magdalena brought the island's doctor to see the children. His words both cheered and depressed Helen.

"I am only a simple island doctor, not one of the city specialists from the mainland or your country."

"But you are university trained."

"Ah, yes, many years ago," he said, sighing as he acknowledged his own limitations and his age. "The world's advances in medical knowledge long ago exceeded my learning; I know when a condition is beyond my skill. If Juanito could go to the mainland, as far as to Tijuana's children's hospital, he could probably walk like anyone else within reasonable time. But it would be costly, Señora San Roque."

He listed the expenses involved: specialists, the hospital, the plane trip and accommodation for someone in the child's family to remain with him. "But," he finished, "if there were sufficient funds the operation could be arranged."

"As soon as we can arrange those details, doctor, Juanito must go," Helen insisted. "I will not have the other children call him a 'cursed cripple.'"

"*Sí*, children can be cruel," the doctor agreed. "So can ignorance."

Helen added the probable costs in her mind. With a reasonable number of sales of her work—and continuing popularity—she could ease the child's affliction and halt the dreadful name-calling. Of course this would mean another lengthening of the contract period.

As for Rafaela....

"I can do nothing for her," the doctor said sadly. "I doubt she will ever speak and perhaps she does not comprehend her situation. You might consult with a mainland doctor, but for this I have never seen a cure."

"I know there is no cure today and perhaps not next year, doctor. But I will not believe she isn't extremely bright," Helen protested. "Look at those wonderfully expressive eyes; you always know what she would say if she could. There is much intelligence in Rafaela... just waiting to escape!"

"You are a woman with great heart, that is plain. Who knows? Perhaps love can accomplish what medical science cannot."

This country doctor was frank in telling her that he was not current with new medical procedures, Helen realized. It made her trust what he did know. She would follow his advice to help Rafaela for the time being. There were exercises she could learn to strengthen the child's weak limbs. The maids and Soledad, as well, could take turns working with Rafaela daily. How much time would she lay aside from her determined goals? It must not be counted, because the child's needs had to take priority.

"You and Señor San Roque will have children of your own and you will not need to torture yourself over another woman's child," the doctor advised. "Your husband will want you to care for his children soon."

A spasm of pain shot through Helen at his

comment, and her expression discouraged further discussion. Aware that he had touched on a sensitive matter, the doctor smoothly changed the subject. He realized it was something between the *patrón* and his lady. The doctor no doubt suspected one of them was infertile and assumed that when they were desperate enough they would seek help. The San Roques were, after all, only recently married.

Helen wondered if San Roque had ever wished for a child of his own. One day, as all men did, he would consider it. The child could never be hers, of course, but she could, however temporarily, substitute these two whose island heritage was the same as his and whom she could unselfishly love in lieu of any hope of her own.

Helen allowed the doctor to misunderstand her problem. She would find a way to provide financially for both Juanito and Rafaela, though it might slow the reduction of her own crippling debt.

SHE BEGAN a gouache painting of Rafaela lying on the terrace, showing the child playing with citrus fruit. In the painting the little girl was perfectly beautiful, perfectly merry. The textures of her skin and hair contrasted with the beautiful bricks of the terrace and the color of the incomparable sunlight reflected from the sky into the sea. A perceptive viewer might detect that the child had a problem and be moved to the same outpouring of loving compassion that Helen felt.

San Roque's features impinged on her flow of creative thought. She could see him, in her mind's eye, in the seascape of the dolphins; and she knew that although that painting was no portrait, it *was* San Roque depicted in the water. The impression she had caught was enough to engrave his likeness and character in her memory forever.

Later she planned to paint Juanito sitting solemnly in his pantaloons, overshirt and straw hat, holding his school books. She had to capture the essential pride of the little boy. He must be very like San Roque had been at his age, she thought, in so many dear ways. The painting would show Juanito with two strong legs. There would be contrasts in the two paintings: Rafaela's inability to look other than merry would be quite unlike Juanito's typical solemnity. The paintings might pay for specialists when the time came.

"It is not healthy for you to work so grimly, Doña Helena!" Soledad chastised her later, upon finding her immersed in office work. "You will make yourself sick and old before the year is rung out! Even Don Luis does not work constantly; he has better sense. Wherever his work takes him, he finds time to swim and he is a great patron of the Mexico City Symphony. You will see in the papers from there that he never misses the important engagements."

Helen had indeed seen pictures of San Roque at the symphony, and she had seen the beautiful women always photographed with his party.

"And he plays chess," Soledad continued, enumerating San Roque's pastimes on her fingers. "He is *muy bueno* at that game!"

"I play that game myself," Helen answered crossly. "I have two chess companions, both excellent, one perhaps better than your master. One is an invalid in Sausalito, California. I played a running game with him all last summer. Since I came here to the island, I have another partner, much superior."

"It is he who is the cause of the second chessboard in your room?" Soledad asked. "Well, perhaps you divert yourself a little but not enough. You must at least take time to eat a bit more."

She rattled the tray of food she wanted Helen to eat. "You must sample what I have made just to tempt you. My best chocolate with almond, egg, cinnamon and sugar, all beaten to a froth." She placed a plate in Helen's hands. "And nibble on my *queso al horno*." The succulent grilled melted cheese and Soledad's marvelous tortillas were temptingly fragrant. "That great chef Don Luis brought to the island is of no value at times when one is in need of morsels. He can only make the fine banquets. It is I who know how to care for my *niña*.'' Fondly she scolded her charge.

Helen tried a mouthful or two as Soledad looked on, threatening, ''If you do not eat it all, I will tell Don Luis!''

''See, I'm eating every bite,'' Helen laughed, demonstrating. ''Tell him nothing!''

''And now you must put your feet up and let me wrap them in a warm shawl. It is good Don Luis comes again tomorrow. You will have to put away the office and the paints. It is all making a deep crease between your eyes and wearing you out.''

''Rest sounds good,'' Helen agreed absently, thinking of the guests that San Roque had warned he would bring with him and wishing, surprisingly and illogically, that tomorrow, and San Roque, would arrive quickly.

CHAPTER ELEVEN

"THERE IS A—PERSON—TO SEE YOU," Agustin Benevidez announced.

"A person?"

Agustin rolled his eyes discreetly heavenward. Helen realized this meant the caller was someone from the cannery, not one of the island's "responsible" persons. Probably whoever it was wanted to find out about the training classes; but why should Agustin bring the inquirer into her office when there were many out front who could answer all questions?

Agustin ushered into the office a defiant, harshly painted young woman who already looked old and wise.

"I am Conchita Martinez."

"Yes?"

"Rafaela's mama!" the woman explained rather impatiently. "Zonia said I should come to see you."

"Oh, yes! You have not been home whenever I called, Señora Martinez. Please sit here and have some coffee with me."

"Zonia says you want to keep the child at the great house," the caller rushed on with a calculating expression in her black eyes.

"Yes, I do, if you are willing. You could see her any time you wished, but we love her and would like to have her there."

Conchita looked around the office with curiosity. "Perhaps you can keep her at the great house—"

"We can take care of her there—Zonia can watch her—and she won't have any fear of accident."

"She was fine at the barrio. She never had an accident," Conchita put in, shrugging.

"But the stairs and porches are dangerous," Helen pointed out.

The woman looked at Helen slyly from the corners of her eyes. "Oh, I know. You will wish to keep her for good luck. It must be the custom in your *gringo* country."

Helen swallowed distaste as she calmly responded, "No, it is not the custom in my country to keep children like Rafaela for good luck. We do not observe that superstition. Rafaela is a dear little girl, and it gives me pleasure to take care of her."

"You want to buy her?"

"Buy her! Buy another human being?"

"Why not? You keep her for a pet."

The woman's callous attitude disgusted

Helen. San Roque was right about some of the people in the barrio, she admitted to herself.

Conchita changed her tactics upon seeing Helen's grim expression. "You are angry, but it is not possible to teach that child to do laundry or scrub floors for other island homes. How will she earn her living and help me? Ah—" she said, suddenly wise. "But you will train her to beg on the quay while you are here in the big offices."

"I—what?"

"To beg on the quay," Conchita repeated impatiently. "The merchant seamen come ashore. They see her. They give her money to bring them luck from the storms."

Helen was outraged into silence. How much would this woman take to go away and never be seen again? She was a monster!

"I doubt Rafaela would excite much interest from the merchant seamen," Helen answered very carefully. "She is too small, too insignificant. She would probably fall into the bay and cause a great scandal. No, I wouldn't send her to beg. What I propose to do is send her to doctors and have her completely cured and then— *then* I will make my investment worth my while. Now you understand?"

"Ah, *sí*! That is the way of the wealthy—to invest in the future." Conchita's eyes narrowed. "What would you do if I let you keep her and she grew pretty and normal—as I was once pretty—and I came to take her back?''

Helen forced herself to look naive and trusting like any *gringa*. "I suppose I would have to face that time when it came.''

"Ah!" The eyes assumed a carefully tragic look. "I will miss my *niña*. She is all I have to remind me of her father.''

"Naturally, I would pay you a small honorarium for your loss. But I have little money because my husband is not as interested in Rafaela as I am. The agreement must be between you and me. You know wives do not have much money of their own.''

"Ah, *sí*! That is why I remain free," Conchita said smugly. "I cannot be hardhearted in bargaining with you, Señora San Roque. I will let you take her now. You pay me only enough to cause my conscience to be assured her absence is for her own good, eh?''

After Conchita Martinez had sauntered out of her office, Helen was almost sick with anger. She wondered how long the woman would remain satisfied before she began to extort more money on threat of reclaiming the child.

She shall never have her, Helen swore to herself.

She was so concerned about the child that she was glad to go home just to see for herself that Rafaela was safely there. All thoughts of San

Roque and his weekend guests had slipped her mind. She had forgotten, too, about the hairdresser, who had arrived on the morning plane.

She took Agustin with her. While under the hair dryer cuddling Rafaela, she dictated some correspondence about the training program for him to type later, and also used the occasion to give him an English lesson.

Benevidez, bitten by the possibility of advancement, had become a vigorous student. Estelita, Zonia's sister, was also dedicated. She did well in class and begged to attend every one.

Scowling, Soledad drove off the secretary and badgered the hairdresser to hurry so that Helen could have a small rest period. At last she made Helen lie down, wearing the wrapper she had donned for her hairdressing session, then covered her with a shawl. "Sleep now, and I will waken you. Close your eyes so that they will not look dull when Don Luis arrives!"

HELEN DID NOT WAKE until Soledad came in with a tray of food. She sat up feeling amazingly refreshed. "I'm ready to dress for the guests," she said brightly.

"Look where the sun comes in the window, *niña*. It is morning!"

"Morning? You're joking!"

Soledad was not joking. Helen had slept through Friday evening and on through the night. No need to worry about the house-keeper's complaining to San Roque about her overworking herself. He must have had to explain it to his guests himself. "My wife overworked herself and sleeps the weekend through!"

"Soledad, you promised to wake me!" Helen accused.

"I would have," the housekeeper answered, her face serene. "But I waited just a bit longer than I might have, because you needed the rest. Then Don Luis came unexpectedly early and said to let you sleep when he saw you were so tired. He went to the office. When he returned you were still asleep and he said I should not waken you until morning."

"What about his guests?"

"What guests?" Soledad asked. "He came alone."

Helen breathed a little more easily. She had escaped a major dereliction, of her duties! Quickly she got up, just as he came into the room. She drew the wrap close about her, embarrassed at having demonstrated such weakness as to fall into an exhausted sleep. Now she stood before him in deshabille with the hairdresser's careful work tousled and unkempt.

"So you have decided to join us?" San Roque asked cheerfully. "You are to have a holiday. There is to be no thought of the company, the office, training or any business matters at all. We will go sailing. You may take your paints if you wish.''

She nodded meekly, glad that he apparently was overlooking everything.

The sailboat anchored off a cove that seemed never to have been visited by man before. On the rocks were sea lions that watched the human invasion with curious yet indifferent eyes. Gulls wheeled screaming overhead.

''Is that a sea turtle?'' Helen used the binoculars furnished her by Vergel to see more clearly. The great creature was on the sand of the short beach beyond rocks that prevented their sailing closer.

''Want to visit him?'' asked San Roque just before diving over the vessel's side into the deep blue water.

''Is it safe to swim among all these wild creatures?'' she asked when she had surfaced after her own dive.

''Do not be afraid.'' He flipped a bit of water at her scornfully.

She was immediately stung. ''I am not afraid!'' she retorted, following him toward the rocks.

When they reached the narrow sandy strip of beach, he pulled her up to join him there. The turtle had disappeared, but the sea lions were still enthroned impassively on their rocks. A small barking seal flapped into the water, and San Roque swam with the small brown creature while Helen stood on the sand watching.

Vergel had been right when he had said the islanders were "all but born in the waters of our island." Watching San Roque swim with the seal, she felt such flush of emotion engulf her that she trembled. The sight of him brought back the same passionate attraction she had felt when he swam with the dolphins. The man and the seal disappeared into the depths, and Helen held her breath watching.

When he broke surface, the relief she felt was so great it brought tears to her eyes. He waved at her then to follow him back to the sailboat, and she found that only the hard work of swimming against the current could bring her back to her senses.

After the meal Genaro fixed them, San Roque got out the chess set.

"Take the advantage," he said.

"Perhaps I don't care to take it. I think I can win without it. I have been taking lessons from an expert since we last played."

"Ah, yes, the man from. . . Sausalito."

"No, he lives in San Francisco. At least his letters come from there. He travels."

San Roque opened with a classic move. The first third of the game moved with ballet precision from classic development and classic defense to the more crucial and complicated middle portion. She was proud of her defense and only at the last did he surprise her with a move she had not anticipated. He had her checked and mated.

"The Sicilian defense is always effective, and Ruy Lopez teaches you much. You must study it more and you will see the one fatal move," he told her. "Evidently your new chess master, Mr.—Castle?—has not perfected your defense yet. When you improve, you will be a challenge."

"I think I was a challenge today," she replied teasingly.

"You are learning," San Roque conceded.

"Perhaps my improved skill should be provided for under the terms of our contract," she continued, still only half serious.

"It is, after all, a challenge we can share in a friendly manner, is it not? A diversion uncomplicated by emotion—as safe as playing the game with an unseen partner by mail or by shortwave radio."

"I think you are a better player than the man in Sausalito," she grudgingly complimented him. "But no better than the one in San Francisco."

"When you can defeat me, then we will see who is the better player, he or I."

A touch of mischief crinkled the corners of

San Roque's eyes. He swept the players back into their chest. "Your eyes are still heavy with fatigue from the sun and water, so perhaps you play better now than I give you credit for. Yes, with some practice you may become a formidable opponent, and since you will be on the island for a long time, I look forward to your improvement."

"I suppose I shall have time to improve, at that," she acknowledged stiffly, reminded of her enforced stay.

"Why do you not go down and rest below while Genaro and I take the boat back into the harbor," he suggested.

"Is going below an order? I would rather like to stay on deck. I might even help." Somehow the thought of leaving San Roque's company after their enjoyable hours together did not appeal to her.

"I can use another crewman, but I suspect you will fall asleep again before dinner and not wake until morning. You attempt too much for your strength, though you believe yourself invincible."

"If I promise not to fall asleep until a reasonable hour, will that prove I am not overworking myself?" Helen pleaded jokingly.

"Do not expect me to be lenient with my crew," he warned. "You can secure the hatch and go aft."

She looked baffled until he pointed to the hatch and explained his terms.

SAN ROQUE HAD NOT JOKED when he said he was strict with his crew; nevertheless the lesson in seamanship proved exciting. A bank of fog began to close in on them as they neared the harbor, and the air became chilled. Helen gave over the helm to him gratefully.

"It is almost the end of the sailing season," he told her. "Soon it will be foolhardy to take the boat out. The season of hurricanes is almost here."

By the time they came in, docked and were approaching the house, the fog had closed over the island. The sound of the lighthouse horn was eerie in the thick damp night.

San Roque handed the equipment they had taken on the boat to the houseman and suggested pleasantly that Helen change into something from Sebastian's collection. "Not one of the great gowns," he told her. "Just something simple. Do not worry about your hair. Salt spray and wind are not necessarily the enemies to beauty that Sebastian and his brother claim."

She was exhausted, and the prospect of changing and dressing was enervating. "I leave the decision on what I should wear up to you," she said from the bath to Soledad.

"You do not even know what is in your

She didn't like to imagine all the beautiful predatory women who no doubt found him fascinating, powerful and irresistible. Dismissing such troubling thoughts, she slipped out of the yellow silk and into the blue velvet housecoat with the studded collar. Soledad handed her her blue mules.

Helen put her most recent letters from the mainland, which she had not had time to read thoroughly, into the pocket of her robe and went down to find Rafaela.

Now permanently bedded down in a crib in a room near Soledad's, the child looked happily expectant as Helen came to lift her up. Rafaela had her own little chair with wheels, which she could maneuver fairly well after only short practice. Her room was brightly painted with happy scenes that Helen remembered being charmed by in her own childhood.

In the library Helen set the child down on the Oriental rug. She placed a firm hand on the sole of Rafaela's small foot and pressed and pulled. She moved the twiglike arms and legs rhythmically, precisely.

"Try to say my name, niña. Say 'Helena.' I know you can say 'Helena.'" She repeated the same thing a dozen times, each time waiting for the child to attempt the name. She cheered every garbled sound, no matter how discouraging it seemed after interminable practice and days of

closet," Soledad complained. "You do not take time to look. What a shame!"

They were only uniforms, Helen reminded herself as she scrubbed salt grime off in the bath. In spite of San Roque's comments, she thoroughly shampooed her hair, then braided it into a thick coronet. The appliquéd floor-length shift in wheat and earth colors was so beautiful that she almost regretted not taking the time to have the hairdresser fix her hair in order to do the dress justice.

When San Roque handed her a bourbon and water, she looked at it doubtfully.

"Soledad will not be offended," he assured her.

"But her carne asada and chiles rellenos deserve every bit as much respect as the chef's grand international specialties. I'd really rather have the Penafiel," she protested.

"You are becoming a real mexicana," he teased admiringly.

She colored slightly and hoped he took it for a touch of the day's sun. Enjoying her drink and his good humor, she ventured to remark, "I speak Spanish all the time now, but you speak to me only in English."

"How odd you do not guess why."

"Odd? But I really cannot imagine!"

"When I speak to a woman, I speak Spanish, the language of love and romance. I do not speak to you in that language, Helen, for reasons you have specified as part of our contract.''

Taken aback by his blunt explanation, she sipped at the drink in her hand to avoid responding. Was that why she spoke Spanish—because she was not free, not herself? Because she had to be formal and careful? As the weeks passed and she felt more and more as though she belonged here, she was forgetting the distinction.

''We should go in to dinner,'' she said coolly in Spanish. ''It's been a long day....''

CHAPTER TWELVE

THE PLANE LIFTED off the island, its lights clearly visible from the library window as it banked and turned to head back toward the mainland. Another week and yet another week had passed. There had been two weekends in a row filled with guests in the strange exhausting mixture of recreation and business that was San Roque' way of increasing his company's profits on large scale, the way that brought outside life the island.

On Helen's dressing table lay another vel case, this one containing a tigereye necklac three ropes of heavy golden stones strung gold, with intricate gold nuggets between of the rich stones. San Roque had suggeste wear it with the rich yellow silk that seem have been meant by the silk worms to be with tigereyes. How easy it was to get usec quisite clothing and jewelry. She closed t and handed it to Soledad to put away.

Helen longed to know how San Roq his leisure time when he was not on th

trying. "*El patrón* will be so proud of you!" she applauded.

She gave Rafaela a rubber ball. "Now, here's something to squeeze in your hand to make it strong." She showed her how to squeeze, trying not to remember how many times she had already done the same thing. "Say 'ball,'" she urged. She formed the letters with her lips and throat and pressed the child's cheeks for the *b* and the *o* sounds. The words were similar in English and Spanish; she used both languages in the game.

Every day she followed the simple routine before going to work, when coming home for lunch and again when she arrived home at night.

At the end of the exercise session, when both were exhausted, she cuddled Rafaela against her shoulder and looked to Soledad for encouragement. "Don't you think she's improving?"

Soledad grunted, her face absolutely blank.

"Well, I'm sure she is! She never gives up. She struggles so hard, I can feel her responding more accurately all the time."

Soledad was not one to give a positive comment when her opinion was negative.

Helen sighed and pressed her cheek to the child's curly head. "You keep my spirits high and teach me lessons every day, my little spider, my *aranita*! Never stop trying!" She continued to solicit the right words from the housekeeper.

"Don't you see how much Rafaela misses Juanito? Can't you hear her trying to say his name?"

Again Soledad grunted as she took Rafaela. "Of course the child misses him. But it is Juanito who has the hard time now, all alone in the hospital."

"His grandmother is there," Helen pointed out.

"But only for a short time each day. The rest of the time he is alone with strangers."

"When the cast is off his foot, he will come home happy and be too much of a boy to spend time with our lonely one here," Helen declared confidently. "He will go to school and become an artist—perhaps a famous artist Cedros will take pride in acknowledging."

Again Soledad grunted noncommittally. She took Rafaela back to her crib and came with a shawl for Helen's feet as she curled on the couch rereading the letters brought on Friday by San Roque.

One letter was from her father, telling of her Aunt Edna's death. The news, hastily read on Friday, had not had the impact then that it did now. The poor old woman had died as she had lived—alone in her house in Oakland.

Helen now could weep. She should have insisted her aunt come to stay with her and her father; at least the old woman wouldn't have died alone. But there was no point in imagining the impossible: Aunt Edna would never have left her own house, even though it dated from the turn of the century and was long overdue for razing to make way for the city that had encroached on it through the years.

The other news in the letter was more crucial, and Helen could imagine how reading it had affected San Roque. Her father reported that Ron had got in touch with him because he needed money: he wanted a loan. Helen's father asked if she had extra to spare now that she had such a fine job.

Her jaw tensed. Poor dad had never understood the message about Ron. She felt angry frustration rise again over a brother so completely audacious. The trouble with Ron was that he was bounded on the north, south, east and west—by his own amorality.

She found she was angry with her father even though he couldn't know why she was there; he couldn't be blamed for assuming she had chosen to stay away. She knew she was angry because, marooned on this island for the best years of her life, those who knew didn't seem to care and those who didn't know, but should, weren't even saying they missed her.

She tucked her father's letter away, wishing San Roque hadn't seen it.

Next she glanced again at her letter from

Chamartin. He praised the gouaches and temperas. He was planning a one-man showing of her work, and not in San Diego or casual Laguna Beach, but in Beverly Hills at a prestigious gallery. She must send everything she could finish before the fifteenth of the month because he guaranteed her success, especially with the marvelous—and he had underlined the word *marvelous* three times—paintings of the Mexican children. She was making a name for herself, he said. He added that a startlingly large offer had been made on the dolphin picture if she wished to change her mind about selling it.

She hastily typed answers to both letters early Saturday morning, when she thought no one else in the great house was awake. San Roque entered the library quietly while she was working, and she sensed rather than saw him there. He strolled over and stood behind her, looking down at the letter to her father. Her hand went limp, so weak she could not seem to hit the right keys on the machine. At first, when he began to toy with her hair, curling it about a long finger and tugging it ever so lightly, she thought it was her imagination—a fantasy. She struggled with the typewriter keys as his touch aroused her more.

Luis ceased toying with her hair and leaned over her, his hands lightly resting on her shoulders. Knowing he was reading the letter as she typed made it difficult to bring up the subject of Ron, but she explained to her father that Ron already had her deep in debt paying back a loan on which he had defaulted. She could hear Luis's muted laughter as she made more and more errors. Her fingers simply would not obey her, but doggedly she kept on. She asked her father once again if Ron understood she could not come home until the loan was paid. "Whatever you really need for the house, or for Mama Jessie, I'll send what I can, if I can...."

San Roque lifted the heavy hair on her neck and kissed her nape, causing her to sigh loudly. "Do you think I would leave your parents to suffer in poverty?" he asked in her ear. "Whatever your attitude toward my feelings, Helen, I am not so callous of yours."

He would never understand how she felt! She would never be able to tell him how she could not bear to let herself love him when he could not possibly feel toward her anything of what she knew she could feel for him. And he had been sensitive to the needs of her family! She turned slightly to tell him so, tears stinging her eyes in her inarticulate silence.

He stared down at her soberly for a long moment, and the palm of his hand came up to smooth away the moisture from the corners of her eyes. "Helen, Helen—why are you so afraid of yourself? And of me? Have I given you any real reason to fear me?''

She shook her head almost imperceptibly at that. He cupped her face in his hands, lifting it so he could kiss her quite gently, tenderly. His caress was without threat or passion, and it evoked a deep response from her that was quite as natural as breathing. Instead of following through however, he straightened and smoothed her hair back from her forehead as one would calm a nervous filly. He then turned her back to the desk and her letters.

"Go ahead and write your letters," he told her. "I will see that they reach their destination." He stopped the stroking that had begun to drive her crazy with longing. Had he continued she would have turned to him and clung to him.

He went over to the great cabinet on the other side of the room, where he kept papers and miscellaneous files, and busied himself there, leaving her alone at the desk.

She wanted to go after him and throw herself at him. She wanted him to hold her so she could tell him what a fool she was and confess all the reasons why she could not love him or allow him to make her completely vulnerable. But she did not know what to say; the words simply would not come. She looked across at him mutely, but busy with his file folders he did not look at her.

If he had turned at that moment she would have called out his name with all the longing in her; but he did not.

Her typing was almost illegible with strike-overs, but she forced herself little by little to finish the letter to her father. She did have to discuss Aunt Edna with him. She asked her father if any help was needed to straighten out the old lady's meager estate. Perhaps Felipe Estrada could offer some advice.

When she wrote Chamartin, she said she had a few more paintings, but he would really have to make do with what he had on hand. She firmly told him not to sell the dolphin painting.

When she had handed the letters to San Roque, he said as he glanced at the letter to Chamartin, "Perhaps you will make a fortune and pay off your debt. You would like that?"

"Of course I'd like that! But if I make the maximum I can imagine, and deduct Chamartin's twenty percent for the show, it wouldn't come near to paying the debt to you."

"You know to the penny how much remains owing. I can see that computer whirling in your beautiful golden eyes."

She flushed. "Of course I know: it haunts me! Give or take a couple of dollars, the debt is down to $220,768. But it would be less humiliating if I were allowed to handle my own bank statements."

"That is what I pay Estrada to do." San Roque vetoed the plea. "The first of January I plan to give you a substantially greater salary. You need not say anything: you are worth every penny. I only wish all my young executives were as competent. But perhaps they need similar motivation."

"I don't find my situation as amusing as you seem to," she said stiffly. "I should think you would be as anxious as I to end this alliance!" And she made an excuse to leave the room.

Alone in the sitting room, she studied the chessboard and planned her next move for Castle, her interesting chess companion by mail. Finally she slipped a terse note—"Q—K8ch"— into the envelope. Too bad San Roque couldn't have taken the envelope with him. She was anxious for Castle to respond, anxious to hear if she had erred or developed a proper defense. She would know in a week. Unlike the player in Sausalito, Castle was prompt; which meant that even though she could not plot her strategy over the weekend, at least San Roque was forwarding her mail as soon as he received it.

CHAPTER THIRTEEN

THE MORNING WAS AS WARM as any summer morning on the coast of San Diego County, except that fog was heavy on the top of the mountainous island where the hills lifted clear to the other side and then fell straight down to the water. There was a crown of heavy clouds that almost never cleared away at this time of the year. The cedars sighed in the morning wind that brought more chill each passing day.

Helen wrapped a piece of cheese in a napkin and took two little rusty brown apples and a canteen for her backpack. San Roque had radioed to the island Thursday night that he expected to spend Saturday in Panama. The weekend was completely hers. She had to admit, however, that she was a little disappointed to be free of his company, which had become a welcome break at the end of her week.

Behind the house, the barely discernible footpath up into the hills had called to her ever since Vergel mentioned the spring and waterfall. She intended to make a leisurely search for it this morning and perhaps paint it.

Vergel had told her the waterfall area was a favorite of San Roque's. The information intrigued her and she was curious to see why it appealed to him.

She was almost at the tree line when she heard Rafaela's plaintive cry and turned to look back. The child had crawled laboriously onto the path from the kitchen and was trying to follow her.

Rafaela grinned happily when Helen swiftly returned for her. "All right, my sweet, you shall go with me and we will have an adventure together!" She called to Soledad through the open door, "Can you make me one of those light slings the Indian women use to carry little ones? I could carry Rafaela with me that way, since she weighs only about as much as. . . a pound of feathers."

In a few minutes, with Rafaela supported securely and comfortably on her back, she began her adventure again, using a good sturdy branch as a walking stick.

Other footpaths branched off at various points from the main one. She had no way of knowing which led to the perpetual spring, but with the prospect of several years on the island stretching before her, finding it today was not that pressing. If she didn't discover it right away, there would be other free days, however few and far between. She took the main path for the first exploration.

Each time she turned to look back, she could see the great house diminishing through the trees. Finally the cedars closed in and hid the house from her view, leaving only other trees behind her and the upward climb before her. The air had another scent here—a heady one of evergreens.

When she came to a clearing she turned and looked back on the entire east side of the island, with the ocean stretching to infinity. She wanted to throw her arms out wide and embrace the whole world here, all twenty miles' length and ten miles' width of it. Did San Roque feel the same intoxication when he climbed to this point?

"Listen!" she said to Rafaela on her back. "I hear water. Do you hear it, too?"

As she climbed higher the sound of water grew louder. She looked down: below in a great ravine a sparkling stream flowed over a jumble of rocks. Tumbling stones amplified the sound of the water.

At the end of the ravine a full-fledged waterfall came roaring down from above, its beginnings veiled by the mountain's crown of clouds. Below the waterfall a doe with a yearling raised her head from feeding and looked up peacefully, fearlessly.

Helen made her way down near the stream, then along the bank above it to the vicinity of the waterfall. The rocks were thick with mountain fern, and the sun's rays danced brightly on the surface of a deep pond. There was even a shimmering rainbow where the water's spray made prisms in the air above the pond.

It was warm so she took off her shirt and faded jeans and made a nest for Rafaela. The sun felt marvelous on her body. Her skin was losing its deep summer tan, but it was still faintly golden next to the worn old white halter and shorts.

"No crawling about now, unless I'm right here to take care you don't fall down on those sharp rocks," she ordered the child.

Rafaela laughed, her intelligent eyes sparkling like the water below them. She picked up a leaf and fingered it with great concentration.

Helen felt she understood why San Roque would love this glorious spot. She unpacked her painting equipment and began working on the scene. After she had been working a short time, she looked over at Rafaela and saw the child napping, as cozy as a little puppy.

When Rafaela woke, Helen laid aside her painting and took her down into the cold mountain stream, where they laughed and splashed and compared shivers in the shallow. She did not attempt to swim because she imagined the bottom dropped off into deep dangerous water. They were alone here and she had to mind Rafaela.

"That's enough!" she said when Rafaela's teeth chattered and the child's skin seemed blue under its naturally dark tint. She wrapped the naked child in the shirt she had brought down to the water's edge to use as a towel. Then, as she carried her up to their little nest, she saw with surprise that they had company—San Roque.

He watched them climb up without making any sign of welcome. His presence aroused mixed emotions in Helen. The weekend was no longer hers; the day was no longer hers. Nevertheless she felt her heart jump crazily and thump with excitement. She smiled with genuine pleasure as she came to where he sat back against a smooth rock quite as though he had been there all morning.

"Soledad said you came up this way. Did it not occur to you that you could become lost in this wild area?"

"No," she said, retaining her normal outward composure. "I wouldn't have got lost. You said you wouldn't be here?" she added questioningly.

"I changed my mind," he said briefly.

Helen wiped Rafaela down with the shirt and dressed the child in her shift. She laid the damp shirt on the nearest rock to dry. Rafaela stretched a wavering arm toward the cheese and apples on the lid of the painting set.

Helen divided the two tiny apples into sections and the cheese into three small morsels and politely offered San Roque his share. He took and ate it as though he had been expected. Watching her feed her pieces of apple and cheese to Rafaela, San Roque grinned. "You shared with me—I will share with you."

From the pocket of his bush jacket he took a package and formally handed it to her. "From Soledad," he said.

As she unwrapped it, a warm spicy aroma burst from the generous bounty of *burritos*. He handed her a second present: letters.

By now Helen was almost used to receiving opened mail, though she never ceased to resent the invasion of her privacy. He couldn't help but realize how she chafed under the indignity.

While San Roque fed Rafaela one of the *burritos* to give her a chance to read her mail, Helen looked first at her father's letter.

Her father's normally uncommunicative report on her stepmother was embellished with a complaint that the house badly needed painting and roof repair, that local children were into the avocado, orange and lemon orchard on the back part of the property, and that he was tired of Mrs. Parish's uninspired cooking.

Well, she thought, he was lucky to have Mrs.

Parish's "uninspired cooking." She wondered how best to stall him on the repairs without adding to his discontent.

She opened the second letter, imprinted with Chamartin's logo, and as she scanned it her eyes widened in astonishment.

"You know about my good fortune with the paintings!" she exclaimed when she could catch her breath. "I can hardly believe it!"

She had been crazy enough to dream of net proceeds approaching $25,000. The enclosed check was for $39,600 after all accounting of costs and fees. "I don't need any of this except for Juanito's hospitalization," she said. "So the rest can go to the debt account."

San Roque accepted the check, placing it in his jacket pocket. "I will sign a receipt for you when we return to the house. But I have an additional surprise for you." He reached into his jacket again and this time brought out a thick package of papers. "When your Aunt Edna died, I sent Felipe to check on your interests and hers. You're sole beneficiary of her estate."

"Estate? I didn't know—"

"No? Perhaps I forgot to speak to you about it; Felipe was using power of attorney. At any rate, Felipe handled it all, since you could not go to Oakland yourself."

"And what did Felipe find?"

"Your aunt had only a very small house there, very old."

"I know that. But why did she leave it to me? I'm not even a blood relative!" She was stunned.

"She was evidently grateful for your faithful letters, and for your willingness to take on the financial responsibility for your stepmother. No doubt she was glad her sister did not have to stay in a county-run home, where she would not get the finest care in nursing. She left whatever she had to you. Essentially that was the little house she had lived in for more than three-quarters of a century."

"I suppose it's in dreadful shape?"

"I cannot say. But there was little of intrinsic value there except for this gold locket and this little pearl ring. There was also some furniture, which was sold at auction for $236.22."

He gave her an envelope containing the money, with Felipe Estrada's neat handwriting listing all the figures. "Felipe found the house had high property value because of its location practically at the center of downtown Oakland. He was able to negotiate a fair price from several merchants, and the check is right here for you to do with whatever you want."

She stared at the bank draft he handed her, hardly able to comprehend the amount: $123,000. "This...this all came from the sale of Aunt Edna's little old house?'' It was unbelievable that such a tiny place in such a dingy area could be so valuable! Her mind refused to accept it. In one morning, she realized, her debt to San Roque had shrunk from a staggering amount to approximately sixty thousand dollars. The new sum, by comparison, seemed almost paltry.

Wordlessly she handed the check back to him.

''At this rate,'' San Roque said with a dry rasp in his voice, ''you will be able to discharge your debt any minute.''

''Hardly,'' she answered in a tiny voice. Without other miracles like this she predicted she would remain on the island a couple of years yet. And her delight at the shortening of her term of ''imprisonment'' was tempered by San Roque's attitude toward her. He sounded condemning and contemptuous, as though all she thought about was leaving. Would he never understand that she wanted to be kept and guarded as more than a hostage for her brother? That she wanted to be. . .loved?

Helen remained silent and confused as a cloud passed over the rock, taking all the sparkle from the water and the warmth from the sky. Shivering, she reached behind her, took her now dried shirt from the rock and slipped it on; but she still felt chilled. San Roque removed his blue denim jacket and put it firmly around her shoulders.

"In the fall weather, warm days such as this are not predictable," he said in a neutral voice. But the warmth left in the jacket from his body took care of only part of the chill. Helen was still unaccountably cold, and she picked up the dozing Rafaela, who was damp and hot in the way of sleeping children. Rafaela warmed her a little more and the cloud eventually passed. She stopped shivering and forced herself to keep from admitting she never wanted to leave the island. Never.

"The only means I have of erasing the debt from now on," she said, "is my salary. I have very little time to paint anymore. It would be folly for me to expect any more great sales—or any more inheritances."

She was surprised at herself—dredging up reasons why she would not be able to pay the debt immediately. Her brother had stolen a small fortune; she had the responsibility of paying it back dumped on her; San Roque had been enormously decent under the circumstances. What had seemed an almost insurmountable burden only two short months earlier had now shrunk by an amazing sequence of events until it was less than a quarter of its original size. She could barely understand her wish that the debt remain an "impossible" sum to repay instead of shrinking quickly away.

How could I want to remain a chattel, she

mused. *Why do I want to stay here when it's insanity on my part to have any thought of.* . . .

"You dropped the other letter," San Roque pointed out.

She picked up the envelope with the San Francisco return address and opened it slowly.

She had won her first match with the chess player in San Francisco! Preoccupied as she was with her ambivalent feelings, she smiled.

"More cash windfalls?" San Roque teased her.

"You know it's just a chess game." Her smile faded a little. The opponent not only complimented her on her game, he wanted a picture of her. He said he imagined her as being middle-aged and stout or perhaps only ten or twelve years old. The typed notes he sent her offered no clues to his own age.

"Are you going to send him a picture?"

"I beg your pardon?" Momentarily she had forgotten he read all her mail. Then she said perversely, "Perhaps I will."

"And if I say I will not let my wife send her picture to a strange man?"

"He's not 'strange.' He's a fine chess player—and my friend."

"And a good hotel contract sanitation man," he added.

"A what?"

"He has a contract to remove hotel refuse, among other things."

"How would you. . .?"

"Naturally I had Estrada check on him. A husband should know with whom his wife is involved."

"Involved! Really, you haven't the right! And it's not true—not the way you make it sound."

"I should think you would appreciate my concern for your interests. Do you wish to know what the man is like? What he does with his life?"

"Not particularly. I am interested only in his chess game." She hesitated. "Well, yes—I would like to know, as long as you made the effort."

"He is of medium height as men are measured. In your high heels I would judge him to be as much as a head shorter than you. He does not take good care of himself: he is a bit heavy, a bit bald and rather pale for a Californian. But he is quite harmless and of good character, if you overlook his habit of drinking a bit too much beer. When we return to the house shall I take your picture to send to him? You could ask him to return the favor."

"I. . .suppose so," she said lamely. She hadn't thought of exchanging pictures with Don Castle, but now she didn't know how to get out of it.

San Roque stood and shucked off his shirt

and trousers, revealing his body magnificently fit with broad shoulders tapering down to slim hips. He walked away in his swimming trunks and disappeared in the undergrowth above the natural dam, leaving Helen holding the child. A few minutes later he appeared on the rock that jutted out above the deepest part of the water and dived from its heights into the pond.

Helen held her breath. The dive was dangerous but executed with the same casual lack of concern he had shown when sporting with the dolphins and sea lions. As brown as one of the ocean seals and as perfectly suited to the water, he climbed the crag easily and dived once again.

Helen looked away at her painting. She had an almost irresistible urge to depict him in it, on the rock; to preserve him as she had in the painting of the dolphins.

She took her paintbrush and poised it over the watercolor pad. Her face grew flushed, her cheeks were stung with changing color and her blood began to sing. Suddenly the brush dropped from nerveless fingers and she was paralyzed by her own senses.

"I love the man," she whispered. "Oh, I do love him...."

She realized she couldn't paint him: it would only become another dolphin painting, one she could not bring herself to sell. At least she now realized why. The dolphin painting was something of him no caprice of reality could take from her. But she had too much sense to expect her love ever to be more than one-sided. She hated knowing her own feelings now that they had been revealed to her, and she could certainly never let him know. The day must come when she would leave this beautiful island, this special country, behind her forever. She didn't want to torture herself needlessly.

She put the paints away.

Every picture she had ever painted was, she knew, a strong statement of herself. It was that quality that Chamartin promoted: the tangible emotion in her paintings and her simple clarity. There were some susceptibilities in herself that she ought never to declare, even in her art—not when the wounds they could inflict would be too devastating.

San Roque completed his swim and returned to where Helen sat with the sleeping Rafaela. She studied him covertly as he put on his denims and island huaraches. At close range he was incredibly tall and rough-hewn, and she was again reminded of the Mexican phrase she had thought of the first time she saw him: *fuerte y formal*. She felt dizzy basking in his beauty.

He picked up Rafaela and wrapped her in his own white shirt. "The fog comes in early this time of year. Already it is too cold for the child. We will go back now."

Silently Helen gathered up her things and followed him down the path through the cedars and underbrush.

"Felipe Estrada, Yolanda Betancourt and her father are with me," he said over his shoulder.

"Why didn't you say something before now?" she asked in astonishment.

"I saw no reason to have to do so." He shrugged at the idea.

"But to leave your guests alone and just wander off and go swimming...."

"Felipe and Paolo are conferring with Eugenio Ochoa. Vergel has taken Yolanda into town. All three have been here many times before; they know how to entertain themselves."

"I hope you don't object," she said hesitantly, "but I asked Eugenio and Magdalena to dinner, since you weren't going to be here—"

"Why should I object?"

"Also, your secretary, Benevidez, and two of my better students from the office-practices program are to come tomorrow afternoon for a special lesson in business English. But of course I can cancel."

"Do that," he said coolly. "I asked you not to turn my home into an office, did I not?"

"Yes—but shouldn't I work if you aren't to be here on Cedros? It would not—"

"You do not know if I will come or not. You

did not know this weekend. I was able to finish my business early. And although I do not owe you an explanation, a good employer knows when to make his employee rest, just as a good farmer knows when to rest his mule.''

He handed Rafaela over to Soledad, who had come out of the house to meet them on the back patio. He continued speaking to Helen. "It is for the good of the other employees as well as yourself. You can burn yourself out with too little relaxation." He brushed cedar needles casually out of her hair. His touch was like a caress and yet she realized it wasn't meant to be.

She raised her hand quickly to her tangled curls. "I'm an embarrassment to you the way I must look. I'll change."

Estrada and Betancourt weren't her worry. They were here on business; they knew how hard she worked. She had no reason to be self-conscious in front of them. But Yolanda.... She had only seen Yolanda that one day at Punta Temereria, and she had not been at her best then, either.

San Roque said Yolanda had been to the island many times before. He did not have to say the woman expected to be the chatelaine of his home, but Helen knew that. What kind of explanation had he given Yolanda for this outlandish marriage contract? Did she know why

Helen was really here? And why had he brought her here this weekend?

"Do not let Yolanda intimidate you," Luis ordered, and Helen stared at him, wondering crazily how he had read her mind. She almost fled before him into the house and up the back stairs to her own room.

She threw two double handfuls of bath salts into the huge sunken marble tub, turned on the gold faucets and climbed in, wishing she could remain there throughout the evening. The only thing that finally brought her out of the bath was her fear that San Roque would burst in and force her to come downstairs anyway.

So, she decided, Yolanda probably knew why she was on the island. Yolanda also knew, then, how vulnerable she was. Yolanda was the queen of the chess game and Helen only an expendable pawn.

For the first time in her life, Helen felt intensely, hopelessly jealous of another woman. The hurt she had known as a daughter always set aside by a father's open preference for his son was nothing compared to this agony.

Again Helen hesitated. Perhaps Yolanda ought to be left the role of hostess this evening while she remained in her room.

No, that would be unkind to Magdalena. Painfully shy among strangers—except Helen, whom she had come to know and trust—

Magdalena had confessed she was intimidated by Yolanda. Finally, Helen thought, Luis would be angered if she deliberately made herself absent.

She brushed her hair fiercely in front of the great mirror and imagined wearing it like that, flowing abandoned over her shoulders. Perhaps she should go down in flat shoes so as not to tower over everyone. Perhaps she should wear the confection of seafoam green that was Luis's favorite from Sebastian's collection. Perhaps she should float into his arms in a demonstration of the connubial affection he seemed to encourage in front of his guests. Perhaps....

Sighing, Helen pulled her hair up to the top of her head, and secured it in a loose knot. Short undisciplined tendrils escaped to curl softly about her face in absolute defiance of her intent.

For the first time she put great care into selecting the correct dress. She wanted to avoid antagonizing Yolanda, so it could not be provocative. She wanted to appear professional and at the same time stylish, to fulfill the demands of her contract with Luis. She wanted to appear womanly in the eyes of his associates, so it had to be feminine. And she needed to feel relaxed, so the dress had to be comfortable.

She finally took down a dark cranberry wool that was the least provocative dress in the lot but had a certain. . . daring. What copper-haired girl in her right mind would choose to wear such a color! Sebastian had been anxious to see her wear it because, he said, she was uniquely able to carry it off. There were beautiful dyed sandals to match.

Helen fastened Aunt Edna's gold locket around her throat to remind her of reality, to give her a sense of herself. She looked at herself critically in the mirror again and was pleased to see Sebastian had been right: the dress was a tour de force. Luis might wonder why she had chosen the simple locket in lieu of perhaps the fire opals; but he wouldn't object, because he knew the meaning it held for her.

CHAPTER FOURTEEN

HELEN STALLED as long as she dared, but at last the time came when she had to descend the stairs. Magdalena peeked out of the library with an anxious face that immediately brightened when she saw her friend.

"They are talking about great cities they have visited," Magdalena whispered confidentially as she met Helen at the foot of the stairs. "As you know, I have never been off Cedros. I thought to come up and help you finish dressing, and Don Luis said I might if you did not mind."

"Thank you; that was sweet of you. But there's no crime in not having traveled," Helen reassured her. "You will travel—when Eugenio becomes important to the rest of Don Luis's businesses. We'll go in and listen, you and I, and learn. Then we can both feel, when the time comes, that we're quite familiar with all the places they speak about."

"Oh, but if I should have to go away in a plane I would be frightened. I am afraid of planes," Magdalena confessed.

"You will not be afraid when the time comes. Later I will tell you all about Tijuana and San Diego. The next time Eugenio goes there I will persuade him to take you with him. You will know everything you need to know and will have a wonderful time, I promise you."

"Oh, Helena, I am so fortunate to have found a kind friend to help me with such matters. It is quite as though we were old school friends!" Magdalena was totally sincere and her timidity visibly diminished with Helen by her side. "Will you go with me to Tijuana? We will be able to see Juanito!"

Helen wished she could be as easily reassured. She had assumed a cool facade, but beneath it she felt quite as timid tonight as Magdalena.

She paused at the door of the library, took a deep breath to regain her calm, then lifted her shoulders and walked into the room looking poised and elegant. Magdalena followed.

Luis put down his Penafiel and crossed the room to greet her. She wished she had the courage to rest her head on his shoulder, look up into his storm-gray gaze and let her own eyes reveal how strongly she felt about him. *That would be the end of dinner and me!*

Luis put his arm around her waist, turned her face to his and gave her a light but firm kiss before guiding her into the circle of guests. "You have all met," he said. Tonight he spoke in Spanish, and to Helen it seemed the most beautiful language in the world.

Betancourt and Estrada immediately made polite flowery speeches of good luck and congratulations. Helen was quite aware of how Yolanda stepped back from her and Luis, rejecting with her body language Helen's role as San Roque's wife and mistress of the great house. She inspected Helen from head to toe in a manner any woman would find nerve-racking, and Helen was not immune to its effect.

Yolanda wore a delicately handcrafted Mexican gauze gown, her blue black hair exquisitely coiffed, and gleaming like the finely polished emeralds at her throat. But her expression told a different story—and with the precision of a surgeon's scalpel. Every word she spoke was calculated.

"I never realized you were so tall." She stood close to Helen to emphasize the difference between them, and looking up at her with liquid black eyes.

"How I envy Helen her queenliness!" Magdalena interjected, not recognizing Yolanda's meaning.

"Luis," continued Yolanda, ignoring Magdalena entirely, "you must lure a hairdresser here to help Helen minimize her problem hair. Also someone to help her with style as befitting your wife. I shall have a serious talk with you on the subject when we fly back to Mexico City. There is no need for her to be gauche, even here at the edge of the world.''

"Do you really think she looks gauche?" he inquired mildly.

Magdalena, who had gone to the local *salon de belleza* to make herself look nice for dinner with her friend at the great house, appeared stricken and then indignant. She obviously took Yolanda's barb to be directed at herself, as well. But her innate courtesy caused her to control her first reaction of annoyance and valiantly try to change the subject.

"Señorita Betancourt has just returned from a trip to San Francisco," she said quickly to Helen. "You have been there many times, have you not, Señorita Betancourt?"

"Our national folkloric group performed there and we were invited by the consul, a friend of my father's," Yolanda responded, readily enough diverted. "Too bad you could not have gone, Helen. I could have introduced you to some of our friends there, but of course with your obligations here...."

Well, then, Helen thought. *I was right. Yolanda knows I can't leave the island. She is going to rub salt in every wound all evening.*

"I would like a bourbon and water," she said firmly.

Luis, who had already poured her a Penafiel,

calmly fulfilled her request with no comment save a steady gray stare. Helen turned away nervously from his gaze.

Felipe Estrada picked up a chessman from the table. "You and Luis still enjoy the game of chess, I see. I remember it was your first meeting ground at La Punta."

"He is still champion," Helen said with a slight gesture of recognition and an uneasy smile. "He gets tired of such a poor opponent." She was not enjoying the drink, but she sipped at it anyway.

It was Yolanda's turn again. "Do you really manage to lose every time? Very clever of you. But then, North American girls are usually clever except when they act aggressively, as they all do. A true man cannot possibly appreciate an aggressive woman. You are so clever not to be that way."

"I hate to admit it, but I am a true North American girl. Very aggressive." She took another rapid swallow of the drink and, seeing Luis's eye upon her, put the glass firmly back on the bar. "As soon as I'm able to do so, I'm going to win every game of chess with him and gloat over every win!" she joked lightly. She was furious that Yolanda would imply she would play a game dishonestly. "I take lessons by mail from two excellent players," she added.

"Chess by mail?" Señor Betancourt asked, laughing.

"Certainly," she said. "One player in Sausalito and one in San Francisco."

"Ah!" said Felipe. "The one in San Francisco—"

She cut him off hastily, "He's a wonderful chess player. I've learned so much from him." She hoped Felipe would not mention to everyone present the information Luis had given her that morning.

"You allow your wife to have involvements with other men, then, Luis?" Yolanda drawled, dark eyes sparkling with malice. "Your wife seems to have changed you from a Mexican to a North American."

"By mail the liaison is safe enough," he said pleasantly, "but you may be right. It is not entirely proper, Helena. Suppose the poor man fell in love with you?"

Felipe, Helen noticed, looked highly amused, knowing what he did about the chess player.

She reached for the bourbon and swallowed the rest almost convulsively, angry that Luis should deliberately bait her about a man he himself had described as harmless. "I think I'll have another drink," she said, holding the glass out for a refill.

Genaro prepared to refresh her drink, but Luis prevented him from doing so. "Here is

Soledad to tell us our dinner is served," he announced.

He ushered Magdalena into the dining room and Felipe escorted Helen.

At the dinner table Helen felt the one quickly ingested drink had numbed her lips. Her meal tasted like sawdust. She sat in rigid silence while Señor Betancourt told more about his trip with his daughter to San Francisco. He compared the cosmopolitan virtues of San Francisco and Mexico City and discussed his decision to purchase the jewelry Yolanda was wearing.

"I knew the quality was nowhere near as fine as work I had seen in Mexico City, but she fell in love with it. The trip made me realize where all quality is to be found: at home."

"The necklace is magnificent and yet does not do you justice," Luis said to Yolanda, his glance lingering on her creamy shoulders and the décolleté where the jewels rested.

Helen realized how pointless it would be for her to hope he might ever have such eyes for her.

"Shall I refer Luis to my jeweler?" Yolanda asked her. "I am sure he would suggest something suitable, my dear, unless you really prefer to wear costume jewelry from your own country such as the piece you are wearing."

Helen silently regarded Yolanda. She reminded herself that Luis had said emeralds looked common, even though it seemed he thought them anything but common when worn by the beautiful Yolanda. She touched Aunt Edna's pendant protectively.

"Helen really needs something to liven up that odd-colored dress, Luis," Yolanda pressed on.

"Is that not the charming little antique pendant I brought back from your aunt in Oakland, California?" Felipe asked.

Helen smiled warmly at him. It was the second time he had tried to rescue the conversation even though—just as the first time—it was a lost effort.

"I knew there must be a sentimental reason for you to wear the little thing," Yolanda said sweetly.

Smiling stiffly, Helen retreated into herself as the conversation flowed over and around her. She wished now that she had worn a more imposing gown—the green one Luis seemed to like, or the silver gray *peau de soie*. She should have shown Yolanda her full power as mistress of San Roque's home. She should have put her time in the bath to better use and done something dramatic with her hair and makeup. Her eyes, naked of shadow compared to the shimmering appeal of Yolanda's, could have been better accentuated.

Each passing riposte of Yolanda's bit Helen

deeper. Nevertheless, she continued to smile, turning the barbs aside gently or agreeing with them easily—a tactic she hoped might take the wind from the other woman's sails. Her agreements roused protests from Magdalena, Felipe and even Eugenio, all of whom rose to her defense.

Luis seemed only too aware of the way Yolanda was baiting her. He seemed even to encourage her. Certainly he left Helen to cope with Yolanda's verbal daggers on her own.

Helen was inexpressibly relieved when Magdalena and Eugenio said their good-nights in the Mexican fashion—a complex formality of compliments, pretty speeches and protests on the part of hosts and guests.

"I, too, would like to retire," Helen said immediately after they left. "I know you'll all excuse me."

"We are all exhausted," Felipe added sympathetically. "We were in Panama City last night, then flew here to the island this morning for a conference with Ochoa. What with your excellent hospitality this evening...."

"I am going to play the piano for you, Luis," Yolanda announced, oblivious to the others. "I have always loved the tone of your piano and it's been a long time since I was here. When I was sixteen you loved to listen to me play. Remember when I was still taking lessons at the conservatory and papa practically forced me to play for everyone? Now I will play again for old times' sake.'' She made a pretty coaxing face.

There was nothing to do but sit while Yolanda proved what an accomplished musician she was. She had the men completely enthralled. At last Helen could remain no longer, and she excused herself from the room with apologies and good-nights.

Entering the blessed sanctuary of her bedroom, she shook her hair free, removed her precious pendant and kicked off her shoes. Moments later, after saying good-night to his guests, Luis came in through the hall door.

Startled, Helen faced him, still furious with herself and equally with him. ''Was it necessary to force such an ordeal on me?'' she asked through clenched teeth.

''You have to face each challenge sooner or later. This was as good a time as any.''

''You could have spared parading me like a...an amazon in chains!''

''Do not be an imbecile, Helen! You were not paraded. Whatever makes you think such a thing?''

''You know very well what gives me such an idea! It would have been kinder of you not to tell Yolanda all the circumstances surrounding my peculiar...status here. The situation is humiliating enough as it is.''

"Humiliating?" His brows came together in a dark frown over steely gray eyes.

"Humiliating! Everything I've ever achieved, owned or hoped to own has been handed over to you to pay a debt that wasn't of my making. I am continuing to pay in good faith. You needn't make me an object of scorn."

"What makes you think Yolanda knows about your reasons for being here on the island?" Luis asked calmly.

"She knows! It was obvious she knows!"

"Now, listen to me, Helen. I told you earlier not to allow yourself to be intimidated by Yolanda, but you let yourself be. As far as the unfortunate theft is concerned—it is a matter of company business that would never be discussed outside of my private office. Paolo would not reveal it to her, any more than he would refer to the most trivial detail of company business with her outside of my presence." Barely controlling himself, he continued, "Surely you do not believe I would discuss our private business with her—or anyone else!"

"Why not? If you and she—"

"Yolanda and I?" His eyes widened. "You believe there is a relationship between us? Is that why you were so far from being yourself tonight? Let me assure you it is not my principle to treat marriage vows lightly with my associates or with the world at large."

She retorted, "You find it strange I could suspect you are in love with Yolanda. It is no wilder a thought than your forbidding me to play chess with a man I have never met, especially when every communication with him passes first through your own hands!"

"You will give your chess partner notice, Helen, if I ever say you must; but at present I see no reason why you should not continue your harmless games, even though the fellow is not the expert you seem to think."

"You have no right—"

"You forget, Helen, I have all the rights."

"Oh! It is futile to try to discuss anything intelligently and calmly with you! It's late and I'm tired. I want to go to bed."

"So do I." As a gleam leaped into his eyes she immediately regretted her words. He stepped closer and Helen felt herself drowning in the gaze of this man who was so unbearably attractive to her.

He took her by the arm and gently pulled her toward him. "You know I have been quite patient with you, Helen—"

"Patient?" Petulantly she tried to wrest her arm free and failed, as she had failed all evening to win even the smallest battle. She was close to tears.

"You know what I mean," he said quietly.

"And you know what I mean! The painting—

the inheritance—you couldn't have hoped to regain so much so quickly unless I were totally determined to see you not cheated of your property.''

"I am not interested in money!'' He made an impatient gesture as he released her arm, much as though he were throwing her from him angrily. "It is our relationship that must change. We have played games long enough!''

"Games! It was your contract, not mine—''

"We have a marriage contract, not one of your sterile chess games by mail. Not a business partnership. Marriage is what we agreed on and marriage is what I intend to have.''

"You agreed—'' she protested, shrinking back. Her devastating longing for him warred with her good sense, and she fought down her desire to fall into his arms. "I . . . told you once before—perhaps not emphatically enough—that I don't wish any man in my bed unless. . . .'' She hesitated, then finished determinedly, "Even if we are legally married—unless there is love between the two of us . . . not just expedience!''

"You know you were meant to lie in my arms,'' he said quietly, and his words sent a tremor through her. "From the first time you saw me it was in your eyes—''

"And for you any woman would serve much the same purpose,'' she cut him off. "You demanded I stay here and pay my brother's debt, and I have no choice but to comply. In this, however, I will not cooperate. You aren't a man who must take a woman against her will, but if you do—'' she felt her face drain of color and looked at him menacingly "—if you do I will hate you until the day you die! That may be a great many years to be chained to a woman who despises you!''

"Putting it to you plainly, Helen, you have everything to gain by doing away with this sterile relationship you have insisted on so far. You have nothing to lose by being a wife. Eugenio would be only too happy to take back the island operation. He dislikes being separated even occasionally from Magdalena, and the separations must increase as his new duties increase. If we were truly husband and wife we could travel together and the world would be our home. You would have everything I could give you—''

"Everything but love and freedom!'' she cried out, agonized by his cold-blooded bargaining for her body, which she would so willingly give to him in a moment if only he loved her.

"What do you call 'love' and what do you call 'freedom,' Helen?'' he probed.

She was thrown off balance by his blunt question and her own terribly ambivalent feelings.

"What difference does it make?'' she hedged frantically. "I'm not free to do anything but pay for Ron's embezzlement! Only after that is completed can I think of love. Not before!''

He was not listening. He pulled her roughly to him, his mouth covering hers with a passion she could not resist. As his lips sought her ears and the hollows of her throat, a wave of weakness engulfed her and her resolve threatened to desert her. His hand found the zipper at her neck, parting her dress, then slipped easily between the fabric and her skin. He cupped one breast gently, caressing the nipple until it grew throbbingly taut. His other hand sent shivers up and down her spine as he firmly drew her closer, molding her body to his and making her achingly aware of his powerful male needs.

How her pulses pounded! Conscious that she could not continue like this without surrendering to him completely, she made one last wild effort to resist him.

"Self-respect!" she choked out, pushing away from him frantically. "Don't take my self-respect!" Because she had broken the spell of the moment for herself at least, she continued hoarsely, "If you don't leave this room I'll scream the walls down!"

He continued to caress her, and in desperation she added, "It would be embarrassing for everyone if Felipe Estrada were to have to come to my aid!"

He stepped away from her instantly, still

keeping a firm grip on her shoulders. His eyes had turned to ice.

"If you do scream, madam, and Felipe does come to your aid, as I believe he would be sensible enough not to do in this house, I would have to kill him. Do you understand?" He forced her back onto the bed, glaring at her still.

She was shocked speechless by his mercurial change from desire to such cold anger and thoroughly frightened by the fury her desperate words had ignited in him. His body pinned hers to the bed and his strong knee pressed against her thighs.

"I will no longer be put off by you," he whispered, and sealed the words with a fierce kiss that crushed her mouth under his, forcing her lips open for his exploration. She was no match for him; there was no way to do battle and she knew at heart that she truly didn't want to.

Sagging under his weight, she went completely limp. He looked into her eyes, but unable to bear his gaze she turned away.

"Do what you like," she told him bitterly. "You have every advantage. I am your prisoner, and it makes no difference that I might want love, not the passion of revenge."

Abruptly he rose from the bed, uttering a string of violent Spanish oaths. When she opened her eyes he was gone.

The connecting doors stood wide. She could

see the interior of his room, but he was not in sight.

She lay on her bed, drained. Her lips, numb from the punishing kiss, began to feel tender and swollen. She thought, dazed, *what have I done? I have sent him straight to Yolanda, who would kill me if she thought it would bring him back to her! I am the world's greatest fool—but how I hate him for making me love him when there is no future in such a love....*

She did not get up to shut the doors—not that she wanted them to remain open, but there was no point in shutting them now and she felt she could not have risen from the bed if her life had actually depended on it.

It was hours before she fell asleep. The doors remained open. The other room remained empty.

CHAPTER FIFTEEN

CLOUDS BOILED UP OUT OF THE SOUTHWEST and brought rain with the sharp wind chopping at the sea. *"Borrasca,"* Soledad warned, nodding wisely as she went about her duties.

Borrasca. A storm out of the tropical ocean to the south was the herald of the hurricane season. As Helen left the house to go to the office, the houseman was putting up storm doors and windows. A hard blow was clearly expected.

"Winds of 125 miles at the center," the man running the wireless reported. "About 275 miles south and coming up fast."

"That's bad?" Helen asked him.

"Not the worst. But bad enough. Winds of that force can wreck the island sufficiently without setting a record."

"Will planes be able to come in today?"

"This morning, yes. Then no more until the storm passes."

So Luis would come this morning or not at all. Would he be able to get away early enough, she wondered.

Eugenio was on the plane alone. "El señor canceled the hairdresser again this week, and also the guests, because of the *huracán* that is coming."

The storm was his excuse to stay away, she thought forlornly. The preceding Sunday had been almost as emotionally exhausting as the sleepless Saturday night. When the Betancourts, Estrada and Luis finally left, she had known instinctively that he wouldn't return to the island this week. He had been icy cold, punctiliously correct and as aloof as Señor Betancourt.

"The storm will probably work itself out before it comes this far," Eugenio explained, "but it is not wise to take its possible arrival carelessly."

"I was in the tail of a hurricane once," Helen mused. "A small one. When it came up into the United States there were millions of dollars in damage and mudslides as far north as Los Angeles. Yet it was hardly classed as a hurricane—merely wind and lots of rain."

"You need not worry: all will be safe. We are used to these blows."

Cedros did not take the threat of a hurricane lightly. Everything all over the island was tied down, covered or taken in; windows and doors were barricaded, and as the wind rose and the rain began, the sky blackened correspondingly.

"I think, Doña Helena, that you should go

home," Eugenio advised. "A stronger wind will make the winding road to the great house dangerous. The *huracán* will pass over Cedros sometime tonight. Until then it will steadily become more hazardous to be away from shelter."

"Tell everyone here to go home now, too," Helen ordered.

Eugenio hurried to spread the welcome news.

Even as she and Vergel left the quay, Helen saw a great slab of tin blow down the street and crash into the side of a building. Tree branches were beginning to fly through the air. She was almost blown through the front door of the house when Soledad opened it for her.

The housekeeper made angry little noises as she removed Helen's raincoat and boots and bustled her into the library. A fire was blazing there, in cheery contrast to the chaos outside.

"I must paint the gathering storm!" Helen said breathlessly.

"But Andreas is fitting the storm shutters," Soledad objected.

"I saw him working downstairs. My balcony is still open. I should have time to do a fast watercolor gouache before he has to do that window."

Helen took her paints out of the storeroom and worked rapidly, fascinated with the panorama of the darkening city as the storm arrived.

"Soon trees will be uprooted, and it will be

dangerous to be near any unguarded window,''
Soledad warned.

Reluctantly Helen relied on her imagination
to work on the painting under electric light.
With the thick cedar shutters in place the fury
outside seemed unreal. The great house had
been built to withstand nature's fiercest storms.
Except near the doors and windows there was
no sound to indicate a storm.

Helen exercised Rafaela, then snuggled the
little one into a floor pillow with a warm quilt
over her as she sat and painted. Suddenly the
lamp winked out and the room was plunged into
darkness. Soledad brought hurricane lamps.

"The electricity often goes in such storms.
For days afterward we may exist without modern conveniences. We should fill the baths and
all containers so as not to be caught short of
water if there are problems with the supply.''

"As long as we are to go back to basics, could
we have cheese grilled in the fire here for dinner?'' Helen suggested.

"Oh, no,'' Soledad objected. "I will make
the proper *cena* for Don Luis, who will be home
at that hour and hungry.''

"He's surely not coming tonight!'' Helen exclaimed, horrified.

"Word was relayed up from the wireless. El
señor instructed Vergel not to meet him because
it will be difficult with the *huracán*. But there is

no need to worry, for he is a fine *piloto*, never fear.''

Helen was unconvinced. ''Good pilot or not, he shouldn't fly in weather like this! He is risking the lives of Genaro and anyone else he brings with him!''

''No one comes with him,'' Soledad pointed out. ''But he wishes to be at his home at a time such as this.''

Helen felt a surge of ambivalent anger that the man would be so foolhardy as to make the trip from the mainland into the face of such a storm. At the same time she was angry with herself for being glad he was coming in spite of the storm. ''The *sopa* from lunch will be sufficient, then, for *cena*,'' she managed to say calmly.

''Leftover soup, Doña Helena?'' Soledad was scandalized. ''Is that the way a *norteamericana* wife takes care of her *marido*? Not in this house!''

Shrugging off the housekeeper's reproof, Helen bundled up Rafaela, put the child safely in her crib and went upstairs to change. She realized that she as well as Soledad felt the importance of making Luis's homecoming special. The howl of the wind and the lashing of the rain now penetrated the shutters, and anxiety grew in her more than she wanted to admit.

She brushed her hair and left it loose, slipping into a white wool crepe gown as sheer as a handkerchief. But when she saw herself in the mirror she changed her mind. Sebastian's wardrobe always seemed to transform her into a provocative woman she didn't recognize. The last thing she wished to do, she assured herself, was appear seductive; but she did want to please Luis, even if she tried to tell herself it was only to avoid spending another disastrous weekend like the last.

She did not twist her hair to the top of her head but fixed it in a loose knot at the nape of her neck. She exchanged the flowing wool crepe for one of her office skirts and a pale gray matching silk shirt. After much thought, she slipped on the flat huaraches. There was no harm in being relaxed. She even put on her old eyeglasses rather than one of the chic designer pairs Luis had ordered for her after the visit of the Argentinians.

Eight o'clock—the hour of *cena* and no sign of him. The storm was rising to a greater fury.

"Is there no way to tell if he's safe?" she asked downstairs, pacing the library as anxiously as a cat.

"I can send Vergel to the airport and the wireless—"

"No!" she exclaimed. "But how long ago did he leave the mainland? Six o'clock? It takes no more than an hour to come here from Guerrero Negro." Helen eyed the antique clock in agitation. "He may have missed the island. It's only a dot in the biggest ocean in the world!"

"You must calm yourself, *niña*," Soledad soothed her. "He will come. He will use the instruments and will not miss the island."

"Anything could happen! Why did he risk his life?"

"I will bring you a pot of strong tea to soothe you. And I will melt some cheese for you."

"How can I eat?" Helen cried, rigid with concern. She tried to control herself, for she did not want to communicate her fear to the other servants. This island was their world, and none of them really understood the terrible danger of flying in a storm. They couldn't conceive how the plane that el señor flew so easily could go off course and head into open ocean. Fear made her turn to ice.

The tea grew cold in the pot, and the melted cheese congealed into a lump on the Limoges plate. Helen felt she could not stand the strain a moment longer, so she sent Zonia to fetch her slacks, raincoat and boots.

"I'm going to go down the hill and find out what has happened," she said. "Don't worry— I'm a better driver than Vergel. I'll take the car myself."

"You are mad, Doña Helena!" Zonia protested. "You will kill yourself!"

"There's no other way to get at the short-wave," she argued. "I have to know!"

Zonia and Soledad failed to dissuade her even when Zonia dissolved into frightened tears.

"Open the front doors," Helen ordered. "I must get to the garage."

But the incredible force of the wind made opening the door almost impossible.

She had not even managed to get out of the house when out of the night stumbled another figure, forcing her inside again.

"It is el señor!" shrieked Zonia.

Luis, soaked, muddy and exhausted, calmed down his household.

"I walked up from the bottom of the hill. There is more than one tree down over the road." He let them help him out of his drenched coat, but he turned livid when he realized he had by only sheer timing prevented Helen from leaving the safety of the house.

"Have you all taken leave of your senses? Soledad, I left Doña Helena in your care and you allowed her to go!"

"Nothing would stop her, Don Luis," the housekeeper told him. "She insisted on driving to the airport to find out where you were. She has made herself crazy with worry, poor child!"

"Is that so?" Luis looked at Helen with an inscrutable expression. "Well, you may all now relax, for I have safely arrived." He sniffed the air. "I smell your soup bubbling in the iron pot, Soledad. Let me have a moment to make myself presentable and we will have dinner."

When he had disappeared up the stairs the servants all sighed with relief that he had not been more angry with them, looking sideways at Helen reproachfully. Helen herself felt faint with relief. The angry pleasure she had felt when she heard he was flying to the island returned. By the time Luis came downstairs, in a beige cashmere sweater over impeccably tailored pale trousers, she was not disposed to be friendly. He looked calm and unruffled, as if he had rested the whole afternoon.

"Soledad is serving dinner in the dining room," she said coolly. "You'll excuse me if I don't join you."

"No, I will not excuse you." He propelled her by the elbow into the room before him and pulled out the chair for her.

"I had my meal earlier," she said, her chin set stubbornly.

"Soledad tells me you planned dinner and then waited. This table is obviously set for two."

"She did not touch what I brought her earlier," Soledad informed him, calmly serving the soup. "She has eaten like a sparrow since you left last Sunday."

"If you do not eat the soup and the *chiles en*

nogales, I will have to feed you as you have to feed Rafaela,'' he warned, laughing at her silently with his eyes.

Helen hastily picked up her soup spoon.

"Do not scold Doña Helena overmuch," Soledad said in her defense, coming back with a delicious casserole of chilies and walnuts mixed with hot diced pork and pomegranate seeds. "What kind of wife would she be if she did not worry and fear for her husband?"

"True. What kind of wife would she be?" Luis asked, looking steadily at Helen, somber eyes glowing in the candlelight.

"Soledad exaggerates shamelessly. She'll say anything to make you feel your machismo," she said calmly.

"She misinterpreted? You were actually disappointed to see me arrive alive?"

Helen shrugged, refusing to look at him.

"Perhaps you felt a thrill of agitation in knowing that should my plane go down you would be quite free of me and your responsibility to your brother—at last."

"I wouldn't wish *anyone* dead," she protested, indignantly throwing down the soup spoon.

"Not even if that death were to leave you a wealthy widow?"

"What in the world do you mean by a . . . a crack like that?"

"As my widow you would be very wealthy.

You would then be free to leave this island, to lead the life of your most fanciful dreams.''

"Shame on you for such an irresponsible statement! There are a great many people who depend on you, and you have been so unconcerned about them that you risked your life. As a responsible employee in management, I believe a good employer should think of his employees' welfare!''

"If I had not returned, you would have been notified to take directorship of San Roque Enterprises. Would that not have suited you— you who are so anxious to run everything?''

Helen stared at him in horror. She took a deep breath and felt her eyes sting at his suggestion that she should think of benefiting from such a tragedy. "You're right," she said, her voice taut with anger, "the idea more than crossed my mind. Are you satisfied?'' She added coldly, "But as long as you are here and haven't gone down with an expensive plane, I'm tired and would like to go to my room. You won't detain me, I'm sure, because as you yourself said recently, 'A good employer knows when to make his employee rest, just as a good farmer knows when to rest his mule.' ''

"You are excused," Luis replied, still with the infuriating little smile on his lips. But as she started to rise he added, "When you finish your soup and the helping of casserole.''

She sat and choked down her food in silence. When her plate was at last empty, he regarded her gravely. "You may retire if you wish. I intend to stay down here for a time. Do not worry; I will not intrude on you unless, of course, you request it."

"Thank you," she said with dignity, and escaped up the stairs with one of the hurricane lamps. She was more terrified of him tonight than she had ever been. How close she had come to giving herself and her feelings away! If it hadn't been for the frightful wind and rain that had crashed into the house with him, forcing them all back into the hall, she would have thrown herself right into his arms, crying with hysterical relief at seeing him alive and safe. It was crazy to feel such passion for a man she had every reason to wish at the bottom of the ocean or his own deepest mine!

It was crazy to love a man who could feel nothing for her except—perhaps—a normal male's attraction to a woman. Even if she were insane enough to wish more from him, there was still the matter of her brother. Until Ron's debt was repaid she simply wasn't free, and that made it necessary to maintain objectivity and keep San Roque at a distance. What a fool she had been never to have suspected how agonizing a one-sided love could be!

In spite of its solidity the house creaked and

groaned with the storm. A tree branch struck one of the side walls with a detached distant thud.

Coming in with another lamp, Soledad noted Helen's apprehension.

"The house is as safe as the vault in the bank Don Luis owns," she assured her, hanging the new lamp from above the bedside table. "This house has been here more than seventy years. And this is only a baby of a storm—nothing like the ones we have seen in earlier days."

"Somehow it sounds worse up here," Helen responded.

"Only because the great wind comes from this side. You can sleep in the other wing if it disturbs you."

"There is no reason, if you are sure this section is safe." Helen managed to sound calmer than she felt.

"Remember to fill your bathtub with water in case our wells are clogged with debris for a time," Soledad reminded her.

"I will. Has the storm frightened Rafaela?"

"No. Zonia is sleeping in the child's room tonight, since it was not safe to go home. As the room is more below ground level than this part of the house, she is as safe as a little rabbit in its warren."

"Go down and stay nearby in case she calls, would you, Soledad?" Helen requested. "Zonia is not likely to wake once she sleeps. We all need rest, for I suspect in the morning we'll have a monumental clean-up task!''

While Soledad took the time to turn down the bed and lay out Helen's nightdress and robe, Helen brushed her hair. She tried not to notice how the housekeeper selected the most seductive of nightwear and opened the connecting doors widely.

''That will be all, thank you,'' Helen said firmly. ''Good night.''

Soledad had taken to using any means at her disposal to make sure her charge was enticing when Luis was present. She even resorted to surreptitiously spraying cologne into the air.

When Soledad left, Helen shut the doors, then put the nightgown on. She didn't want the housekeeper to suspect her employer's marriage was not the blissful union she imagined it to be. Better to play along with Soledad's game, she decided.

She wrapped herself in her old blanket robe, which was warmer than the diaphanous one Soledad had chosen, and padded barefoot into the storage room, ignoring the beautiful but impractical marabou mules at the foot of the bed. From the storage room she took out the half-finished painting of Rafaela. There were background details to stipple in that would take her mind off the storm and the man downstairs.

The light of the hanging lamp sufficed for her purposes, though it was not the best illumination to work by. She reminded herself that before electricity came to this island a few years earlier everyone had made do and huge numbers of people in the world still did. But it was late and she was tired, and soon she decided to pack up her things. She returned the painting and equipment to the storage room, then came back through the bedroom.

Before she reached the bed there was a deafening thud, and something crashed through the heavy shutters causing the window to explode inward. Glass shards rained down on her; the room filled with the shattering storm window and her own terrified screams.

"¡Luis! ¡Ayudeme! ¡Luis!"

The door to the adjoining room burst open almost as she cried out and Luis was at her side in an instant. He swept her up as she stood terrified amid the shower of shattered glass and debris. He carried her swiftly from the chaos into his own room and laid her on his bed.

"Lie still!" he commanded, bringing the lamp closer to better examine the injuries she had sustained. Blood trickled into her eyes, blinding her with its sticky gushing warmth.

"Luis... I can't see!"

"Hush! Hold still, *querida mía*—there may be glass in the wound. No, thank all the saints!"

he concluded after a quick inspection. "It is only a very small cut on the scalp, clean and small. Surely there will be no scar." He brought a basin and dampened towel and sponged her face gently. "It has almost ceased bleeding, *querida*. There is nothing to alarm you now."

She struggled, but he held her gently, soothing her, as he pressed a cloth to her hairline over the cut.

"What happened?" she cried.

"The storm drove a large tree branch through the shutters like a spear. The shutters and window shattered. What were you doing out of your bed, *querida*? You could have been killed!"

"I was painting," she explained lamely.

"Painting! I forbid you ever—" he began, than unexpectedly he laughed softly. "No, of course I do not forbid you to paint. But I forbid you to be close to a window in a storm!"

As he spoke, another branch thudded against the wall, and Helen shrank, shivering, against him. He held her and stroked her hair tenderly. *"No tenga miedo, querida. No tenga miedo!"* Softly he kissed her eyes, her face, all the time whispering soothingly to her.

Helen found herself sinking into a delicious state in which she had no will of her own except the desire to be close to him. She felt his hard muscular body pressed against hers and was breathlessly aware of the musky aroma of the shaving lotion he had used after his bath on his return home. Strangely, the touch of his lips burned her at the same time that the contact shot icy chills throughout her body. When his mouth claimed hers insistently, she was more than ready to answer his passion.

Her mind emptied itself of all past determination to resist. She opened her soul to the exquisite excitement of every nerve in her body as his passion guided her own. Her fingers fluttered to the nape of his neck, then her arms crept up around him. She was astounded by the wonders of surrender. He removed her robe, then slid the gown from her shoulders. It slithered down around her ankles, releasing her. His lips traveled down the curve of her breast to tease first one nipple and then the other into full glorious arousal.

As they lay on his bed, she sensed lightning flashing white through the room, striking her body with first cold, then hot fire. Only dimly did she realize the lightning was within her, as well, emanating from every pore. Sensitive to Luis's lightest touch, she felt possessed of a new vitality. She had never before experienced or imagined anything like it.

She could feel the heavy embossed silk of the dressing gown he wore imprinting its design on her body. Soft and rich though it was, it hindered their intimacy, so she pushed it aside in order to feel nothing but his body close against hers. His robe joined her gown and robe on the floor.

Her breath seemed to leave her body in the dizzy sensation of complete delicious contact. She was quite calm, as though in the eye of the storm. She allowed herself the supreme luxury of exploring the surface of his neck, shoulders and back with her fingertips, mourning that she had not been daring enough to do so weeks—months—before. She could almost cry for the wasted moments that had gone before this.

He took her hand gently, kissed the palm, then guided it down his body until she had no doubt that he was experiencing at least as magnificent a passion as she was. She gasped as he carefully raised himself on one knee and separated her thighs. Although she was a virgin more inexperienced than most, she was not naive; but never in her wildest yearnings had she imagined lovemaking to be as wonderful as this moment.

She moaned, calling out his name mindlessly as he entered her. She convulsed and arched toward him, and the sudden shock was as though the entire universe had exploded within her. She wanted to give him every joy, but in that timeless moment she could only feel the heaven he had given her.

For a moment, after she woke, she did not know where she was. The room was silent, but the sounds of morning filtered into her consciousness. Already the shutters had been removed. Light streamed into the room, gray, cool, wet light, as rain without wind came down softly over the island.

He was no longer beside her, but the clean masculine tang of him lingered as clearly with her as the memory of his physical presence. How they had slept the night comfortably in such a narrow bed as his she could not imagine, but the memory of that glorious entwining of their bodies made her catch her breath. She remembered the glow of ecstasy and felt betrayed...not by him, but by her treacherous weak self.

She drew the bedclothes up to preserve any modesty she might have retained, though she knew with a rush of color that all had dissolved in last night's passion. Her gown lay in a heap on the floor, and in the other room she heard Soledad utter concerned little cries at the sight of debris only just now discovered.

When Soledad entered the open doorway between the rooms, she halted. Agitation forgotten, *"Bueno!"* she said with utter satisfaction. "It is an ill wind that does not bring blessings!"

With almost motherly pride the housekeeper greeted Luis, who came from his shower unselfconsciously wrapped in a towel. The white of the towel around his waist contrasted with the mahogany of his smooth skin and the fine dark wet hair that etched his muscular legs and formed a pattern from his chest to his navel.

As calmly as she could, Helen said, "Please, Soledad, bring me my velvet robe and slippers." She added casually, "We'll be surveying the storm damage this morning, so we'll eat downstairs in the dining room."

Soledad laid the robe across the bed, put the slippers down at the side and went out smiling.

Luis crossed the room swiftly to Helen, but she moved faster and eluded him. In almost one gesture she donned the robe and had the room's only chair between them.

The happy anticipatory expression that had softened Luis's harshly hewn features vanished, to be replaced by one of bewilderment.

"No!" Helen said.

"No?" He threw the chair aside and grasped her roughly around the waist. His grip on the hair at the nape of her neck was not painful, but it forced her head back so far that she could neither close her eyes nor struggle.

"I thought we had put away all games, Helen. What is this, that we begin again?" he demanded.

"You're hurting me," she protested faintly.

"I do not want to hurt you. But answer me

quickly. What has happened to change you from the woman you were last night?''

''The light of day. I'm the same person I was yesterday in the light of day. Last night wasn't meant to happen, Luis. It won't happen again!''

''Of course it was meant to happen...from the first moment we laid eyes on each other!''

''Don't you understand, Luis? I cannot be a wife to you until that debt my brother laid on me is paid. I'm not free. I won't cheat you by using sex to get out of my responsibilities.''

''Damn the debt! It is canceled!''

''No. Not for me. Not until I've paid it back in honest cash. I could never feel anything but a bought-and-sold kind of...harem slave. I couldn't stand it!''

''You know what I want. What we shared last night is what I want from you. *All* I want! By what possible reason could a mere financial debt make you deny what we have shared?''

''Not like this, Luis. Not like this!''

He released her slowly. ''*¡Jesus Maria!* Can this be?'' His face registered his total disbelief; his features had never looked so harsh.

Helen's golden eyes asked for understanding, but she saw she had angered him deeply. He muttered a dire Spanish oath and followed it with a rapid string of maledictions. Then he stalked over to the connecting doors, threw them open and looked inside the main room.

"Everything has been cleaned up in here for you." He gave her the smallest of formal bows and spoke coldly in English. "You are welcome to return to your self-imposed prison."

She was afraid to pass by him as one would fear to pass too close to an unchained lion, yet pass him she must. As she had feared, he halted her with one hand on her shrinking shoulder.

"Helen—if you persist in this mad fixation, I cannot stand by and suffer, too." He returned to the soft Spanish language. "Do not drive me away. I cannot continue to come here, see you and not claim you as my wife at every opportunity!"

"Please try to understand...." Her voice was a mere whisper.

"I am only a man."

"Luis—don't make this more difficult for me than it has to be."

"The responsibility lies with your brother, not you," he went on. "Do not take his guilt on yourself any longer."

She continued to look at him in silence, pleading for understanding.

He sighed, and still in the language that was his own, he said quietly, "Except for the most pressing of business reasons, Helen, I shall have to remain away until you come to your senses. Are you prepared for that?"

"No. Of course I'm not 'prepared.' But we do what we must do."

Again he sighed. "I can forgive you for that. But you said once that you would never forgive me for taking you against your will. If I stay, we must inevitably be one. You risk sending me away in such anger that I may never forgive *you*."

"You need not leave the island; it is *your* home."

"If you will not live with me as my wife, I will not stay to be tortured. And—Helen, I have told you plainly that I will have a woman for my own. You risk much in sending me away."

"If you intend to find another woman quickly, then I won't stop you!" she threw at him, resenting his implication that she was a mere convenience; that any willing woman would do. She knew his threat was a promise: he would go straight to Mexico City and Yolanda.

"Do what you must do, Luis," she said in a low voice. Her lips were white around the edges from the pressure she had to exert to keep them from trembling. "I do what I have to do. As all the islanders say—it's in the hands of God, isn't it?"

As she passed through the doors he sighed, then closed them behind her.

She was once more alone in the big bedroom and knew that when she went downstairs he would no longer be in the house. She would remember Luis's face forever the way she had last seen it—grim and unforgiving.

As soon as the road was freed of the trees that blocked access to the house, and he had investigated for himself the extent of the damage from the storm, he flew to the mainland.

CHAPTER SIXTEEN

A GLAZIER CAME UP FROM THE CITY to replace the window in the big bedroom. The houseman and two of his cousins worked tirelessly to clean away mud and debris from the grounds. Fortunately, the wells were not clogged and there was no trouble with the water or electrical system beyond minor problems.

The islanders congratulated themselves that the hurricane had spent most of its fury before hitting Cedros. Quickly the word spread that there was little damage except for one section in Barrio X. Part of the bluff structure had collapsed, along with the crazy makeshift stairs.

"A miracle that only two people were killed," Zonia reported, her black eyes wide. "Rafaela's mother and the man who was with her! He was only a sailor from one of the freighters, not one of us. And who will miss her? Rafaela has already forgotten her."

Helen could not bring herself to be as callous about the passing of Conchita as Zonia, even though the woman had not once come to the house to inquire after her child since the day she had been brought to the house.

"The poor woman couldn't cope with Rafaela's problems or her own," Helen defended her. "Were there any other relatives?"

"None." Zonia shrugged it off. She went on brightly, "Now you do not have to worry: Rafaela is yours."

What would Luis say about that, Helen wondered. No doubt he was too angry with her to be interested.

Helen inquired about Zonia's family, who lived only a short distance from the barrio.

"They are all fine. They were not even in their own homes to be frightened during the storm. Estelita took them all to Chuey's house when the storm began, and they were as comfortable as birds in a sheltered nest."

"Perhaps now the corporation can do something about the barrio and back some of the costs of providing new homes in a safer area for those who lost theirs. The island has many more suitable places for housing."

"But they will not leave!" Zonia objected. "They have their pride; the barrio is their home. It has been there more years than I have lived, more years than my mother or grandmother! The residents are used to storms. They will rebuild that old portion of the barrio." Seeing Helen's frustration, Zonia added soothingly,

"Perhaps the corporation will build some new stairs. I think el señor has arranged it already."

Zonia's prediction was fairly accurate. Except for the annoyance the residents felt at the lack of stairs, life seemed to go on cheerfully in Barrio X and they were already beginning to make repairs. There was a large supply of cinder blocks and wood planks stacked for use, which Helen felt sure came from San Roque Enterprises. By the end of the week everything was back to normal in the barrio.

Helen saw to it that Conchita had a decent burial and attended the funeral mass. She lit a candle in the church, in gratitude that Rafaela had not been with her mother and the sailor when the storm came.

Luis did not come back to the island at the end of the week. There was no word from him for her; there weren't even any business memorandums bearing his slashing signature. The only difference was that among her usual censored mail and the company papers were Mexico City newspapers, which in themselves were a message. Pictures of Luis and Yolanda were prominently displayed in the large society section, and each of the pictures seemed meant to strike Helen to the heart.

The captions were explicit: "Señor Luis San Roque, director of San Roque Enterprises, and Señorita Yolanda Betancourt Ibanez, with her father, Paolo Betancourt, the corporation's legal counsel, at last night's performance of...."

Helen died a little inside as she crumpled the papers, stuffed them into the office fireplace and watched them burn.

"Are you ill, Doña Helena?" asked Agustin Benevidez, coming in with a contract to be signed. "You look so pale and thin!"

"I am only...preoccupied," Helen explained. Agustin looked inquiringly at the papers burning but did not question her further.

Juanito still remained in Tijuana. The specialists at the hospital were giving special therapy lessons to the boy's grandmother so that she could assist in strengthening his mended foot.

Soledad went about her business looking more and more long faced and reproachful. There was no more excitement in the great house. The island had returned to the empty routine of the days and years before her beloved Don Luis had taken to coming home every week. Christmas apparently would be enlivened only with a celebration for Rafaela and possibly for Juanito if he was sent home for the holiday.

Helen tried not to think about Luis; but even during the day, when she was pressured on all sides with responsibilities, that wasn't easy. His name was on every letterhead, his initials on every memo. His picture, handsomely framed next to his father's, confronted her the moment she walked into the main building each morning. She was reminded whichever way she turned that her loneliness was of her own making.

She briefly wondered what Luis thought of her new chess partner's letters. The susceptible Don Castle seemed to have developed an unfortunate emotional attachment solely through the chess games, and without the slightest encouragement from her. In a way, she was grateful that Luis sent her the Mexico City newspapers with those dreadful social photos that explicitly revealed his activities—his pursuit of Yolanda. Don Castle's naive crush might serve a purpose, if no other than to preserve her pride. Luis should know she was not without her own admirers.

Nevertheless, she could not allow the chess player to continue in his fantasy. She was careful to reassure him that she enjoyed playing chess with him but made frequent mention of her husband's considerable skill at the game. "Would you like to play with him by mail? I think you would find him a far more challenging partner."

Perversely, she knew that the letter could potentially serve her in more than one way. While it would cool down Don Castle by reminding him that she was married and loyal to her husband, it would also probably encourage him to respond that he would prefer to keep her as a chess partner. Such a boost to her ego would not displease her—but it might certainly trouble Luis.

Oh, it's all so impossible, she thought, tearing up the letter and trying to write another, even more circumspect and discouraging one to Castle. But at the same time she did not want to reveal herself more than was necessary to her husband, the censor. She wished Luis had not so smugly told her about Castle's personal characteristics. How he must be amused by her discomfiture!

CHAMARTIN AGAIN ASKED that she reconsider the sale of *The Master of the Dolphins*. "I have two offers at present," he wrote, "both for prices you can hardly afford to refuse."

She sent an immediate note back to him saying that she would not sell the painting but would begin another of the same subject, in tempera. Tempera, she felt, had such clarity and glow that the reproduction of the original scene could be even more beautiful than the first watercolor.

She prepared the gessoed board carefully and separated eggs so as to use the yolks in binding pigment. Her tempera paintings sold better than her gouaches and watercolors. This painting could not fail to be a success. Was she greedy to think of money accruing from the painting's sale? Not really, she assured herself. She had to finish paying Ron's debt.

At first the picture progressed smoothly enough. The scene was accurately remembered: the beach with its intriguing sweep to the point, the curve of the water and the gleam of its dancing current against the sky. Then came the arching forms of the silhouetted dolphins; as in the first painting, every line was perfect motion. But oddly, without the man swimmer the painting seemed empty.

Technically the composition was correct, accurately remembered; but somehow the whole thing was wrong, wrong, wrong!

She worked on it a little each night, always giving up in frustration. She finally scraped the tempera off the board and began again.

Her second attempt was no better than the first. It was the same unfinished, empty composition. Some essential ingredient was lacking. Perhaps, she thought, it was the difference in medium that made it seem so joyless.

Her only option now was to sell as many paintings of other subjects as she could. If she could pay off the debt within a couple of years, there might be time yet for . . . love.

ON THE QUAY, Agustin Benevidez was not just her star pupil but also a gem of an employee, needing only the polish of training to sparkle and outshine any other. He was the type of person who absorbed new ideas and education like a sponge and could see beyond the tradition that bound so many on the island. He needed only opportunity to help him break out of the routine mold, and with Helen's help it was clear he would do so.

She gradually added more responsibility to his duties. He found a building in which to house the growing classes and taught a basic class himself. He enthusiastically endorsed the acquisition of modern equipment for the company offices. The new building would contain all the old typewriters and machines plus some new items needed for student practice.

Benevidez set up the lease for the new building and made arrangements for its remodeling. After approval arrived from Mexico City, he began advertising to attract teachers of Japanese and German, the two other languages that would be useful in the business. Each selected instructor was to have additional skills, so that he or she could serve in a number of areas.

Agustin assisted Ochoa and Helen so ably with many phases of the growing programs that they relied heavily on him.

"What do you think of Estelita Sanchez?" she asked him one day.

"The sister of Zonia Sanchez, the maid at the great house?"

She nodded.

"Miss Sanchez types well," he said, practicing carefully in English. "She types better than any of the women we now employ and has learned the shorthand—"

"Learned shorthand," Helen corrected him.

"Learned shorthand," he repeated carefully. "Her English is. . . almost as good as mine. But she is still only a *maquilladora*."

"She does not wish to remain a *maquilladora* and she has studied diligently without hope of recompense from us. She deserves a chance. I want to hire and train her as my secretary."

"But, Doña Helena—have I not served you well, as I have served Don Luis?" he asked worriedly.

"You have served so well that I have requested, and had approved, your promotion to assistant island operations manager. There will be need for two secretaries—one for me and one for your present job. You will train that new secretary so well that Don Luis will not regret your leaving the post as his secretary at all."

In her mind she prepared for the day the debt would be paid and she would depart. It was important that she plan the delegation of her responsibilities for when that time came. Luis would have to think well of her as a former employee, even if he did not think that way of her as a woman. The thought stabbed her to the heart.

"Doña Helena!" Benevidez was momentarily overcome with pleasure, but he was also practical. The business of appointing his own secretary, who would serve el señor's office when he was present, took precedence over celebration.

"José Bello is the student who has made the most progress—other than myself. He is under our employment."

"Yes, I thought of him, too. You will take much responsibility for the training program from now on, Agustin. Do what you can to encourage other businessmen and contract traders to subsidize the program. San Roque Enterprises should not bear the entire burden of cost, since the program benefits the entire island and the traders, as well."

"Perhaps we should charge students not working for the company. That will ensure they finish each class they begin. Some of our first group dropped out, which is most wasteful."

"That seems a reasonable idea and can be worked out so as not to exclude any serious students," Helen agreed. "By the way, Agustin, one of the teachers I just hired is a Mr. Teiko Akigawa. He saw the ad you placed in the Yokosuka paper. He will teach Japanese, and also computer programming and word processing. That should please Señor San Roque, for he stressed the need to know Japanese."

"May I also take advantage of the computer class?" he asked eagerly.

"Of course!" she laughed.

Agustin withdrew, leaving Helen to cope with her daily piles of mail from the main office and company connections off the island.

Luis had not withheld her mail, regardless of his anger toward her. Was he taking the time to read her personal letters? Or did he simply rip them open to let her know she was still subject to their contract?

She thought about sending early Christmas cards to everyone she had ever known. He would have to open the envelopes and look at each card. Then later he would have to inspect each reciprocal card, as well. The tedium of it might cure him.

Why do I dream up petty ways to antagonize him when I really only want him to pay attention to me, Helen scolded herself. *But I confess I want his attentions on my own terms. So I am a fool!*

Luis had probably given her mail over to Felipe Estrada to take care of by now, just as he had Felipe take care of the finances. He seemed to have erased her from his mind. She desperately wanted to hate him but succeeded only in finding fault with her own stubborn self.

Monday's mail brought the usual neatly typed envelope from Don Castle, with another chess move. She would have to resign the game to him. No matter what Luis had told her about Castle's limited job and his drab existence, he was a master chess player.

She unfolded the piece of hotel stationery from the St. Francis Hotel. On it Castle had typed:

You seem to have fallen off your game. Do you want to continue? I love you.

D.C.

Dear Mr. Castle:

Things are difficult for me at present, as I have many responsibilities and concerns. I know I am playing badly, but you are an excellent teacher. I would like to work on a game using Alekhine's defense, if you will be patient. I cannot send you the picture you requested. My husband does not approve.

Sincerely, Helen San Roque
(Señora Luis San Roque)

There was still another plea from Chamartin on the dolphin painting. The offers he was receiving and relaying were by now so large Helen found it difficult not to tell him to go ahead and sell it so she could send the money to Luis.

Regretfully she typed yet another refusal:

I will send a tempera version of *The Master of the Dolphins* as soon as I find time to finish it. Perhaps you can sell the tempera for an even better price than the watercolor you have.

Regards, Helen

She pushed the call button for Estelita to take her letters out so they could go with the plane.

Estelita waited as Helen signed the rest of the letters and memos dictated and typed that morning, and both looked up when Agustin knocked and entered. "Our company plane is coming in. Señor Estrada says over the wireless that you should meet him at the airport."

"Is Señor San Roque with him?" Helen's heart leaped into her throat.

"No. Don Luis is in Argentina with the new contracts, Doña Helena. I do not think he has planned to come to the island, but there must be some strong reason for the arrival of Don Felipe."

"Tell Vergel to take me to the airport immediately."

They joined the line of red cabs whose drivers were also aware of the plane's arrival. Estrada came off the plane directly, without any briefcase in hand. His dark earnest features displayed concern as he took both her hands in greeting.

"Your father's housekeeper contacted us, Doña Helena. She reports that your stepmother died in hospital yesterday morning."

"Yesterday morning! Oh, poor Mama Jessie!" Helen was deeply saddened, immediately aware that she could not go home to comfort her father. For all his faults, he had deeply loved Jessie, who came late into his life. Jessie had also garnered Helen's love and respect.

"She's out of her misery and at rest at long last," Helen said to Felipe, trying to take some comfort in that knowledge. "We've expected this day for years—ever since the accident. It's a blessing, really."

"We are sorry not to have reached you sooner, Doña Helena. Your father did not understand the message from the hospital that his wife had had a 'cerebral accident.' He thought it meant the hospital had not taken proper cautions and that she had fallen or was otherwise injured. He became so upset and incensed that he suffered a heart attack. Mrs. Parish, his housekeeper, was so concerned about him that she delayed relay of the message about your stepmother."

"Oh, no—not my father, too!" Helen felt faint.

"Don Luis instructed me from Argentina to take you home to Garnet Beach. We can be there quickly."

"You're sure it is all right for me to go—leave the island?"

"He sent me, Doña Helena," Felipe repeated. "And I am to assist you however possible."

"Then I must send Vergel to the office—no, I will go to the office myself." Helen, stunned by the terrible news, found it hard to make even the smallest decision. She could think of nothing but going home to her father.

"Vergel will take you to the great house and Soledad will pack for you, Doña Helena. I will stay at the office and take charge there as necessary. You can stop by the office on your way back from the house. We will have sufficient time, for the plane must be refueled."

"Yes. You're right, I suppose. That's best. I won't need to take very much," she added distractedly. "I still have a few things in my room at home in Garnet Beach."

Felipe helped her into the car and directed Vergel. "Don Luis would have come himself, but then there would have been further delay, since he is still in Argentina. You understand we had to reach him in Buenos Aires."

"It's all right. I understand." She was grateful that Luis had been kind enough to let her go home in this emergency. Would he really have wanted to join her? She wished he were here under any circumstances. She needed his personal strength, the strength only he could give her at this time.

With Soledad's help, Helen packed a small bag and bade Rafaela goodbye. "Soledad—you will remember to exercise her every morning and afternoon, won't you? You know the way we have done all the exercises? Please don't neglect her. Talk to her as much as you can; one day she will surprise you and answer!"

"Do I not talk to her?" Soledad demanded.

"I mean special conversations that encourage her to answer. We must not give up."

"You think I do not know how to take care of the *niña*?" Soledad grumbled. "I, who have taken care of Don Luis and countless other children in sickness and health? You know I will see to the child!"

CHAPTER SEVENTEEN

WEATHER EXPEDITED THEIR TRIP north. Felipe rented a car at the airport outside Garnet Beach, and they drove straight to the hospital in La Jolla where Helen's father was a patient.

Helen saw little of her hometown because of the location of the hospital, but even driving through the fringe of Garnet Beach on the way to La Jolla, she was struck by the changes that had taken place in the short six months she had been gone.

A whole new shopping center had mushroomed west of the airport. The hills were dotted with new construction of homes with a view of the sea. There was even a new wing on the hospital in La Jolla that dwarfed the rest of the complex. Three new skeleton stories rose powerfully to the sky, signaling the future.

The doctor, wearing a worn green coat, noticed Helen in the lounge of the unit as soon as she arrived.

"Your father has had a massive coronary," he said bluntly. "He's comfortable now, but—"

"Can I see him?"

"Yes. But I want no one other than immediate family, and it's important not to excite him. If he wants to talk, let him but ask no questions and don't encourage him to continue. Just keep him calm. Reassure him." The doctor rubbed his jaw wearily. "We're doing all we can, Mrs. San Roque," he explained. "There is always hope. If he doesn't have another attack within a week...." His words dwindled away, and Helen understood that there was little chance at all.

Her father's eyes were sunken far into his head, and one of his hands picked feebly at the hospital coverlet. She took his cold hand in her warm strong one and held it tightly, willing her strength into him. "Hey! I'm here, daddy," she said when he opened his eyes. "Mrs. Parish said you wanted to see me, so I came right away."

His lips moved. He searched the room with glazed eyes, and his expression was disappointed when he finished. She leaned to him and he whispered, "Ron...?"

"He'll be here," she assured him. "He'll come."

"You tell him I want to see him, Helen."

"I'll find him if I can, dad. But I don't know where to look."

Her father gestured feebly, defending his son. "Don't tire yourself," she cautioned.

"You have to tell him, Helen! Tell him I... have to see him and...it's wrong, what he did to you. He's got to fix it with you. Find him, Helen. Tell him to come, tonight."

"I would if I could, daddy—"

"He doesn't want—there's something keeping him away because he's afraid. But you can make him come home, Helen. You're smart. You have him come...so I can talk to him."

With the greatest effort her father dredged out of his memory the barest sketch of an address—the name of a friend through whom she might contact Ron in San Francisco. "Don't fight with him, Helen," he said pitifully. "He's had such a hard time—"

"I know, daddy."

Her father had always made excuses for Ron. A motherless boy was sad to see, but the motherless Rons always seemed to be excused somehow. It was time to put a stop to it; time that her brother stood up for himself.

"You sleep, daddy, and I'll try to find Ron and bring him here to see you."

Her father shut his eyes. A smile wandered over his drawn old face. She knew he believed she would take care of everything.

Outside, Helen confronted Felipe, more troubled than before. "My father looks bad, Felipe. I don't think he will be with us long, but he longs to see my brother."

"Then we must see that your brother is brought here immediately."

"Felipe—" she began, relying on his discretion and hoping beyond hope that he would not see himself as her husband's agent in exacting payment of the debt. "My brother may still be afraid that Luis will want to apprehend him and...take revenge."

"But why would Don Luis do that?" Felipe asked, bewildered. "Your brother has been paying back what he took from the fund. Why should Luis seek simple revenge? He is a businessman, not a bandit!"

"You say he—my brother—has been paying back the debt?"

"But surely you knew? Luis said himself that arrangements were made through an intermediary. I thought you were that person—"

"Oh!" So Luis had let Felipe think Ron was paying the debt himself. It appeared to be safe for her brother to come here, then, to see their father on his deathbed. She must trust Felipe, anyway.

She gave him the details she had got from her father. "Please, Felipe, we must get Ron here quickly or it will be too late." Thinking of Luis, she felt a rush of gratitude that brought tears to her eyes. He had, in spite of everything, spared her reputation among his colleagues. If only he were here so she could thank him for his kindness, his generosity, when he was the wronged one and had so much to be vengeful about.

WHEN SHE SAW RON she could hardly contain herself. He did care. Thoughtless and unethical he might be, but he did love his father, who cared so deeply for him.

Ron stared coldly at Felipe, who melted into the background with a murmured courtesy but remained in the hall in case Helen needed him.

"Well, you knew I'd come if it was life or death," Ron said a little uncomfortably. "I hope you weren't overreacting."

"I wasn't," she said, tears in her eyes. "Dad's dying."

When they went in to see the old man, she knew Ron had to realize what his coming meant to his father. The look on their father's face was one of pure joy. He took both their hands. "It's been lonely without you kids and Jessie," the old man whispered. "I'm sorry about everything. I haven't been fair to either of you, but I tried...."

He could speak no more, but he did not let go of either of their hands, and as the day faded the old man's life ebbed and he quietly followed his Jessie. For the first and only time Helen could remember, Ron bent his head and wept. Helen took him in her arms and hugged him tightly.

They went back to the small ranch house the

family had called home, and Mrs. Parish tried to make them comfortable.

Helen looked around, noticing details she had not been able to see in her first anxious days back in Garnet Beach. The house had recently been painted inside and out. There was new wall-to-wall carpeting instead of the threadbare throw rugs she had longed to replace for years. The fence that had inadequately kept little boys out of the fruit orchard had been torn down completely, and the new fence made the property look inviting and secure.

"You can thank Ronald for the improvements," Mrs. Parish beamed. "He had it all done not too long ago. Your father always did think you were a good lad, Ronald, sending money to make the old house look nice."

Helen stared in surprise at Ron, who looked exceedingly uncomfortable. At last he said, "Listen—I didn't send it. This place—it isn't worth fixing up. Dad must have had some nest egg."

"Your father said if anything ever happened I was to see you were given these papers, Helen." Mrs. Parish brought out the locked box her father had always used as a house safe. Inside were his marriage licenses and will, the insurance policies and her own and Ron's birth certificates and adoption papers.

Helen handed the papers to Felipe to go over.

"Your father's hospital bills were almost entirely covered, but there's a big loan on his life insurance," he reported after a swift glance at them.

"Maybe that's how the house was renovated," Helen suggested.

"Actually," Ron said casually, "he helped me out. Said it was a gift. I have a paper, so you'll know—"

Helen couldn't help wondering aloud, "I can't think how he got the money to fix this place—"

"I was told by Don Luis to see that matters were made comfortable," Felipe quietly interjected.

Luis's generosity again! Helen was ashamed of how he had done their job for them without a word to make her feel more in his debt.

"The insurance is worth very little," Felipe continued. "This other set of papers takes care of the funeral and cemetery arrangements. And this is your father's will."

The will was simple. It made provision, of course, for Mama Jessie, but it stated that if she predeceased him everything he had left in the world, after the bills were paid, was to go directly to his daughter, Helen, with the exception of his gold watch and army medals, which were bequeathed to Ron.

Helen yearned for San Roque to lean on at

this moment of confused responsibilities. "I don't understand the will at all," she said to the two men. "Dad always said he intended to divide his property equally, but that isn't the case. How could he not have left half of the real property to Ron? This will was written only a year ago!" She put a hand on her brother's arm. "He was getting old. This property here must be quite valuable on today's market. Why—each acre should be worth as much as thirty-five thousand dollars. There must be something we can do to make things right."

Ron interrupted, "The will's okay, Owl. And the lots are worth about fifty thousand dollars each, except for those on the other side of the hill with the ocean view. They'll be sixty thousand."

"Whatever the value, Ron, I'll share. Dad would want it that way."

"Maybe," he said. "But you look as though you're not doing too badly without anything in the way of an estate from the old man. That dress you're wearing—real pretty. You can't be as hard up for cash as you made out to dad all this time."

"You know where my money's been going, Ron." She bit her lip, not wanting to discuss Ron's debt in front of Felipe.

"Not all of it's going there, for sure," Ron said without reticence, looking her over with brotherly criticism.

"You know, you might make a pretty good model, Owl," he added.

"That has nothing to do with anything, Ron," Helen said reproachfully. Wasn't that just like Ron to hedge, she noted sadly. "By the way," she continued, "my name is Helen." She was no longer willing to accept his insulting nicknames for her, especially now that San Roque had convinced her of her beauty.

Ron regarded her circumspectly. She could almost imagine him thinking, *is this the sister I once knew?* She was, but she *had* changed—and so, it seemed, had he. In some ways he had acquired a measure of maturity.

"Okay...Helen," he said firmly, "I get the point. Now about the property...."

She could hardly believe her ears, but without taking another breath she launched into the discussion once again. "We always were equal in dad's sight and shared when we were kids. He was getting old, and I think the will must be a mistake. Can't we just preserve the house and the property around it, and perhaps find a buyer for the rest? We could split things evenly, and withdraw from your share of the inheritance enough to pay back the debt to Luis. Then we can put that episode behind us for good."

"I have a better idea. You can get Felipe here to find one of those house-moving firms to move the house off the property. Then you can have the house and I'll take the land.''

"You need a roof over your head, Ron. You know how you—"

"Don't you understand, Helen?" he blurted finally. "Dad didn't leave you the house and the land. He couldn't. It wasn't his to leave you."

She gave him such a blank look that his impatience surfaced.

"Remember six years back, when you were still in school? After the accident?"

"Yes...?"

"Dad said you'd have to drop out of school, and then you didn't have to?"

"Yes...?" Certainly she remembered that difficult time. "He and Mama Jessie said things would be all right after all, and I could go on and graduate. Then I did, and dad insisted I go on to graduate school—"

"That's right. Well...the money came from me."

"You?" She was totally confused. "But—"

"I had a good deal going at the time, and it turned out pretty well. So I gave him the cash. Well, I didn't exactly *give* it. It was an investment. Dad signed over the property to me. He made me give him life estate, but the property— all of it—is mine."

"I just don't understand—"

"The property hasn't been dad's to leave to

you or anyone for six years. It's mine. I let him live here, so I've been supporting him, if you want to look at it that way. But now—you can take the house off if it would make you happy, though I'm not sure it would be worth the trouble. The developers won't want it.''

''Felipe?'' Helen appealed to him faintly.

Ron took some papers from his breast pocket and handed them casually over to Felipe, who after scanning them said with regret in his voice, ''I am sorry, Helen. What your brother says is true; the property seems to be his.''

She was reeling with shock upon shock, though why anything Ron did should surprise her was a good question. She really did not need to ask for a repetition of what he had said, or proof. Ron was telling her simple facts. He'd had cash at a bad time in her father's life and had taken advantage of him to get control of the entire piece of prime coastal property, which even then had been in line for a tremendous development boom. Her father had allowed him to do it because he wanted her to finish her education.

''Dad never was very good at business,'' Ron remarked, shrugging.

''But the property was worth a great deal more, even then, than the expenses for my schooling,'' Helen protested.

''Sure. But that's how any smart man does

business. Ask your great San Roque: you get it cheap, sell it dear. Dad and I both took a chance on the property's escalating in value. You got your inheritance a little early; I just had to wait. But I'm into a deal now, based on the property's current value, and I need every dollar of the cash. That's the way it is. I've got some higher-ups breathing down my neck on the deal.''

Helen, sick at heart and bewildered, asked weakly, "How could you lend your father three thousand dollars and take property worth three hundred thousand?''

"I only gave him twenty-five hundred," Ron said complacently.

"But—it would have been worth forty thousand even then on a bank loan! How could you cheat someone who loved you, trusted you?''

"I didn't cheat him. He understood what was happening.''

"I think you did something very wrong," she said firmly. "But since I have paid your Mexican debt except for sixty thousand, will you pay the rest from the sale of the property? Then I can write an end to it, too.''

Ron's eyes sparked. "You're smarter than I ever thought you were, Helen! You could give me lessons in wheeling and dealing. You mean you earned that much money in the past few months?''

"The proceeds from the sale of Aunt Edna's

house provided most of it," she said with her usual compulsive honesty.

"So—you got yours from Aunt Edna. You can't complain because I got mine from the old man."

"You're twisting everything until it gives me a headache," she complained, putting her fingers to her temples. "I'm not pressing for what I've paid back already—just for the balance. Please?"

"You've managed fine so far; you manage the rest," he said coolly. "San Roque would be just the s.o.b. I always said he was if he didn't let you forget it. He could make you a present of ten times that much and never miss it!"

"Don't you understand, Ron? My life depends on clearing this up!" Ron's maturity, she recognized sadly, was not fully realized.

"Don't sound so desperate. No one's threatening you with a cement bathing suit for a swim in the bay!"

"I beg you—"

"You're begging up the wrong street. I have my own problems, and when it comes to money you're in a lot better shape than I am! I'm not kidding about cement bathing suits: if I don't get this cleared fast I could be wearing one. So you see, you're not in such bad shape as a lot of other people."

"It's all so futile," Helen said in a low voice. "You'll be in just as serious straits within another six months; you always are. Can't you learn, Ron? If you'd just do some honest work and put half as much effort into it as you put into getting into trouble—"

"Don't preach!" he cut her off. "You always were a preacher even when you were a kid," he added, cheerfully unregenerate.

Mercifully, Felipe Estrada had taken Mrs. Parish into the yard, where he wasn't witness to this painful conversation.

"I'm glad dad isn't around to hear us talk about this," Helen said quietly. "But if he were, he would ask you to pay the last of your debt. We need to be true to each other, Ron."

"Sorry." He actually looked regretful. "But when it comes to money, I haven't any choice. No choice at all. Cement bathing suit—remember?"

"What will you do the next time?" she asked softly. "When I am not around? When dad's not around? When there's no way out?"

"Hey!" he said cheerfully. "This is *it*, Helen. No more chances. You got my word."

He came over and dropped a fleeting kiss on the top of her head, standing a little on tiptoe to do it. "Ciao!" he said. "I gotta split and see how to convert this fast."

Helen watched him go in a daze. She'd had

too many shocks to grieve or be angry. As Ron left, Felipe considerately came in.

"I thought there might be something I could do to assist..." he offered kindly.

She gathered her wits and her spirit. "Not about the property, Felipe. Apparently—well, Ron will be selling it, but I'll need to put an ad in the local paper to find a private buyer for the house. And I'll have to put the furniture in storage...."

The furniture and Mama Jessie's ring, like Aunt Edna's personal belongings, weren't worth a great deal and were in fact a sentimental burden rather than a blessing. Mama Jessie would have hated strangers putting grubby fingers on her cherished cherry-wood table. The Coalport china had never been used except for Thanksgiving, Christmas and family celebrations. "You'll take care of it someday, Helen," Mama Jessie had said more than once. "You'll hand it to your own children, too."

Someday. If she ever had any children to hand the china down to, which appeared unlikely.

CHAPTER EIGHTEEN

CHAMARTIN'S SAN DIEGO GALLERY was the most elegant of all the galleries on the fringes of great green Balboa Park. The gray-and-white columned building wasn't too far from the city's main art museum and catered to an impressive international clientele. Featured on its elegant walls were the best works of modern artists: Wieghorst, Kingman, Pollock.

Helen blushed to see her own works in such prestigious company. Only three small watercolors were left now besides *The Master of the Dolphins*, which was spotlighted in the gallery's best section. There was a neatly lettered Not for Sale sign near one corner of the painting.

Helen was astonished by the picture's impact. Though an elegant frame could enhance the most modest picture, the impact of this painting wasn't due to the frame. The picture still gave her a tremendous surge of emotion that transcended the circumstances under which she had painted it.

She felt her knees weaken again just at the

sight of it. In spite of her steady maturation as an artist, her pleasure with the medium of gouache, the gallery's praises of her tempera and the success of her acrylics, this painting was the star of her works, probably the best she would ever do.

"A strangely compelling picture," Felipe Estrada commented beside her. "Of the dolphins that can be seen all summer from Punta Temereria, no? But the man in their midst—the swimmer—a curious fancy. Strong emotional impact...very powerful, very dreamlike. Unusual."

Did he know it was San Roque? Helen gazed at the picture without responding.

"There are stories, you know," Felipe continued. "The dolphins were said to have swum with the ancient Greeks. They helped shipwrecked sailors to shore. Was this your inspiration when you placed the swimmer in their midst?"

"No," she said, and didn't explain further.

"But of course he is not shipwrecked. He is swimming among them, enjoying being there. An excellent picture. It has a strange effect on the viewer."

"Let's see if we can find the gallery owner," she said hastily.

Chamartin was genuinely delighted to see Helen. He welcomed Felipe warmly, too.

"I've come about *The Master of the Dolphins*," she said with little preamble. "Do you think I might sell a tempera of the same subject to the party making the highest bid on the watercolor version?"

"I can't say without checking. But possibly— your temperas are your best medium. Perhaps the buyer wouldn't want the tempera sight unseen, but I'll get in touch with his agent."

"I find it hard to understand how anyone would pay as much as I've been offered," she confessed, a little embarrassed. "I feel I'm stealing money from him—or her. You wouldn't believe what a short time it took to paint: one little afternoon."

"It is not the time spent on a painting that determines the price. Most people in this world could wear out a factory of paints and never come near to creating such a masterpiece. Don't apologize! I know the value of paintings and that one has value—even though the price being offered at present is unusual for someone with your limited reputation."

"That is what I really want to ask about. Just who is offering such a price for the work of a relative unknown?"

"The agent is Japanese—Fumiko Watobi. The Japanese and the Arabs are buying practically everything they see these days. Money is no object."

"Yes. I've worked with the Japanese on Cedros. Please call this agent—Watobi?—and find out about the tempera."

Chamartin placed the call to Watobi, who said he would have to contact his principal and return the call later.

"You two shall be our guests for lunch and tour some of the sights here," Chamartin told Helen and Felipe. "He will call us back at four o'clock this afternoon."

After lunch and the tour they returned to the gallery to receive Watobi's call. Chamartin relayed the buyer's reaction to the suggestion of substituting the tempera painting for the original watercolor: "He is interested only in this particular work."

Helen sighed and bit her lip. "Tell him...." She hesitated, then plunged. "*Why* is he willing to pay such a high price?"

Chamartin asked the question, listened to the answer and reported, "The picture is wanted by a tuna-canning company connected to the big San Diego cannery. The parent company will use the picture as the base for a worldwide logo." He covered the phone mouthpiece with his hand. "The design will appear on the labels of their cans. Shall I tell him you won't sell it at any price?"

Helen felt ambivalent, torn between outrage and a desire to laugh wildly. Her precious painting, the one that meant so much to her for its emotional value, would be so commercialized that no one would ever know it had been intended as a serious work. She found it amusing that she had actually been naive enough to believe someone simply wanted to own the painting because it was beautiful.

She struggled one last moment with her decision but knew her mind had been made up when she came to the gallery. "Tell the agent, Mr. Watobi, that the artist is willing to sell—provided the buyer pays seventy-five thousand dollars."

"Helen, that's crazy!" Chamartin responded, his hand still covering the mouthpiece. "You really want me to say you won't sell at all."

"I'd rather not sell. But I need the money, and that's my price if he really wants it."

In ten minutes the astonished Chamartin reported the painting's sale. "You have seventy-five thousand! With my twenty percent you'll net sixty. The certified check will arrive here in the morning."

"We'll stay over. I want to take the check back to Cedros with me."

"You forget looking for a hotel. Stay with us—both of you!" Sally Chamartin insisted.

"I wouldn't want to put you out—"

"We won't hear of your going to a hotel when we have such a big home!"

Later, at their home, Chamartin broke open a bottle of champagne to celebrate. "How does it feel to know your prize painting will be seen only on billions of cans of tuna?" he asked Helen.

She smiled with effort. "I might have wished it had a more loving home. But why shouldn't tuna cans be beautiful? Perhaps the company knows more about what is suitable for a can of tuna than I know about what is good for a buyer of serious art."

She closed off her feelings about the painting and concentrated on the sixty thousand dollars she would have. Along with the five thousand from the house, it would more then cover the rest of Ron's debt to Luis. She already felt the burden lifting. She was becoming her own person again, able to face Luis without any barrier between them.

Now she could go back to the island, open her arms to him and say, "I'm free now. I'm free to say I love you. I've loved you since before I ever knew your name. I can be yours on any terms you want me."

Or was it too late? Had it been all an illusion? He had never said he loved her. She would know when next they met. . . .

"Felipe, will you get in touch with Luis?" she asked at the first opportunity. "Tell him that we're flying down and that I'm bringing the money with me to finish paying my brother's debt. I would like to give it to him at the house—make a...a kind of ceremony of it. Some people burn the mortgage papers; this is *my* way of celebrating. That is, if he'll come," she added.

"You can speak with him yourself, Doña Helena," Felipe responded. "He is now in Mexico City."

"No," she said, suddenly quite shy. "Just give him the message."

She felt her old insecurity bubbling back up to the surface. To him she was only a tall redhead without a thing to recommend her except a bit of talent in administration and office practices. That did not qualify her to be loved by him—to be his wife in the fullest sense. She had no reason to believe Luis truly cared for her; and yet she couldn't help hoping.

She remembered a girl she had known at college who had half-seriously listed all the requirements of the type of man she intended to marry. "He must be rich, handsome...taller than I am, of course. Great teeth. You know the kind of teeth I mean: white and perfect. He has to know wine and headwaiters. Art, literature, the theater. Politics. Business. Oh, yes, he has to be good at that. And witty. Has to know everyone and have everyone know him and look up to him. Powerful, physically. Sexy. In other words, absolutely perfect. But he doesn't have to be handsome. Not pretty, I mean.''

A third girl in the group had laughed heartily and said with more wisdom than most girls her age, ''Judy Ann, what makes you think this perfect man is looking to marry any one of us in this room? He's going to latch on to a girl whose father and mother are in *Who's Who*. His wife will look like Miss America, have been to a Swiss finishing school, ride to the hounds and call a lot of famous people by their first names. She'll be oversexed, rich and social. Anyone here meet this description?''

Which lets me out on every count with Luis San Roque, Helen thought miserably.

What happens when the poor simple imperfect girl falls in love with the perfect man? She comes out with a broken heart, or a reputation as a gold digger or adventuress. *But I love Luis, and I'll hope for a miracle. Once the debt is paid—we'll see what happens.*

CHAPTER NINETEEN

As THE PLANE made its normal landing approach, Helen could see the line of red cabs returning from the airfield, where they had gone earlier to meet the regular morning plane.

Coming out on the run from the city of Cedros was the company car with Vergel almost certainly at the wheel. One or two island cabs, perhaps more, followed him. The drivers always hoped to load baggage from the company plane, or even to have a well-paid fare back to the city. Today Vergel was not alone in the car.

Agustin Benevidez came forward full of importance. When Felipe and Helen stepped off the plane, it was Agustin who ordered the bags placed and made all arrangements with the expertise Eugenio Ochoa had once demonstrated in such areas.

Taking Helen aside, Agustin was effusive in his thanks. "I cannot tell you, Doña Helena, how very grateful I am for your patronage. I always knew that once el señor saw my loyalty and abilities in their full perspective he would reward them. You have brought those abilities to his personal attention, and I am most grateful! Also, you were quite right about Estelita Sanchez and José Bello: both are excellent personnel.''

His rapid monologue continued unabated all the way into Cedros. Parts of his chatter confused Helen, until he said, ''Who would have guessed six months ago, when you first came, that I would be the manager of the operation on Cedros today! My wife could not help coming this morning just to polish the new brass nameplate on the door of the manager's office. She tells me I must continue to take English lessons and become more proficient in Japanese, and converse as much as possible in those languages. I prefer the English, as that is the language of Mexico's nearest neighbor to the north. But one ought to learn the best methods of doing business. Thus one rises quickly in one's career.''

''I did not know you had been appointed manager!'' Felipe interrupted. ''You did not tell me, Helena.''

''There have been many other things to occupy my mind,'' she reminded him.

So she had been replaced! Luis had said she was to be promoted, but there had to be another reason for Benevidez's new position. She felt vaguely apprehensive and told herself not to jump to conclusions.

"How has the school in the new building progressed since I have been gone?" she asked calmly.

"Ah, the school! Two instructors arrived, and the new director. Everyone is much intimidated by him, for he is an important man. New students from the mainland have been accommodated on the top floor. The planes daily bring new equipment to work with."

"Agustin—" Helen cut in, "I am not familiar with all the details of the new developments because I have been occupied in San Diego. Just what has Don Luis arranged with respect to the new director?"

Agustin was only too pleased to inform her. He explained that the new director had run a similar school in Mexico City, had formerly taught at the University of Guadalajara and was an *abogado* who knew business law. "Soon this island will be full of educated people, just as the big cities are!"

"I suggest, Felipe," Helen said, fearing what she would discover about her status once she arrived at the house, "that since there have been so many administrative changes in the island's operation since you last paid an official visit, you might want to stop by the office with Agustin. I'll go up to the house and send Vergel back for you later."

"Yes." Felipe looked resigned to the prospect

of a long stay at the office. "I feel sure Agustin will find much to keep me busy."

"He'll wear you out," Helen promised. "He'll show you every letter, every file." She said goodbye to the two men at the quay with a pleasantly light smile that was purely superficial. She was glad to be alone for a while and conjecture on what surprise might be in store for her at the great house.

Since Agustin had been elevated to her former position and someone else had been brought in to take charge of the training program in addition to the teachers, was she now expendable? Had she realized her one-time goal only to see it all end here?

Three days before Christmas was no time to be out of a job, mourning a father and somewhat disillusioned by a brother. But the possibility that she would soon be preparing for a Mexican divorce caused her the most concern.

There was no job in the company off the island for which she was particularly qualified or wanted to apply, and her reason for employment here would no longer exist once she turned over the certified checks. She feared, as well, that she had ruined any chance for happiness with Luis by her lack of compromise.

What could be worse than being fired, broke and five thousand miles from home on the wildest peninsula in the world?

Considering that question, she conceded that she might be in all the same circumstances and still owe $263,000 someone else had stolen, with no way to repay it. She might not have some proven commercial talent to fall back on. Well, she thought, she would have to rely on that talent—feast or famine. If her past sales had been flukes, she thought Chamartin would at least give her a job in the gallery. Somehow she would manage—and she no longer had the sword of debt hanging over her.

The real tragedy was that she would have to leave her beloved Cedros. She cared about her students and the people she'd worked with. She was fond of Soledad, and she loved Rafaela dearly. She would miss everyone on the island—and most of all she would miss Luis, whom she loved with an intensity that frightened her. She felt sure she must somehow bear this tragedy, but she did not know how to begin.

Her sight was blurred as Vergel whisked her up around the last turn in the winding road to the great house, but she blinked the tears back fiercely. After all, she had known all along that this was the only logical ending to the whole affair. Here came that ending, racing to meet her. She had to face it—and Luis.

Soledad opened the door, forgot herself and put her arms around Helen with a sob of delight.

"*¡Niña!* You are home! *¡Gracias a Dios!*"

"I've missed you, too, Soledad!" Helen hugged the old woman and laid her cheek on the housekeeper's gray head.

"Don Luis is in the library," Soledad told her, taking her bag and shoving her ahead as she would a child.

"Leave the bag in the hall. There's something in it for Rafaela that I brought from the north."

There was no sense in having the bag lugged upstairs and then back down if she was to be summarily dismissed.

She took a deep breath before entering the library, remembering how she had first seen Luis in this house, and how she had been stunned by everything he had said. Nothing could stun her this time. She had prepared herself for the worst.

Luis looked just as forbidding as he had that first time. He sat in the same chair, behind the same mammoth desk, and he didn't rise, just as he hadn't risen the first time.

"Well. . . you have finally returned," he said.

"I appreciate your trust in me, allowing me to leave the island in spite of our contract," she said quietly, finding the words hard to say.

He looked at her silently as she came up to the desk.

"I have brought the rest of the money," she said, placing the international bank draft on the desk before him. "There may be more here than I still owe you, Luis. When it is computed you can adjust the amount however you want to." She knew how stiff and awkward she sounded, but she hoped she had some dignity to preserve when all else was gone.

He gave the draft a brief glance before pushing it slightly aside. "Agustin met you as I instructed him?"

"He did. He is overjoyed with his promotion." She added sincerely, "He'll be conscientious and increasingly efficient in his new position, I'm sure."

Did her treacherous high coloring betray her? She managed to look him calmly in the eyes as he asked her, "Are you satisfied with my selection of the school director?"

"I haven't met your new director. Agustin has good instincts, however, and he is satisfied."

She hated the cat-and-mouse game he was playing with her. Wasn't it enough to say she was fired?

"The contract terms of my employment have evidently been completed. Since you have placed Agustin in the one area I was covering and an outsider in the other, I assume my usefulness to San Roque Enterprises is over." She made her voice even.

"You have done a fine job as far as cultural

restrictions permitted. You do understand that such an arrangement could not continue?''

Helen nodded at that, adding, ''I hope you'll furnish me with suitable references should I ever need them.''

''You will not need my reference. Your paintings will make your name for you.''

''Which means I *am* to leave the island.'' It was a statement, not a question.

''No one will stop you if that is what you wish to do. There is a place for you on the island—''

''I don't want you to *make* a job for me,'' she cut him off stiffly. ''Since I have been replaced I will leave as soon as possible. I wouldn't want to be an inconvenience. But...I would like to resolve the matter of Rafaela.''

''What about the child?''

''I am very fond of her. I would like to take care of her, see that she is given a chance to develop as far as possible. I would like to take her with me, adopt her. Can that be arranged?''

''No.''

''Why not?'' She was stunned by the cold finality of his refusal. ''She has no one else! Her mother is dead. I love her. I would—''

''Mexico does not appreciate well-meaning foreigners from the north coming to take our children as though they were an exportable product. Besides, Rafaela belongs on this island. It is her world. Everyone in this house loves her and takes care of her. No, you cannot take her away.''

She felt her face was now truly white, her lips trembling. Even Rafaela was to be denied her. Nevertheless, she knew Luis was right. It was presumptuous of her to think she could take Rafaela away from the world she knew. The wound went deeper as Luis made it clear there were no concessions.

Helen feared she would burst into tears. They burned just behind her eyes and she struggled to contain them.

''I'd like to take a few things of mine with me,'' she said, trying to maintain her dignity. ''Mostly my painting equipment.''

''And your clothes. After all, they cannot possibly fit anyone else.''

''The clothes are beautiful, and I have enjoyed wearing them, but they were, if you remember, uniforms. I can't take them without paying for them, and I can't begin to afford them. Perhaps...I might select a few that approximate the difference between the balance of the debt and the bank draft?''

''You always make such a thing of money!'' he complained in a voice heavy with irritation. ''In your perversity you refuse to be on the receiving end of anything in life. If you cannot dole out the favors, you turn to ice! It is most unbecoming.'' He agreed to her request with a casual gesture. "Whatever you think is right will suit me. Do you want Genaro to pack the large fish painting in the upstairs storage room?"

"Yes, if it's not too much trouble," she responded politely. "And my paints—they're in a box next to the painting. Would you have him carry them down, as well?"

"You are an extremely gifted artist, Helen. I might buy one of your paintings as an investment. Not, however, that particular painting upstairs."

"Why not?"

"It seems rather empty to me. No, I do not care for it at all."

"It isn't finished," she said defensively. "Anyway, it isn't for sale. I want it for myself."

"Strange!" He looked at her thoughtfully.

"What do you mean, 'strange'?"

"Obviously you remembered Punta Temereria, where the dolphins can be seen most of the year. But do you not have a similar painting in that San Diego gallery? I remember the correspondence between you and the gallery owner. It seems odd to me that you want to keep two of the same subject."

"The painting in the gallery has been sold."

"Sold? I was under the impression that you would not sell that one under any circumstances!"

"I needed the money. The draft on the desk is

mostly from the sale of that painting. Surely Felipe told you? He always keeps you totally informed."

"Felipe told me you sold a painting. He did not describe the subject of the painting, except to say it was very beautiful. From the size of the bank draft, I believe the sale price is astonishing for one as new to the art world as you."

"A. . . a Japanese tuna company bought it for the logo for one of their products," she confessed.

"Aha! The painting you set such store by will now be thrown into every trash can in the world?"

"You needn't put it that way! Tuna is an honest industry—and commercial art isn't evil."

"Of course not. I merely wonder at your apparently insatiable need to realize a cash value from everything. You easily sold a painting that one would gather had meaning for you. I find this attitude singularly cold and unfeeling. As much as you talked of cherishing the work, you willingly prostituted your art when the price was right. You seem to let any reason for living take a poor second place to money."

Helen stared at him without answering. His voice was as cold as ice, and there was no answer she could give. His words stabbed her to her heart. She longed to tell him, *I did it to clear a barrier between us!* But instead she had only raised it further.

At last she managed to say, "May I go? You'll be free of the crassly commercial Helen Forster as soon as the regular plane leaves the island this afternoon. Can I assume you'll take care of all other details through your lawyer?"

"All details will be taken care of. But you may want these," he added, opening the drawer of the desk. He handed her a packet of bank statements and the power of attorney she had signed the end of August.

"Thank you," she said stiffly, then headed out of the room. She couldn't spend a moment longer there and maintain her facade of dignity. The tears were going to start any minute and she didn't want to reveal her weakness in front of Luis.

She bumped into Soledad at the library door, Rafaela in her arms. The child struggled to reach out for Helen, her expressive face full of joy.

"L-lena!" the child crowed triumphantly. "Lena!"

Helen stepped back in amazement.

"She has said nothing else ever since you left! All the time, night and day, she has called you. She even has other words. Not easy to understand yet, but she is speaking." Soledad was overflowing with the excitement of the child's accomplishment.

Tears of joy in the midst of misery streaked Helen's face as she took the child from Soledad and fiercely hugged her.

"*¡Hola, niña! ¡Diga! ¡Don Luis!*"

"L-lu-is!" the little one repeated cooperatively, beaming.

"Oh, Rafaela, Rafaela!" Helen hugged her enthusiastically. "How beautiful, how wonderful you are!" She handed her reluctantly back to Soledad and bent to open her suitcase.

"This is for you, darling." She gave the child the doll she had carried from Garnet Beach. "Beautiful Annie—I've told you all about her. She was my doll when I was little like you, and she shall be yours now. You must learn to say 'Anabella.' I always loved Bella Anabella and you will love her, too." She kissed Rafaela, promising, "I'll come to see you again a little later, my darling, but just for now, 'Lena' is busy."

She almost pushed Soledad away with the child to keep from breaking down entirely.

Soledad carried Rafaela and her doll back to her room, and Helen dashed tears from her cheeks as she stumbled up the stairs.

SHE WENT TO THE ROOM off the upstairs sitting room where she kept her painting equipment. Undraping the dolphin tempera on the easel, she brought it out into the sitting-room light.

Luis was right, of course, as usual. This painting was empty. The technique was flawless—her best. The memory of the point was accurate, even dreamlike, and the composition was artistically correct. But the painting had no spirit, no soul: it was emotionally flat, a mere exercise.

She knew now why she had left Luis's swimming figure out of the second composition. It had been too risky for her to express the way she'd felt when she painted the first picture. The need to keep Luis from knowing how she really felt about him, the need to salvage her pride....

"Oh, damn!" she said. She could never put him in this painting now. And she knew the painting would not sell to anyone, not even a tuna cannery. She began to cry, great snuffling, nose-reddening sobs that were dredged out of her misery.

When she could stop crying long enough to function, she began stacking her things in a pile for Soledad or Genaro to box. Then she sat on the floor and cried a bit more.

She had come to Baja for a summer opportunity. Some opportunity! She had lost her heart forever, she had no job, no home and she would never see Luis again.

She began looking desperately for a handkerchief. In rummaging for it, she bumped the packet of bank statements off the table.

She picked them up and looked at them distractedly, wiping her eyes on the tail of her shirt. Only the last one hadn't been opened, and for some perverse reason she slashed it open with one of the palette knives.

The statement covered the period of November 18 through December 18. She scanned the sheet indifferently at first, then in a puzzle. There was nothing on the brief one-page accounting but deposits.

Her salary had been deposited. The money from Edna's house was shown deposited. The auction money was there, and the painting sales. There was no withdrawals indicated, not even for Mrs. Parish or for the nursing home.

The daily-balance portion began with an enormous amount and ended with that amount augmented by the month's deposits.

Her tears dried as she tried to decipher what kind of a bank error was involved. The recap also mystified her. Total number of checks drawn: none. Amount total of checks: none. Service charges: none.

She hunted for her glasses, which she had removed when they had become too wet to see through. She cleaned them and put them back on. Frowning, she quickly looked through the other statements, but they read in the same manner clear back to the summer, where her own transactions were all recorded just as she remembered making them. There had to be a large continuing error. She would have to go downstairs and confront Luis about it.

Just what I need, she thought. *A monumental continuing bank error!*

She went out through the big room toward the hall door, but halfway through the bedroom she halted. She hadn't seen the south wall of the master bedroom when she came in because she had headed directly for the sitting room, her mind on the unfinished painting, her paints and her misery. How could she have missed the sight of that wall? It dominated the whole room.

In the gallery, *The Master of the Dolphins* had stunned her with its impact when she saw it framed for the first time in a suitable environment. There it had been possible to believe someone could pay an exorbitant price for its exotic, fantastic qualities.

Here the painting had a different quality. It exuded the energy and bemusement she had felt as she painted it. It was a statement of the open passion that had risen up in her when she had glimpsed Luis in the water and on the beach.

The sight staggered her.

The bank statements fluttered to the floor. Slowly she bent and picked them up in a daze.

Everything began to click into place like a crazy, unbelievably wonderful puzzle solved.

The Japanese tuna king—it would have been

easy enough for Luis to ask any Japanese business associate to act as go-between. He had known all along about the painting and would have satisfied his curiosity about it.

All the money, the money she had made such a fuss about! She had proved she meant to pay the debt. He had gone to great lengths to keep her on the island when he couldn't have cared about the repayment of the money at all.

He had not cared about losing the money. He had cared about her! *Had he cared all along about her?*

She hardly dared the luxury of believing. It could not be that enormously simple. It must be a fantasy she only wanted desperately to be true.

She sat on the bed staring at the painting, crying again like the little fool she felt she had been all along. The connecting doors between the room and Luis's study opened, and he came in, closed the door and stood looking at her.

"Did you really think I would let you go?"

"I don't know!" she sobbed, crying harder than ever.

"Never, *querida*!"

With his arms tightly around her, his kisses tasting her tears, she knew how foolish she had been.

After some time she drew back a little—very little—and asked him, "How many of my paintings did you buy, Luis? To make me think I was such a successful artist?''

''Besides this one, which you so often refused to sell? Only three.''

''Only three?''

''But they were good paintings!'' He defended his purchases stoutly. ''They were particularly suited to our corporate offices. Perhaps not great art, but suitable! The price set by the gallery was not out of line, so why shouldn't I have bought them? They were pictures of the holdings of the firm—the sheds at Punta Temereria and the wharf on Cedros. They were done by the wife of the owner—and many company owners have bought lesser paintings for the same purpose!''

He kissed her again, then said teasingly, ''Ah, but it cost me a great deal of money when I was determined to have this one.''

''A Japanese tuna factory owner!''

''Actually, a Japanese tuna factory owner did wish to buy the painting. He and I bid against each other for some time.''

''I realize you have been laughing at me all this time. But I don't care!''

''*Amada mía*, I have never laughed at you.'' His lean brown hand caressed her cheek. ''Believe it! I never laughed. I have been filled with love, passion, admiration. Also irritation, frustration—much frustration—and every possible emotion a man feels when he is unfortunate enough to be in love with a woman like yourself!''

"Unfortunate enough!"

"You know what I mean. Have we ceased playing games at last?"

"You never told me you loved me. . . ."

"Would you have listened?"

"I have been too busy telling myself I was unfortunate to have fallen in love with a man who could never love me. But I do love you, Luis! Incurably!"

She lifted her face for another beautiful kiss to which she could surrender with every fiber of her being.

Much later she asked, "What about Ron and the money he stole?"

"The debt has been paid as far as San Roque Enterprises is concerned. Each payment was entered on the books by Estrada when he received it. What difference does it make to me if my money is in this account or that? But I confess I am more angry that he stole from you than from me. Before I learned of this from Estrada, when he called from San Diego, I had some small fondness for the criminal ways of your brother—since they brought you to me."

"Luis! What do you mean by that?"

"*Querida,*" he answered softly, kissing her throat, "he was a fortunate accident for me."

"A fortunate accident. . . ?"

"My darling, the last thing in the world I expected to see when I came out of the water at Punta Temereria—where I had thought to have a peaceful relaxing hour in the sea and forget the pressures of business facing me—was a tall redheaded goddess waiting for me. I knew in a moment who you were. I would have taken any action in the world to keep you with me from that moment on. That your brother chose to abscond without you was a godsend. It gave me an opportunity and reason."

"You mean our marriage was never intended to be a simple legal method of holding me here until the debt was paid? You never intended dissolving it?" Helen asked, astounded.

"God forbid! I meant the marriage to bind you to me forever from the very first. Marriage is no light matter to me; I am an old-fashioned man in that respect."

"What about Yolanda?"

"Aha!" he said with his teasing smile as he wound her hair around his hands and held her close to him. "What of her? You were jealous? Did you not know that if I had ever loved Yolanda, I would have married her long ago?"

"When you sent those Mexico City newspapers with the frightful pictures. . . ." She burrowed her head in his neck and held him to her tightly.

"I told you I was tired of being patient, *querida esposa*. I thought to frighten you a little and perhaps bring you to your senses." He nipped at her ear with his gleaming white teeth.

"It was cruel of you to give her hope if she could have none," Helen reproved him with her old spirit.

"Had you been with me, you would have seen many others in the group. One of the others was always her escort. The pictures were arranged by the photographers or myself for the best social effect. They served a small vengeful purpose, my sweet: to make you as miserable as I was. Desperation makes us all do strange things, as well you know."

"Never again—*nunca más*—will I give you reason to be vengeful!"

"Nevertheless, my tactic did not seem to have its desired effect, and I had to devise other means. I chose to remove you from your job, which I thought would give you time to paint. I would have bought each painting at any price to end such stupid games. As it happened, this one painting served to solve the impasse."

"Tuna-can labels!" she murmured, laughing.

"The first time I saw this painting—when I went to the gallery to learn why you were so adamant about keeping it—I knew it had been with you as it was with me, and I was content." He kissed her hair and her eyes. Then he gave her a mischievous look. "But I must tell you of one more small deception."

"You are Don Castle," she murmured, answering his mischief.

It was his turn to look surprised. "How long have you known?"

"Not long," she confessed. "When I was in San Diego I tried to call him. I wanted him to tell me of the best book on chess that I could buy, to bring as a Christmas gift for you. It *is* almost Christmas, you know. No one at the St. Francis in San Francisco had ever heard of Don Castle. Then I remembered that *roque* in Spanish is another word for 'castle,' specifically for 'rook' in chess. I thought then, my darling— but I wasn't sure. I never had time to be sure... until now. I didn't think of it again." She shivered. "I really thought you were sending me away—"

"I am neither your father nor your brother, my darling. I am your husband and lover forever. I will never dismiss, never reject, never abandon you. *Nunca más.* Perhaps it will take a lifetime for me to prove it to you. It is a fair exchange. You give me all your love, and I will take on the task. I have already proven my patience, no?"

"Oh, Luis...Luis!" She could not contain her joy at being in his arms, being caressed so gently and yet so passionately. "I shall become like Magdalena and despise having my husband gone from my side even for one night.''

''You need not suffer separations. You will travel with me. Perhaps I will delegate some responsibilities, and with my duties dwindling away I can stay here on the island more of the time. We shall enjoy the sea and investigate every cave and cove. I love you, not San Roque Enterprises.''

From the open window came the sound of the church bell announcing noon on the island.

''Should we rescue Felipe from Agustin?'' he asked, showing no inclination to leave her side.

''No, my darling, there is plenty of time after the hour of siesta,'' she murmured. ''In this house, too, we can observe the island custom of connubial love at noon!'' And she blushed as his mouth claimed hers.

Harlequin Presents...

The very finest in romance fiction

Get all the latest books before they're sold out!

As a Harlequin subscriber you actually receive your
personal copies of the latest Presents novels immediately
after they come off the press, so you're sure of getting all
8 each month.

Cancel your subscription whenever you wish!

You don't have to buy any minimum number of books.
Whenever you decide to stop your subscription just let us
know and we'll cancel all further shipments.

Your FREE gift includes

Anne Mather—Born out of Love
Violet Winspear—Time of the Temptress
Charlotte Lamb—Man's World
Sally Wentworth—Say Hello to Yesterday

What the press says about Harlequin romance fiction…

"When it comes to romantic novels…
Harlequin is the indisputable king."
— *New York Times*

"…always…an upbeat, happy ending."
— *San Francisco Chronicle*

"…a work of art."
— *Globe & Mail*, Toronto

"Nothing quite like it has happened since
Gone With the Wind…"
— *Los Angeles Times*

Enter a uniquely exciting new world with

Harlequin American Romance™·

Harlequin American Romances are the first romances to explore today's new love relationships. These compelling romance novels reach into the hearts and minds of women across North America...probing the most intimate moments of romance, love and desire.

You'll follow romantic heroines and irresistible men as they boldly face confusing choices. Career first, love later? Love without marriage? Long-distance relationships? All the experiences that make love real are captured in the tender, loving pages of the new **Harlequin American Romances.**

What makes North American women so different when it comes to love? Find out in the new **Harlequin American Romance!**

Send for your introductory FREE book now!

Get this book FREE!

Mail to:

Harlequin Reader Service

In the U.S.
1440 South Priest Drive
Tempe, AZ 85281

In Canada
649 Ontario Street
Stratford, Ontario N5A 6W2

YES! I want to be one of the first to discover the new **Harlequin American Romance** novels. Send me FREE and without obligation *Twice in a Lifetime.* If you do not hear from me after I have examined my FREE book, please send me the 4 new **Harlequin American Romance** novels each month as soon as they come off the presses. I understand that I will be billed only $2.25 for each book (total $9.00). There are no shipping or handling charges. There is no minimum number of books that I have to purchase. In fact, I may cancel this arrangement at any time. *Twice in a Lifetime* is mine to keep as a FREE gift, even if I do not buy any additional books.

Name _____ (please print)

Address _____ Apt. no. _____

City _____ State/Prov. _____ Zip/Postal Code _____

Signature (If under 18, parent or guardian must sign.)